THURSDAY IN THE SKY

and other tales

H. R. Brown

Copyright © September 2021 H. R. Brown

All rights reserved.

ISBN-13: 9798477087921

Also by H. R. Brown:

The Howling of Satan's Temple (and other tales)
Roid Rage (and other tales)

For my nephews..

(when they're old enough)

contents

Two Dead Men	7
Thursday in the Sky	17
The Flag, the Femme & the Fiery Apocalypse	56
Zero	70
Essence	108
Sim City^3	121
Make Up	137
04:22am [TRANSCRIPT]	140
Opinion Poll	155
Evolution	182
Zero (reprise)	193
Abortive	200
The Hive	210
Scribbled Notes Found at the Sci-Fi Convention	272
Sunny Uplands	280
Happy Holidays	337
There Was an Explosion	348
About the Author	352

TWO DEAD MEN

The enormous, ruined starship floated in the inky shadows of deepest night. Caught in orbit around a small moon, which itself was slowly orbiting the dark side of a stupendous gas giant, the starship *Hyperia* had been lost in the endless night of space since it had fallen into this path, over a hundred and fifty Earth years ago.

The ship's massive fission engines were gone, destroyed in an almighty collision. All remaining energy cells were dead or virtually so. The damage was extensive. Only a few dozen of the ship's two million functions were still nominally active, but had automatically powered down to save energy when the dying *Hyperia* had fallen into its shadowy orbit.

Locked in two separate escape pods, frozen in stasis-sleep, were the two great adversaries, Jorgen and Hadrik. The two fearsome warriors lay silent, entombed in darkness.

Dead, to all intents and purposes, Jorgen and Hadrik had both boarded the escape pods when it seemed the *Hyperia* was doomed. This was before the auto-pilot had found one last gasp from the auxiliary engines. The final burst had been just enough to achieve a stable orbit, rather than a fiery death.

The remaining escape pods had jammed due to the damage and debris caused by the impact when Hadrik had rammed his smaller starship, the *Dinomenes*, into *Hyperia's* engines.

Jorgen had been the one with the upper hand in the encounter, but Hadrik, nimbly skipping his ship's destruction by a few seconds via a stunning escape through a mini-portal - directly onto the *Hyperia's* bridge - suddenly turned the tables. He lobbed a couple of grenades at his old enemy Jorgen, the first second he was through the portal, then fled for the mid-section as the grenades went off on the bridge and the *Dinomenes* exploded into *Hyperia's* engines at the other end of the ship.

Staying alive on the imposing, grandiose *Hyperia*, had never previously been a problem, but these few seconds of decisive action from Hadrik changed everything. Yet Jorgen, ever wary, weary, paranoid and scarred by his years of war with Hadrik, saw his peril immediately when the sudden wormhole opened onto his bridge. He barely managed to leap out of harm's way, narrowly avoiding the explosions with his catlike agility. Many of his bridge staff did not have such reactions, and paid dearly for it.

The air was filled with sirens, screaming, smoke and fire. The engines were gone, as was the bridge. Further impact damage and debris wracked the *Hyperia*, who's decks listed crazily out of control as the gravity generators shuddered and flickered. Amid the chaos those who still could, evacuated the ship. Jorgen and Hadrik, chasing and blasting at each other through the wreckage with wanton, raging hatred, caused yet more destruction as the last of the crew escaped.

These sworn enemies both had the latest tech; mini-portal manipulators to track each other directly through space-time, and Sword guns to blast each other with. His dynamic use of his mini-portal (or more accurately; mini-wormhole) manipulator had allowed Hadrik to assume the upper hand, at least briefly.

'Swords' were the latest form of designer blaster gun, the kind usually owned by the biggest and baddest of those who ruled the known galactic systems. The name was short for Subatomic Weaponised Omega Ray Disruptor. The Sword would vaporise a living human from half a mile away, within seconds of impact. Dying in such a fashion usually involved a moment or two of screaming agony.

When the *Hyperia* began its death-dive towards the small moon, Jorgen and Hadrik, bitterest of enemies, both finally decided the best chance he had of killing the other was to remain alive to do so – which meant getting to an escape pod.

Both men found an intact pod, sealed himself within and looked to fire it free of the *Hyperia*. Both men found his chosen little life bubble fused to the body of the *Hyperia* due to the impact of burning debris from the collision of the *Dinomenes*.

Hyperia's power was gone, and as its central computer fought to stay alive it sucked power from all available remaining sources, including the jammed escape pods. Each man scanned his computer portal for info, and found all the remaining escape pods were equally fused to the body of *Hyperia*. Each man then knew he was dead.

Then the auxiliary engines began to die, but in so doing, they flared wildly for a short time, altering the dying ship's course. After some moments of recalculation, the computer then showed the Hyperia had achieved a stable orbit of the moon they had been heading towards. However, the orbit of the Hyperia was in darkness, blocked from the local star by the stupendous gas giant.

This orbit meant freezing to death, before long.

Surviving in an escape pod in deep space means not just evading the vacuum, it means large supplies of food, water and oxygen. Unless the human body could hibernate in some way; unless it could survive for long periods without much sustenance, escape pods themselves would have been an expensive way of delaying the inevitable. The stasis chamber was a coffin-sized box which, when activated, froze time for everything within. This meant a person could seal themselves within, activate the system and blink and find the rescue party opening the chamber, but that blink had been frozen for twenty years.

The *Hyperia* had been designed and built by engineers of brilliance and sophistication, so each escape pod contained a stasis chamber.

Before committing to removing himself entirely from the fourth dimension, both Jorgen and Hadrik took up his portal manipulator and searched the vicinity frantically for the other, hoping to shoot him dead via the wormhole created by the manipulator. They both understood the odds of finding the other via this crazy, fledgling technology, but each knew it were possible and that hatred would lead the other to try it too, before it got too cold.

Had they known it, they were within forty yards of each

other, on opposite sides of the ship. Hadrik was in a starboard-side pod, facing out towards the stars, and Jorgen was in a port-side pod, also facing out.

How cold was too cold? Hatred is a powerful thing, as is fear of hatred. Eventually, the endless scouring of inky black nothingness and the severe cold ended the search for both men. Both were shaking madly before giving up on hatred, for now. Within a few minutes of each other, they were both within their pod's stasis chamber, both were activated – and *zip*! Time froze for them both.

Thus it was that virtually all remaining activity on the *Hyperia* died. The ship was left drifting slowly around the small moon, dead and in total darkness.

The battle between *Hyperia* and *Diomenes* was the penultimate act in a war which had raged beyond control throughout several star systems, and ended the lives of millions.

The trail of devastation the pair left behind them made a mockery of all human conflict before and after. Such was the utter destruction meted out in the violence of the war that those left behind were so few, so traumatised and so scattered amongst the stars, that many would never again rejoin the league of human worlds.

The ancient, beautiful Astral Cities of the Mirrored Moons, orbiting the shining emerald gas giant of Pollyanna IV were ruined, punctured by the cold vacuum of space and destroyed.

The warm, sultry, hazy, evergreen summers and seashores of

Mysteria II were ripped from orbit and spread across the infinite night of cold, dead space. One day archaeologists will ponder the asteroid belt which once was Mysteria II. Why are there so many parasols and camper-vans in an asteroid field!? Closer inspection will reveal rivers of human bones.

The lurid cascades of multi-coloured neon which lit the fabled star-ports and trading hubs riding the Rings of Pangloria VII; these were shattered, wrecked and left glowing only in fire. The utopian ideals of universal night-life for all sentients, died with them.

All gone. All torn apart by the dreaded Planetary Anchor Gun, a working version of which was used by both armies. All those glorious homes of humanity were ripped from their orbits and sent spiralling into gravimetric oblivion, along with others, as the armies of Jorgen and Hadrik tore each other's territories apart, over long years of intensive intergalactic turmoil. Millions upon millions were dead, and millions more grimly waited their turn to try to help return peace to the universe, though basic arithmetic and statistics showed surely it meant their deaths, and those of most of their families.

And yet, after the *Hyperia* was struck and almost destroyed by the *Dinomenes*, peace finally returned to the cosmos. The blazing wreckage of the *Hyperia* fell into a cold, dead orbit, carrying Jorgen and Hadrik with it. Upon hearing the sudden silence from those channels which, for decades had carried only death, destruction and the promise of more – the guardians of the remaining undamaged systems simply raised flags and allowed the rejoicing which everyone felt to bubble over in a week-long party.

It has been said that no party in human history ever beat this one, however the term "week-long party" has always been contended. Some didn't manage a full week, millions were injured and incapable. Others gave it a week, others more or much more; rumours have it of a bohemian tribe, somewhere out there beyond the stars, for whom the party has never ended.

After this rejoicing, the remaining worlds stuck peaceful agreements with each other. The echoes of war were allowed to fade. Jorgen and Hadrik were dead, they were gone, and no more need die for them or their futile cause.

A hundred and fifty years passed of relative calm, give or take the odd planetary insurgency, coup or revolution. War ceased to be interstellar in this period of our history.

And yet, frozen in the deep night of space, a battered, broken vessel was finally about to pass the horizon of night, after more than one hundred and fifty years of darkness.

From the dead of eternal night to the broad day of full sunlight, within minutes.

Severely damaged though she was, the *Hyperia* had ten thousand solar panels, at least six thousand of which were still operable. When the she finally cleared the horizon of the gas giant, the rays of the local sun suddenly bathed her. Warmth began to return to the frozen ship. Power began to flood the cells. Systems began to re-initialise.

Before long, Hadrik popped, shivering, from his stasis

chamber and onto the floor of his pod. He squinted in the bright sunlight, then crawled into the big patch of it which was coming through the main portal. He slowly began to feel warm again.

Jorgen had a similar awakening, freezing and shivering in the sudden warmth and bright light.

And each man soon remembered his enemy.

Before long Hadrik stood again as he had before, facing out towards the stars, booting up his mini-portal manipulator. Jorgen, in his pod, did likewise.

Now power was no concern, both men channelled it into his manipulator to boost the signal and the reach. Both blasted out wormhole fissures fiercely, as both had come to realise the other must still on board, somewhere. And each knew time was against him.

After some time, when their machines had both thoroughly warmed up, it became inevitable. The snaking wormholes found each other, and locked on.

Suddenly, for the first time in many years (not counting their sleep in the stasis fields), the two oldest of adversaries faced each other down the conjoined portal.

Each man focussed on the other with the strangest of expression; it was part snarl, part venom, and part grudging respect.

"You killed my mother."

Hadrik said it quietly, but with absolute conviction. He *knew* it.

"I did no such fucking thing," Jorgen growled, "I've told you that in good faith, as have many others, a million fucking times!"

Hadrik shook his head.

"But you!" Jorgen was yelling now, "You fucked my sister!"

Hadrik's jaw stiffened, and whilst he was quietly saying "I loved Zoe, man, what happened was not my fault.." - Jorgen was still yelling;

"You did! You fucked her – and then you killed her! You killed her you bastard, and now I'm gonna fucking kill you!"

Hadrik and Jorgen saw the flash of death in each others eyes down that wormhole-connection, and with a roar for death or glory, each went for his Sword, aimed it at the loathed enemy and fired...

Both fired successfully.

Thus it was that the greatest battle ever fought in human history, finally ended. A tale from eons into the future, lost in the cyclical oceans of universal time. Multi-wormhole broadcasting from decades ahead of Hadrik's and Jorgen's time, looking back at a long-lost, bloody, barbaric, imperial age, sent broadcasts into realms they were never intended to reach. The early inter-galactic, multi-wormhole and mini-portal broadcasts did not always fire correctly. This ensured the tale of Jorgen and Hadrick accidentally became part of the distant past, as well as multiple futures.

Thousands of years of 'Chinese Whispers' since then have now passed, and ensured all that remains today, of this legend of our distant future, is the nonsense children's rhyme it once gave rise to:

> "One fine day in the middle of the night,
> Two dead men got up to fight,
> Back to back they faced each other,
> Drew their swords and shot each other."

© H. R. Brown, 19/01/2017

thursday in the sky

It started out a normal day like any other. There were two, ten-minute snoozes, before the alarm went off for a third time, then Jim Hackett had to force himself up and out of bed. He had left just the right window of time in which to pull on his office clothes, splash water around his head and shoulders and down his neck, comb his hair, grab his bag and his lunch, get out of the house and to the bus stop in time for the 597.

Breakfast was coffee with a biscuit, a satsuma and an apple, whilst he sat at his desk and began his first case of the day. His desk was a nugget of ever-decreasingly personal space amidst a hundred other such nuggets in a large, open-plan office.

His work was the usual stuff: Pick up a case. Are all the relevant boxes ticked? Yes = Progress the case to the next level (where it becomes someone else's problem); No = Chase the relevant department(s) for the outstanding info and re-diarise the case to reappear in the work flow once again, in two working days time (i.e. Monday, this being Thursday).

After a couple of cases had been chased-up, Jim went for a second coffee around 9:30am. He found four of his lady co-workers all giggling next to the hot drinks machine. He ordered his coffee and heard Irene say -

"Hey let's try Jim's!"

"Try my what?" he asked, turning to see what exactly they were doing.

"We're all feeling each others boobs for a laugh!" said Tina, "Can we feel yours?!"

Jim's eyes widened in surprise; he wasn't one to miss this kind of opportunity.

"First of all ladies," Jim said, "I ain't got boobs, moobs or even tits; these are *pecs*! Second of all – Yes you can, absolutely!"

Jim then found himself being felt-up for an enjoyable moment or two by all of them, in a manner excessively inappropriate to the minimum accepted standards of office behaviour and etiquette. He wondered if he was still dreaming, so decided to push his luck further; "But.. I'm not seeing any girl on girl action!" he said. "Where is it?!"

At this, Tina and Irene clinched each other in a lively, and equally inappropriate manner. Susie and Gina whooped and danced, and carried on rubbing Jim's chest.

Jim knew this situation was all wrong, but it felt so right. Like some of his wilder and more youthful weekends, years ago.

"Oh, I've gotta get me some of this!" he found himself saying, before he grabbed Tina's sizeable assets from behind.

The whooping and laughing and merriment increased as Jim's chest was fondled from behind again by Susie. Gina joined in by grabbing hold of both Jim and Irene.

"Group grope!" said Jim.

"Yes!" said Gina, "*Group grope! Group grope*!"

The chant was taken up by all; "Group grope! GROUP GROPE!"

Then Jim, his mind on fire and going through the current buzz words for those continual managerial allegations, protestations and demands of Progress in the Workplace, yelled out:

"Going forward!"

- and the chant was shattered into shrieking hysterics all round.

Jim had snogged both Tina and Susie and had grabbed at least five individual breasts before he and Susie began to seriously focus their attention upon each other. Their kissing slowed, heated and then ran to fever. They pulled at each other for greater purchase, tongues wrestling, hands going into bra, boxers and knickers. His shirt and her blouse were coming dangerously loose when they caught each others eyes again. Something in the spell was broken then. They stood panting and flushed, still holding each other, then both began to giggle at what they had been doing. As they took a breather and glanced around them, they began to go into hysterics.

They had set quite a trend. There were now ten or twelve of their colleagues becoming similarly entwined, all around them. The scenes! The tongues, the greedily grasping hands and fingers, the loosened elastic, the flapping fabric; the steamy, lusty impropriety of it all!

There was a good deal more hysterical laughter between them, at the absurdity of what they both believed to be 'their creation', before the fact of their recent clinch came back to them; they looked deep into each other.

Susie smiled at Jim. Jim smiled right back at Susie.

"I think we've both kinda wanted to do that for a while," she said.

"I certainly have," he admitted, "But, oh babe, I know part of me is gonna hate myself for saying this but I do have to say it..."

"Say what?"

"Ahh! Godsdammit, OK – here it is – don't you already have a fellah?"

Susie's smile went flat and her eyes went moon. "I do," she said, "Oh, God Jim, I'm sorry, I never meant to lead you on, it's just..."

She floundered, hands in the air, her hair still askew and more charming than ever, gesturing at the embryonic orgy which had broken out around them.

"Oh, I know," said Jim, "Absolutely no worries my dear! This is all completely mental and random, isn't it? I mean -" he lowered his voice "- This is not exactly your normal, everyday, office scene, is it? What the fuck's going on?!"

A bra hit Jim in the face, causing he, Susie and a few of the other revellers around them to burst out laughing again. Susie took his hands and kissed them, each one. Jim responded in kind.

"I only came here for a cuppa!" she said, which sent them both off into hysterics again.

"Me too," he gasped, wiping his eyes, "Think I'm gonna leave this lot to it."

"Good idea, me too," she said, picking up her cup.

They turned to go but Jim couldn't quite leave it there.

"You know, if that boyfriend of yours ever treats you bad or if he's ever daft enough to dump you -"

"Oh yeah!" said Susie, "If he ever messes me about then you and me's gonna finish what we started today, mister!"

Jim laughed, "I'll pray for his urgent incompetence!"

Jim took his coffee back to his desk, avoiding the four or five of his younger male colleagues who had started an impromptu bit of a footy match, up and down the office aisles. They yelled at him to join in, but he refused.

"I'm having a coffee first!" he yelled back at them, after the football bounced off his back. He grinned as he realised that he had managed to spill not a drop, then grinned some more at the memory of his recent antics. He glanced backwards in the direction of the coffee machine and saw that at least three couples were definitely at it now; Mick Denning was banging Irene up against the coffee machine; Gina was riding John Burdy, who was sitting, straining, in the eating area; and Rick and Phil were quietly hard at it in the corner.

Jim's smile became a chuckle. He felt not as elated as he knew he would have, had he banged Susie against the coffee machine, yet he did feel vindicated, proud and more; he knew beyond doubt that he had done the right thing. His karma was in perfect balance.

At his desk, Jim looked in confusion at the spread of papers in front of him. Of course! It was his current case. It felt like ages since he'd been sitting here, doing this shit. He laughed. "What? *Why*?!", he said out loud. A quick glance around the office told him for sure that no-one else was doing any work. Somehow, he gathered the presence of mind required to put all the sections of the file together, put them back in the folder and then he pushed the folder to one side. He hit 'save' three times on the electronic part of the file on his screen.

Now, he was able to relax!

As he sipped his coffee he leaned back in his chair, the better to take a more leisurely look at what was now going on around him in the office. He noted what he had seen already; the football game which was in the hearty process of making quite of a mess of the place; the orgy by the coffee machine, of which the same might be said...

He noted that a several other random couples around the place were also getting it on; on the floor, on a desk and against a wall. Some other colleagues sat staring into space, or talking excitedly to each other or on their phones - or web-surfing. There was also a group at the far end of the office who had found a frisbee and were playing it to each other in turn. The pattern of the frisbee enthusiasts' movements seemed highly likely, in terms of mathematical probability, to coincide with those of the footballers, sooner or later, but his attention then became focussed on a matter more serious. There were at least two - no, *three* - colleagues in different areas around the floor who simply sat at their desks and sobbed. As he examined the situation Jim realised that a couple of others were slumped on their desks, either to hide the sobs or because they were unconscious.

All of this was worrying, yet his own mind told him not to worry about it; this was *awesome*! The fact of the mad, liberated and just generally strange behaviour of everyone in the place was one thing, Jim reasoned, but how was it tolerated? Where were the bellowing floor managers? Where the screeching, lightening-fast, office-wide silence; spawned of the recently and spectacularly unemployed? This entire reality was askew, unless it really was a dream, a completely crazy, scarily-real, lecherous, libidinous dream, which said some very worrying things about his general state of mind. Jim tutted, shook his head, sighed, then bit himself extremely hard on his own forearm.

"Aaarref*fuck*!" he scoffed in pain and irritation, actual blood drawn and tasted. So; not a dream.

Think, he told himself; *look*. He arose from his desk, rubbing his forearm, cursing under his breath, taking the remainder of his coffee with him. He moved carefully but assuredly through the office, noting in close-up many couplings which the darker part of himself told him he should be filming on his mobile, but his greater soul made him move on, taking only a mental note (or so he thought).

It wasn't long before he noticed movement and lights coming from within the blinded windows of conference room three, just off to one side of the office. He remembered in a flash; the team managers meeting was

going on in there. Appalled and elated in equal measure, he walked quickly and quietly over to the door and peeked in, through the gaps in a badly drawn set of blinds over one of the windows. He sipped at his coffee and watched.
He realised what was going on and he had to stop himself laughing out loud - all the managers were in hysterics; some were half-dressed and it looked as though there had just been a food fight.

The thought occurred that knowledge was power and that if anyone got in trouble for the craziness sweeping the office, they might need help in the form of leverage. He took out his mobile phone and began to film the proceedings, as best he could, through the gap. His luck was in; another food fight broke out - with what food remained on their complimentary trolley. All the remaining sandwiches, sausage rolls, bajis, spring rolls, etc. - all went everywhere and the meeting collapsed once again into a joyful mini-riot.

After not many minutes of filming this, Jim went from elation to boredom. He now had plenty of leverage to spare everyone else in the office with what he now had on their managers. He chuckled, and added the video files as attachments to a draft email which was quickly saved online. Then he packed his phone away and floated off, serenely, into the heart of the office. Whatever spell it was that everyone seemed to be under today, it was OK. Karma remained constant.

Without knowing why, Jim arrived at Diane's desk. She wasn't sitting at it, she was lying upon it, smiling, eyes closed.

"Hello Jim," she said without moving.

"Whoa! How did you know it was me?!"

"The force is strong in my family."

"Seems like the force is playing around with everyone today."

"I know. Do you know what I'm doing right now?"

"Go on."

"I'm communicating with the dolphins and the whales," she said, "I've found their psychic frequency. They're magnificent, beautiful, noble creatures and I want to grow fins and a tail right now so that I can join them."

"Good for you my dear," he said, before becoming instantly determined to play her at her own game - "I was speaking telepathically to aliens from another world myself, just earlier."

"Oh were you?" she said, "What did you say to them?"

"I welcomed them to earth's orbit," he said, quickly warming to the task, "But I warned them the human race may not be ready to meet them yet. Bit more evolution required."

"Interesting thesis. But have you done the Phd required to prove it?"

"The proof's in my guts my dear. I know it to be true. And I wasn't gonna be the representative for my entire species without an absolute dedication to the absolute truth!"

"Fair enough," she said, her eyes open now, "So what happened?"

"They're gonna swing past the gas giants again," he said, loving his own inventiveness, "Especially Saturn's Rings and Jupiter, maybe do some mining in the asteroid belt and on various moons. They'll swing on back here to check us out again in a few years time."

"Imagine surfing the cloud belts of Jupiter," she said, "Imagine surfing that red spot!"

"That red spot's a gigantic tornado, it could swallow planet Earth three times over! The sheer size of it, the pressure of gravity, the freezing, poisonous gases, wow, yeah, I'm getting vertigo just thinking about surfing it. Ooh, no love. Anyway, enough about that. Tell me dolphin and whale news; what's the word from Poseidon's Realms?"

"They sang to me. It was lovely."

"No specific messages?"

"Oh yeah, they did have one! They told me I should go for a swim, actually. I'd forgotten."

"Sounds fun."

"Yeah, that's it," she said, lifting herself into a sitting position on the edge of her desk, "I'm gonna go for a swim! There's the baths just over the road, I'll be able to hear them much better from there!"

"You do know there'll be no actual dolphins at the swimming baths, right?!"

"Yes I do know that, thank you. But I know I'll be able to

hear them better when I'm in the water myself. They want me to swim and enjoy myself; it's part of the process."

"Then I want to you swim and enjoy yourself too," he said, "You go have a swim my dear!"

"Aren't you coming?"

He hadn't thought of that. He found himself caught; the scope of his gaze upon her cast quickly - yet quite clearly - down and back up again. Betrayed by his own biology before he could even think to stop it. He saw her in a bikini, himself in trunks - then remembered he had none with him.

"Ahem, I only meant for a swim, Mr Hackett," she said, grinning.

He grinned as well. "Apologies my dear, I never dreamt you meant anything other. You must go and swim, I have other plans and I must attend to them."

"You go take care of business Mr Hackett. But what business is it?!"

Jim looked around the room in agitation. The horizon he wanted was not here. Part of him knew why, knew that he just had to see the wood amidst the trees - but he could not.

He sighed.

He shrugged, turned back to Diane and was struck again when he noticed the generous rise of her breasts - and it hit him. The thing with Susie; the distraction of Diane's attributes (even though he knew she was off the market with a happy family); the growing irritation that everyone else around him seemed to be finding some great epiphany - be it joyous or morose - and yet he had found nothing to strive for; *now* he knew what the problem was.

"I have to find her." he said, simply.

"Find who?" Diane was now packing her things up to leave.

"I have to find my princess," he said.

"What?! Who's your princess then?"

"I don't know. But it's been too damn long since I had a woman, and I'm getting no younger, and I do want to find someone for keeps someday, and right now is as good a time as any, so I'm going to go and find my princess! I'm gonna find the One."

"Oh Jim! Oh, that's so romantic!"

As quickly as Intergalactic Ambassador on Behalf of Humanity had become his main and current role, so now did that of the romantic. "Really?" he said, "You don't think it's just desperation talking?!"

"Romance, Jim. That's what a woman wants. You go get her! Just don't go marrying her before I've had a look at her for you."

"Oh, I can promise you that!"

"In fact, you've not said why you're not coming with me - how do you know your princess isn't a mermaid if you've not met her yet?"

"Good point," he said, pondering what else in a bikini he might encounter, were he to go with her, "Very good point. Look, I tell you what - things round here today are a bit mental, right?"

"Agreed."

"And I don't know what's going on or why - but whether or not things are the same for other people outside this office, I don't feel too good about you going off to the baths on your own when everything's crazy like this. Why don't I walk you there and check it out - then I'll see if I fancy it or not?"

"A capital arrangement, Mr Hackett! Shall we?"

"Yes! I'll just get my stuff."

When they got downstairs and into the lobby, Jim and Diane found the security guards there leap-frogging the barriers. They were laughing and whooping and constantly setting off the alarms. The switching off of these alarms was a duty they were taking in turns. They also stopped intermittently, to flash the security cameras.

"Oh, this is freedom!" said Jim, after they had watched the guards for a minute or so; "This is total and utter *freedom*!"

"Yes it is babe," said Diane, "And we're not gonna beat 'em, you know."

Jim looked at her, the sudden, childish delight spreading as far as his face would allow - "Might as well join them!"

"*Yes!*"

They leap-frogged the barrier, laughed it up with the security guards and then for good measure - and as an act of communal triumph and solidarity - they both flashed the security cameras as well. As Jim and Diane exited the building, the guards all gathered around the desk to replay, freeze and zoom in upon their new footage. It would be several weeks later before Jim would grinningly explain to Diane why it was that the she heard the guards all yelling 'thank you' at them, as they left. Within seconds, she would offer the riposte that any one of the guards could have been gay and checking out his own offering to the proceedings. She would add that the oldest, ugliest, hairiest guard was actually a woman with an unnaturally deep voice. Jim would wish he had kept silent.

Outside, their movements became strangely furtive as they passed out of the courtyard, over the street. Other folk passed them in the street but they seemed furtive too, everyone avoiding each other. Jim said as much to Diane as they approached the baths entrance.

"Of course they are, we are, we *all* are!" she said, "Everyone's tripping this same shit! It's in the air, I can smell it, I can feel it on other people - can't you?"

"There's definitely something in the essence of today," he said, "I'm just not ready to process it all yet. Feel like I'm on a journey that hasn't even got going yet. I'm trying not to think about it too much."

"Gotta talk to my dolphins n' whales!" she said, and then she walked through the doors of the swimming baths.

As he followed her in, he felt the air change. Suddenly, totally uncertain of anything, he saw Diane approach the counter and yell out - to an apparently absentee staff - an enquiry as to what it was she had to do in order to go swimming around here. Jim looked past her, past the booth and through the giant windows behind, which let shine in the full glory of the pool, the mini-pool and diving area, with the sun again behind them through further glassy reaches on the other side of the complex.

A mass of writhing pink bodies rolled and splashed around all areas, in and out of the water. Some were screwing, some just playing but he couldn't see any swimming costumes. As he watched, gaping, Jim saw one naked couple, the gentleman wearing the lady as a frontal rucksack, attempt a leaping screw-dive from the top board. This was followed by great whooping cheers all around. When they surfaced again, quite separately and in some apparent distress, the cheers grew louder.

Jim was still standing in the doorway and he became aware of a prescience (his own or else somehow suddenly perceived from elsewhere) - a realisation that this, now, was a nexus point between the universes. Either he followed Diane into this, only his second direct experience of an orgy in his life, or he held fast and sought his princess elsewhere. He looked towards the multiply diluted sun, re-reflected on water and multiple panes of glass and it was not enough.

He ran out of the building, realising as he did so what a bright and sunny day it was outside, despite being early November. He stopped in the car park and shivered in the stark, sunlit chill. He looked directly at the sun for inspiration and begged it for an answer; would he find his princess in that flesh pool?

The sun itself shimmered and flashed around its edges, as if highly put-out at the impudence of the question. Then it held, seemed to freeze in time for a second, before another white-blue wave shimmered and shuddered across its surface, and then zapped into space. Jim knew he was the only one on earth who had seen it because it told him so as it warped to earth within a second. It hovered in the air before him; a quivering little slice of the sun, wrapped tightly into a ball of white-hot light, about the size of a football.

Jim fell to his knees before it.

It looked into him and asked him a question. He stood up. "I don't know," he said aloud. He tried to reach out and touch the ball of light, but before his hand was within a foot of it, he had to gasp and snatch it back, amazed at the intensity of the heat coming from it.

The ball of light buzzed again fiercely, hinting of the hideous mauling by fire to which it could treat him, if, by the window of his eyes, he should lie to it.

Jim rubbed his chin and looked again through the windows of the swimming baths, at the flesh pool inside. This was day one of a new era, and suddenly he was quite well aware that a naked encounter with a willing girl would be far more conducive to a rapid intimacy than randomly setting off to seek one around the town would prove to be. He smiled and nodded and his new Sun-sphere friend winked at him, in a flicker of cosmic rays, then flew towards the baths. He ran after it.

"Wondered where you'd got to," said Diane as he found her still in the lobby.

"I had to seek advice from the Sun Goddess," he said.

"Any luck?"

The hovering Sun sphere crackled a warning at him, so he spoke carefully;

"Loads actually, I think she listened!"

"Good for you. But I tell you what - I'm thinking this might not be for me you know. Think I might go home."

"Why?"

Diane had been trying to buy a costume from the vending machine, but it was apparently broken.

"You know, everyone else in there is stark-bollock naked anyway," he said, "Haven't you seen?"

"They aren't *all* naked, I've definitely seen a few with cozzies on. But anyway; I ain't going in there naked! There's too much shagging going on and that's not what I'm here for."

Jim surveyed the lobby and instantly came upon a solution. "There's no-one at reception or in the back office," he said, "They've all abandoned ship - we can sort this."

He found the wall socket and unplugged the vending machine. He then hoisted the nearest metal waste bin into the air. Diane, realising what he meant to do, yelped with laughter and covered her face. It took three attempts for him to finally break the glass, then two more to make a hole large enough for him to reach a costume-packet, without touching the sides.

He beamed as he handed her her requested costume. "There

you go my dear," he said, "Now you must go commune!"

"What're you gonna do?"

"Well, I won't be needing a cozzy, I don't think."

"Ooh! Well just don't be trying to poke me with it!"

"I'll be very careful. But don't worry; you aren't my princess!"

Diane leaned closer to him. "Seriously though, do you really think you're gonna find your princess in here?!"

"I can't answer that. I can only live in the moment and play and laugh and hope and live and let live. Anyway, the Sun Goddess showed me that I should come back in here, and since then I've been able to help you in your mission too, so I know it was the right call. Now I'm gonna go find a spot in the bloke's changing rooms for my clothes!"

She smiled at him. "You playing safe?"

"Oh yeah!"

She looked at him oddly. "Where you gonna hide it?!"

Jim clenched his right hand, pondering. Yes, that would work. "In my fist!" he said, grinning.

"Were you in the boy scouts or something?"

"Never!"

The bright and brilliant Sun sphere was still hovering, waiting for him, and was becoming increasingly irritated with the dalliance. He could tell. He turned and followed it.

The Sun sphere took him into a trance, in which he passed calmly and serenely through the dishevelled mess which was everywhere in the mens' locker room, for he was now part of the Sun sphere and it was part of him. It knew not fear, or anger, it knew only the truth; and it led him precisely where he needed to go.

In this weirdly heightened, dreamlike state, Jim wrapped shoes inside his clothes and stuffed them into locker number 12. He now wore only the locker key on a band around his ankle, and carried one condom in his hand. When he followed the Sun sphere into the main pool area, he felt over-dressed. There were many cozzies discarded at the sides of the pool, and hundreds of naked men and women were writhing and splashing and dancing and singing and screaming and laughing all around the place. Then the steamy scent of sex hit him like a speedball, alerting him and wiring him directly into the immediate potential of this glorious flowing imagery.

Still, he did not make a beeline for the first attractive and unoccupied girl he could see. The Sun sphere, following his orbit directly and ever-wired into and unto him, had other plans. Jim knew and understood nothing about these plans, other than that they were exactly the right choice, and so he followed the Sun sphere. It led him halfway round the pool, past all sorts of salacious sights within the general throng, before it stopped. He looked askance at it, but it offered no further movement. It simply hung there in mid-air; a miniature star, all his own. He realised that here - this spot - was where he was meant to be; the rest he would have to work out for himself.

He slowly turned and looked around. He had turned from twelve through five o'clock before he saw her.

She had auburn-hair and was laid out on a lilo on the side of the pool, propped up on raised elbows. She was a cute little thing, breasts like full-blossomed peaches and a lovely little tuft of sandy-coloured, candy-floss hair at the top of her long, lithe legs. He wondered what she had done to secure such a lack of male attention, when she fixed a piercing pair of blue eyes upon him and said,

"Oh yeah? There's not been one man in here all day who's got what it takes. What makes you so special?"

Jim tried to ignore the blood which was clearly rushing to his loins.

"All I can tell you, gorgeous, is that I set off on a quest earlier today. A quest to find my Princess. I don't even know who she is yet, but I've been communing with the Sun Goddess and She, She has led me to you."

This clearly gave the girl pause.

"That's slightly interesting, I suppose," she said, blue-eyes narrowing, "I've known for ages now that if I wait exactly in this spot for long enough, the right guy'll show up. So far, at least fifteen have tried and failed. What makes you the right guy?"

Jim was truly stiffening now as he contemplated her, but he hadn't a clue what to say. He began to open his hands out - to ask forgiveness for the very creep and presumption of his own flesh - but then he remembered what he held. A smile crept over his face as he showed it to her. As she saw what it was, she smiled too.

"OK," she said, "That does make you the right guy. Come here."

And Jim got down onto the floor with her and they took hold of each other. They explored and they kissed and grasped and licked. Their passion grew as they relaxed within the increasing intimacy which flowed and surged between them, as they began to melt into each other. Their frantic movements became a tide, as they harmonised and became as one.

The Sun sphere looked on and it shone more brightly than it had before.

Later, they simply lay, wrapped around each other, bathed in the afterglow. The Sun sphere shone down upon them, though only he, Jim Hackett, could see it.

"What do you think happens when we wake up?" he asked her, "Is this my dream or yours?"

"You must know we're actually awake though!?" she said, " It was a comet that passed in the night, that's what's happened. It's made everyone evolve overnight!"

"Maybe you're right," he said, "I've noticed some weird shit in the skies, certainly."

"What, like the Sun Goddess?!"

"Well, yeah."

"What's she like?"

Jim knew he had to keep the Sun sphere a secret at all costs, so he said, "I'm not sure I can describe her physically, which is a shame - although she ain't a patch on you babe! It's more like she spoke to me telepathically, she showed me an inner light and it's been leading me down the right path ever since."

"All right Yoda! You're not that righteous. You barely know me and you've already fucked my brains out."

"Well, you didn't seem to mind. In fact, I think you'd have minded more if I hadn't."

"Yeah, well, I think my boyfriend might just mind about it, a bit."

A horrifying thrill of risk ran through Jim as he realised what she had said, and he pulled away from her. Oh shit, he thought, oh why did I entrust my karma to the Sun sphere? What the fuck *is* the fucking Sun sphere?!

He controlled his breathing first. "You never said you had a boyfriend."

"You never asked."

Jim sighed and then smiled at her. "You're right. Well thanks for a wonderful time, Peaches," he said, "All the best to you and your fellah, I won't bother you again."

"It's no bother," she said, "Can probably fit you in for one afternoon a week, if you fancy some more?"

Jim stood up and blew her a kiss. He retreated with an "Au revoir, mademoiselle!", and wandered back around the edge of the pool. He ignored the Sun sphere, which nipped ahead of him and yet clung to his orbit, anticipating every turn he made. In anger and sudden revolutionary fury, he swung his fist hard at the Sun sphere, raging, careless, knowing full-well it might cost him his hand in molten flames to do it.

The Sun sphere buzzed and nimbly zipped out of the way. "Well fuck you then," he muttered, although he wanted to scream it, but he also wanted to retreat from this public shagathon without any further attention, and without throwing any more punches at what looked like thin air, to anyone else who might observe him.

Where's my good karma now? he wondered.

"Oi, dirt-bag!" a familiar voice yelled at him.

He grinned as he found Diane at the side of the pool, half in and half out.

"You do know, don't you," she told him, "That you've got a used johnny hanging off your cock, and that it's full of cum? You do know that, right?"

"Yeah. I'll get rid in the changing room. Think I'm gonna be going. Will you be OK?"

"You're going? What about you and the Princess?! I saw you, you were like a fuckin' porn-star with her! Is she not your Princess then?"

"No. I found out - *afterwards*; she's some other poor bugger's princess."

"Oh. I see, right, well, you're better off out of it then."

"No shit Miss Marple!"

Diane rumpled her lips and for the first time in he knew not how many years, Jim felt an unexpected and strange pang of shame at the pity of another. "You OK?" she asked, as if to highlight the feeling.

Suddenly, nothing was sacred to Jim and the Sun sphere was most certainly not.

"Do you know," he said, "I'm being followed everywhere by a sliver of the Sun itself that sliced off and transmitted itself here, to Earth, just earlier today? It's been directing me around, telling me what to do - but it's fucked things up!"

The Sun sphere buzzed at him and it flew into a dangerously close position, warming the hairs on the back of his neck almost to boiling point.

"Aaarghh!" he yelled, "Did you see that? Did you? It attacked me!"

Diane nodded at him. "I saw your karma take a nosedive, is all I saw," she said, "But I can't see what you're seeing."

"Didn't think so. That's why I didn't mention... Hang on; you can *see* karma?!"

"It's all about positive waves and negative ones. You're generating angry waves right now, but you've externalised the source of your anger which is why the negativity will carry on until you realise what it is that you're really angry about. You see, what you're angry about is part of your own character. Anger generates outwards, away from the source of the problem. You need to let it go and look inwards."

"OK. Maybe you're right." The Sun sphere buzzed angrily at him and he ignored it. "I'm gonna go put some clothes on."

"Don't forget to lose that johnny first! See you Jim."

"Laters my dear."

The Sun sphere followed him still. He flushed the DNA evidence, showered, dressed and left the building and still it hovered near, shining brightly upon him. Outside, the golden sunny morning had grown into a cloudy and troubled afternoon. A swift breeze blew the scent of rain down the stone streets. Jim could hear the distant noises of bad karma; people were screaming and shrieking and from all directions came the sounds of hysteria. Jim wandered towards the town centre, knowing this to be a bad idea with every step, yet completely unafraid.

As he walked serenely towards probable peril, the Sun sphere was changing as it sailed along with him upon the breeze. It grew larger, and is it grew it darkened. Before long it had swelled to the size of a beach ball and turned a fierce, seething red.

"Yeah, you don't like the sound of that, do you?" Jim grimly grinned at the enlarged, swollen, boiling orb of fire. "But you won't stop following me, will you?" He was coming into a busier section of town where many people were, so he resolved to stop speaking to it.

As he passed the various shops he realised that they were capitalist no longer; people were walking freely in and out, taking whatever they fancied. No-one was manning any of the check-outs, anywhere. Jim chuckled and wondered if he should join in, but decided against it. This was not for any particular moral reasons; he simply didn't need anything right now and didn't want to burden himself unnecessarily. He was vaguely aware that windows were being occasionally broken too, but these things happen. As he wandered through this free-for-all Jim wondered if our collective greed, once harnessed and nourished across an entire population (as only true, fervent capitalism can) might be unstoppable, under the right conditions.

There was a large, buzzing chaos ahead. It scrolled along the landscape towards him as the marching apparatus of flesh and bone beneath him bore him along, flowing, into its sphere.

The throng was an unhappy one. Such are things written, he realised, as he drew to a standstill. But what was the problem?

A whirl of screams, the commotion of many people dashing around, blue flashing lights and sirens of randomly-parked emergency vehicles. They had the look of slumbering creatures, eyes bright, awaiting orders and yet somehow scared by the disorder.

He realised the reason of the commotion when he saw what was hanging from a lamp-post.

The young man was probably a teenager. Fat, freckled and ginger. One shoelace undone. Tongue lolling out horribly to the left beneath eerie, white eyes, without pupils.

Some of the people did not dash around trying to remember the form for such occasions, hollering and fighting invisible demons. Some were on their knees praying; including one ambulance man, a fireman and two police officers.

Some of the emergency services were better at doing their jobs than others. Two firemen were working on getting their ladder to the boy to cut him down, although they hadn't yet realised that they were swinging it the wrong way and were about to skewer somebody's upstairs flat window. A couple of the police were asking questions of those who were in the vicinity and not wearing uniform, though there was a manic desperation in them as they did so.

The large red sun sphere growled at him and its lava seethed. It had swelled to the size of a small house. Jim looked at it. He took in the entirety of its new dimensions, leisurely. That was now a gigantic ball of fire he was looking at. He became afraid of this seething red orb. No point showing fear though. Act like it's your dog, he reasoned to himself, it's following you around like one. He then ignored it, and turned to let the entirety of the scene in the street wash over him.

Kid dead. Hung himself from the lamppost. Bullied? The craziness of today, combined with a sustained bullying campaign which had been ongoing since months before today, that might have done it. But then...

Smash. The window went, and the two firemen dived onto the ground for cover from this new foe which shattered glass and threw it at them. That their own ladder had done the damage would take a minute to compute.

Without even fully understanding what it was he was doing, Jim scanned the scene surrounding the hanging boy bit by bit, weeding out anyone unaffected by it. Then he weeded out - from the affected - anyone who wasn't directly involved with the live drama of the scene. Six people remained. There was himself; an elderly couple whose horror and concern he judged meant then had simply stopped to watch; and three teenage lads skulking around a corner, keeping furtive eyes on the proceedings. He couldn't hear them, but their movements said that two of them were trying to hold off the giggles, one rather better than the other.

There it was.

Jim stared at them sternly and raised his hand to point. He held the pose like a statue. After a few moments, others in the crowd had seen him and they followed his gaze at the three boys hiding, badly, around the corner.

The three boys realised. Their smiles fell into pure terror, it lit them from within. Others in the crowd began to point at them; one man's surmise quickly becoming a truth without words nor need for them, as the three boys whirled around and fled from what had suddenly and silently become a street trial.

"Get 'em!" The cry went up, and the hunt was on! Jim dropped his arm in horror. A couple of dozen or more eager citizens, police officers and firemen all sprang, valiantly, to the challenge and raced after the young men in a baying mob.

As he stood watching the raging mob flow like an inevitable river of doom after the three hapless targets, Jim noticed blood dribbling down across his vision. The terror and the guilt raced like burning ice through him and as he looked at the Sun sphere again he saw it had become yet more enormous, perhaps the size of a castle.

The gargantuan ball of blood-red fire crackled and seethed in deep, brooding waves. It was like blood washing over his eyes, the heat waves coming off it were thick and relentless. He screamed and fled the scene.

Then it was that every grim and darkening street frowned at him and rumbled ominously at the very presumption of his passage. The more he felt venomous eyes upon him, the faster he pushed himself to run and keep running, to escape this hell of harsh concrete and cold neon and the thought of what might be happening to those three boys.

The giant scarlet orb sailed through the sky behind him, in majestic serenity. Jim Hackett wasn't looking, but he knew it followed him. He could feel the warmth coming off it. That just pushed him to run harder. Streets flowed by him at alarming speed.

Echoes and shades of that flight would haunt him to the end of his days. What was that he had just done to those kids? He asked himself the question over and again.

What the fuck did I just *become*?

Darkness was falling now. Ghost streets flowed past him as he left the town, putrefying and dead. Other fugitives from the madness also scurried hither and thither, heads down, avoiding others. Jim kept his head down too, wanting it all to be over, wanting to be away from others where he could do no harm and have none done to him.

He ran on. The evidence of civilisation grew sparse as he progressed into the countryside. The giant red ball followed him; a calmly seething behemoth of red fire, gliding through the air.

At a quiet, unused spot at the side of a broken, dead house, Jim collapsed on the pavement and tucked himself into a niche, to be out of the chill breeze.

Then it was that his thoughts ran into an awful brooding.

There was worse than this madness to face, and he knew it. He always avoided thinking of it, the *worst* of things, because the signs were everywhere. He saw them many times a day, every day he lived and they scared him. So he never really thought about the very worst of things, because they were too grim to face. But now, so suddenly it seemed, he could no longer avoid facing the thoughts he always avoided.

The news said it every day, incrementally more frantic in tone, piece by piece, laying out the creeping, inevitable gathering of the Four Horsemen. The world was facing unprecedented numbers of humans, a decreasing land mass to sustain them and the end of fossil fuels to power their civilisations, not to mention ruinous climactic change. It was a horrifying, boiling kettle and it spelt out not millions but *billions* dead.

He hurled back his head and bawled at the sky. What made the human race so suicidally fucking insane? He screamed the louder as he understood that he meant that quite literally; the human race is fucking insane! The violence of his emotion hurt so good he began to sob as well.

Was it a Catch 22 situation? Does an ever-expanding population with ever-expanding needs make essentially infinite demands of what is, essentially, a *finite* planet?

War. Famine. Pestilence. Death. The brothers are coming, he told himself. They're riding inexorably towards us, and they bear with them the only possible answers.

Jim had no idea how many hours he sat in that little niche of cold concrete, losing his mind to visions of hopelessness.

***

It had become night now.

The giant red fireball, in whose hot gaze he bathed, shuddered. It told him, in a message contained within the rhythms of its heat waves, that it might spit at him, if he wasn't careful.

Jim looked at it askance. "Am I wrong?" he asked it aloud.

Then something happened to the giant red ball of fire. The seething red burned out, the outer surface of the star shuddered and evaporated off. The remaining, collapsing star became a cloudy, planetary nebula, before settling into a dull, white dwarf star, now no bigger than a golf ball.

Jim understood the basic theory of the life of a star, and what this meant to him was a life cycle which was decaying. And whilst this star had followed him all day and into darkness, he knew it to be tied to him, by both karma and the cosmos. That it's life now ran short filled him with a colder, more immediate dread than he had felt before at the vague notion of an impending apocalypse.

And so he raised himself again, weary as he was, from his cold, quiet, sheltered corner. Again he ran from the horrors, but they lived in his mind and so he made himself focus outwards.

The land warped, bubbled and frothed as it flowed crazily around him. The sky pulsed lightening shades of electric blue and strobed in alternate, night-time shades of purple, indigo and navy. The road became a river beneath him and he skimmed its surface, effortlessly.

The white dwarf star followed him still.

And yet he felt the road betrayed him. All roads lead to Rome, he reasoned as he glided along it, and Rome was an empire. All roads lead unto the heart of empire! The heart of empire was the last place he wanted to be.

He left the road behind and he climbed a mountain, though it shook in fury at his insolence and tried at many sharp points to eat him whole. He resisted its ferocity, determined as he was, and through yet more hard hours of toil, he fought his way to the summit.

A whirl pool of lights caught him up and spun him away from the mountain top at warp speed, into a quiet place, dark, but somehow warm a nd green of grass.

He lay down now on the grass, and felt more at peace. His eyes closed. His mind wandered, entranced, through various landscapes of breath-taking kaleidoscopic beauty. Infinite patterns of complex geometry danced through everything in gorgeous colours. He came upon beautiful silver shores leading to the Poetry Garden at Cosmos Dawn, wherein he dallied for a weird and wonderful lifetime, before finally, he felt himself back within his mortal skin.

Still he felt the pulsing which flowed through him and through all life. Jim was an atheist, but now he understood God was a force of nature such that its tendrils flowed through all living things on Earth. He finally understood that the dimensions we perceive are only a portion of the truth; the truth is that our Universe is just a part of the skin of something infinitely more huge and complex, which lies behind and beneath everything we know.

Realising this, he was suddenly aware, meant that all was over. He looked up to see the white dwarf star turn dark above him. This was the last stage; the Black Dwarf stage. Once the light had completely left it, the Black Dwarf was dead. It dropped from the sky to the ground. Jim leapt to catch it, but it was gone. He scrabbled at the grass where it had fallen, but there was nothing left of it to find.

He had always known it would die. Still he stared at the patch of grass upon which had landed the corpse of a star he had known for its entire life, from birth to old age and death. He knew this to be the end and was simultaneously terrified and delighted. Then it happened; he felt his heart stop. He accepted it, his head lolled back upon the grass and he knew no more.

***

When he came to, Jim Hackett found himself shivering under a bush, in a field, under a cold grey sky.

There was much retching, groaning and gasping as he sat up, rubbed his freezing limbs and raised his damp body from the ground.

He staggered a little, looking around him. The good news was that he could tell by the landscape where he was, which was a spot in the countryside only a couple of miles from home. The bad news was that the events of the preceding day were all rolling in a jumbled mess through his mind; harrowing, amazing, horrifying and stupendous as they were, they threatened insanity.

Walk. Just walk, he told himself. Whatever the fuck happened yesterday, I have to get home. Right now.

As he walked, he slowly warmed up. He then wondered what day it actually was. His watch said Friday, 6:30am. He winced at the sight. Even if he was due at work, he shouldn't have to be up until after 7am. Work? Jesus. He already knew he was going to call in sick; there was no other option. Then he remembered the footage he had recorded on his phone.

Amazingly, his phone was still in his pocket. There were many missed calls and texts. He skimmed his inboxes and all the subjects looked worrying, so he decided to read them later. He went straight to the camera file, forgetting he had saved the files online already. His face lit up as he found the two film files, containing a total of just under two minutes of joyfully riotous footage from yesterday's management meeting. Finally, something to make him feel good again! Whatever else had or hadn't happened yesterday, he was definitely taking today off.

***

7:17am. Jim staggered through his front door, locked it

firmly behind him, drew the curtains closed, and put the kettle on. But the kettle wouldn't immediately quench his nagging thirst, so he filled a mug with water from the tap and gulped it down. He then took milk from the fridge and gulped until a cold headache nearly hit him. Then more water.

He gasped, breathed deeply for some time, then the kettle boiled. He made a cup of tea and went into the lounge to check the news. He was almost afraid to watch, but when he risked a peek at BBC News 24, the first line had him hooked;

"...it's thought that the terrorists actually used... sorry; they *could* have used up to a hundred gallons of the stuff across the UK, with the result that as much as eighty percent - or possibly *more* - of the population has been affected."

Jim froze, hooked, whilst the haunted-looking news anchor continued:

"Once again, it cannot be understated; do not use water from any tap. Terrorists have poisoned most of the major water supplies of the UK with a highly-illegal, super-strength, class A drug. To avoid being affected by this, all water must be boiled before it can be drunk. Bottled drinks should also be fine, as long as they're properly sealed until use."

Jim looked at his cuppa, felt smug for a split second, then remembered his previous thirst – and he retched. The overwhelming horror of his immediate situation was thankfully doing the required job for him – but rather too well. He leapt up and made for the kitchen sink as best he could. Cornering from one room to the next was too much – it came hurtling back up his throat and he clamped his mouth shut firmly as his cheeks filled and he grunted, aghast, nostrils frothing, and raced for the metal bowl.

He just made it.

After much purging, Jim was dribbling, howling, crying, spitting and cursing. He knew it wasn't enough. He couldn't do a day like yesterday again, and he knew that even if he got all the tainted water out of his stomach, some of it had already been absorbed and could do him a serious cerebral disservice. He scowled as he understood the inevitability of what he now had to do, then did it; he took two fingers and made sure that his stomach truly was as empty as possible.

Feeling utterly dejected, Jim perked up a little when he realised his tea was still hot, and more importantly; safe. He settled back onto the couch again, sipping occasionally.

He watched the news for a while, and it answered many of his questions about yesterday's insanity. He was able to glean the following facts:

- He, and most other people in the UK, had been affected by an exceptionally strong new drug which can make people dangerously and unpredictably high in extremely small doses.
- As it's full, scientific name contained a ridiculous 47 syllables, the drug had been nick-named 'Thursday in the Sky'. This was in reference to both the day it had struck, and to an old Beatles song (which was officially not about LSD, but unofficially; pull the fucking other one). This nickname was naturally and immediately coarsened to 'TITS' by some.
- The drug's effects were a drastic combination; similar to those of LSD, magic mushrooms, MDMA and viagra, all rolled into one.
- Infidelity had allegedly sky-rocketed, all across the

UK.
- Many gallons of this drug had apparently been dropped into most main water supplies by a new terrorist group named 'Brutal Truth', claiming to be formed of an unholy alliance between extremist offshoots of both Isis and the Hacktivist Alliance.
- There were massive amounts of damage, countrywide; to the people – both physically and mentally, and to roads, railways, airports, buildings, property and infrastructure.
- The UK was now facing a huge clean-up operation and billions of pounds worth of damage, not to mention the potentially gigantic cost to the population's mental-health.
- 'Brutal Truth' had put out a video explaining their actions but the Beeb were not allowed to show it.
- Jim made a mental note to watch this video on the net later, to find out what the hell 'Brutal Truth' actually thought they were doing; their name being quite at odds with the crazy dream world into which they had apparently transported the majority of the UK population.
- Besides not drinking tap water, no-one should bathe in it either – Thursday in the Sky is absorbed through the skin as well as by mouth.
- All waterways in the country were being purged of the drug, but this operation was ongoing, and all viewers should regularly check the news and not use unboiled water until further notice.
- Anyone suspecting they were affected by the drug - but otherwise fit and well - should remain calm and stay indoors; hospitals were overwhelmed and unable to cope with all the afflicted and injured.
- All armed forces had been mobilised, along with the Fire, Police and Ambulance services.
- To sum up, Thursday in the Sky had been an

epidemic of destructive madness, sweeping the
country like a tornado.

Jim switched the news off, his head still reeling. Absorbed
through the skin? He thought of the swimming pool, and
the sweetness of the peaches he'd enjoyed on its shore. The
thought was tempered by the memory of his shower
afterwards; how much of the drug had he absorbed then?
He had a flashback of scenery warping and bubbling around
him as he sped through it.

Enough was enough. He went back into the kitchen, filled
the kettle and switched it on. He needed to build up a clean
supply.

As it had turned out, he had escaped Thursday in the Sky
quite lightly; he was all in one piece and his home was
undamaged. Despite his earlier urge to hide away in his
house until he felt fully recovered, he realised that he and
most other people had been victims of the same crime; he
now understood he had nothing to feel ashamed about.

He thought he'd better check his phone and do some
replying and reassuring to folk – not to mention he needed
to check that everyone he knew was OK.

He brought up his inbox and noticed something he hadn't
earlier; the first text was from Susie. His eyes widened as he
remembered what had happened with her yesterday, and he
opened it:

"U might just b in luck
Mr! Caught the boyf
cheating on me. He can
blame TITS all he

wants – last straw – he's
gone. Call me!
;-)"

Jim laughed out loud in pure delight. He thought of the strange terrorists' and their weird new attack method, and this further, wonderfully unlikely consequence of their actions, and he laughed again.

"Ahh!" he said aloud to no-one, giggling, wiping his eyes, "Thanks guys!"

© H. R. Brown, 16/11/2013

The Flag, The Femme & The Fiery Apocalypse

It was May 2015, on a warm evening. The golden evening sun trickled through the trees onto the verandas of the renowned California establishment where the legendary 1–4 Club were gathered, when –

"America is the greatest nation on earth sir, and I shall prove it to you!", yelled Bullroarer Jim, rising to his feet in anger at the presumption of the Frenchman, Nonchalant Jacques.

Seated all about the large verandas, the other club members fell quiet and watched with a gathering glee. Such altercations were rare at the 1-4 Club, as it was the most exclusive on planet earth; a.k.a. the Supreme Global Masonic Lodge for Gentlemen Billionaires.

"Prove it how?" asked Nonchalant Jacques, singularly unimpressed by Bullroarer Jim, as he knew Jim would be instantly removed from the club for the evening, if he actually started a fight.

Bullroarer glared down at the still-seated Jacques, his legs upon another chair. "I will prove to you sir, that America is the greatest country in the world, because we have the best system of government in the world. And we have the best system of government sir, because it has three separate branches, count them; *three*! All act as checks and balances against the others, to deliver the best outcome for all."

"This is not proof," sighed Jacques immediately, "To begin with, suppose you are correct to say the best way to judge which nation is the greatest on our planet, is by determining which nation has the best *system* of government, many might disagree with this to begin with. But assuming you are correct; you supply me only with details of which I am already aware; no actual proof of your governmental system's... infallibility."

"And what would you call proof?" said Bullroarer.

"What would be the biggest test your government could take, and survive?" said Jacques, "This is where it becomes interesting!"

"Now wait just a god-damn minute, I won't allow -"

"Hush, hush!" Jacques waived him down, "I meant no form of attack or warfare, I understand the rules of the club as well as you do. I was merely going to suggest you get someone elected to an important position, like that of a Senator, for example, who is of unsound mind. A madman! Or as demonstrably mad as you feel you can get away with. If your system of government cannot then find a lawful way to contain and dismiss him from this position, within say, a year, then I win. If he, she, he-she or she-he is not dismissed within a year, then I say your governmental system, she cannot be the best."

"One year!" said Bullroarer, "No sweat, not even an issue!"

On seeing Jacques' raised eyebrow, Bullroarer again found himself nashing his teeth at the Frenchman's insolence. So he said -

"And never mind a Senator; I say we could put a madman in the fucking Whitehouse and he'd be gone within a year too!"

Jacques feigned surprise at what his goading had brought to the table.

"You go from the proposed expulsion of a mad Senator," he said, "Straight to the proposed impeachment of a mad President! I respect and admire your death-or-glory style, mon ami! But, what are to be the terms of the bet?"

"If I win," said Bullroarer, "You get a tattoo of the USA flag on your right shoulder, six inches by four!"

"I'll accept four inches by three," Jacques countered, "I have thin arms. And if *I* win..."

"Yes?"

"I want either your 1957 Ferrari 250 Testa Rossa, or that sweet little latina mistress of yours, what is her name now...?"

"Elena," said Bullroarer, "And if you win you can have her. You'll find - if you manage to keep *her* for a year - she'll cost you more than the car!"

Jacques was grinning again. "You are speaking to a Frenchman, mon ami!" He held out his hand to Bullroarer -

"Hold," called out Kaiser José . All eyes turned to him. Kaiser José was one of the grandees of the club.

I should here note; the grandees are The Council of the 1-4 Club, of whom there are only ever twelve; decided by democratic vote of all members, and to be unelected only by "death or doubly-doubly-diagnosed, serious mental illness" (This stipulation was as noted in the 1-4 Club Constitution; the alliteration was believed to be the work of Taff Gareth, an original member of the club who had made his money in the Welsh coal mines and fancied himself a poet. Of his poetical works, sadly, not a shred survives, yet his meaning in the passage above has almost unanimously been accepted as meaning that four separate diagnoses must be in agreement before a grandee may be expelled).

The 1-4 Club had existed since the twilight years of the Victorian era. It was named for the mathematical idea behind its creation; a club for the cream of the cream. It was not for those people who are 1 in 100 (the one percent), not for those who are 1 in 10,000 – it was for those who are 1 in 100 million (i.e. [1 in 100] raised to the fourth power). For the first fifty years, the 1-4 Club had in fact been known as the 1-3 Club; for those who were 1 in a million, but the population explosion of the twentieth century had changed matters.

"Now gentlemen," intoned Kaiser José, "Whilst house rules have always been 'sky's the limit', are we truly prepared to install a lunatic into the position of the most powerful man on earth? Do we all understand the potential this scheme has, of destroying our own species, and all of us included? The President of the United States is elected for *four years*. Checks and balances notwithstanding, and putting aside the virtually impossible task of convincing the American people to vote for such a man, do we really want to take the risk?"

Jacques shrugged. "A bet is a bet, although we have not yet shaken hands on it... I do enjoy the thrill of risk – even if that risk becomes the survival of our race. I will take the bet, if Bullroarer Jim is still willing. Although I say again Jim, are you sure you would not prefer to bet on a mad Senator being expelled, than a mad President being impeached?"

Bullroarer looked hard at Jacques. "You aren't ever allowed to cover over this tattoo with another one, or have it removed, agreed?"

Jacques nodded, "Absolutely! And if I win.."

"I'll ditch Elena in public, within 24 hours," said Bullroarer, "Say, in a restaurant. I'll walk out straight away. You'll be in the restaurant too, to reach out, help her, give her a shoulder to cry on; you can take it from there, yeah?"

Jacques nodded, smiling, reached out his hand -

"Hold!" said Kaiser José again, "I rule this must be voted on by all present. More than three quarters of the 1-4 Club are here tonight, so a two thirds margin is required. Are my fellow council members in agreement?"

The were nine other council members present, eight of whom agreed.

"Then it is decided! To allow Bullroarer Jim and Nonchalant Jacques the right to place a bet which may end up causing World War III, we must to the lines gentlemen, to the lines!"

The voting lines were at the end of the glorious verandas, at the edge of the grassy fields beyond. These were simply two, parallel, straight lines, three metres apart, marked upon the field and each one a hundred metres long. Each line was clearly marked once every metre, and the ascending number set in one hundred plaques, set in the earth between the two lines.

When a bet was taken, the two opposing blocks of votes simply assembled on each line, one by one, without any spaces, so votes could instantly be taken and numbers verified by all concerned. Each opposing side would soon call out anyone attempting to cheat, for it would necessarily be done in plain sight. The grandees always cast their votes last, once they were satisfied everyone else was in place and all was fair and above board.

The current membership of the 1-4 Club was only 178 members; it had never exceeded 189, but if ever it did, the lines would simply be extended.

Tonight 135 members of the 1-4 Club were present. Once all had reached the field, Kaiser José pointed to the first line and called out, "This side to allow the bet, and the possible destruction of civilisation."

He pointed at the other line; "This side to deny the bet, on the grounds that it might cause the destruction of civilisation."

The voting took place quickly, and no-one cheated; there was never any point trying to cheat - unless one only wanted to waste everyone's time. No-one with the kind of financial portfolio required to gain access to the 1-4 Club was in any doubt as to the monetary value, per hour, of his time; it was never worth wasting.

Once the grandees had also taken their places on the lines, the vote was 94 in favour of allowing the bet, 33 against and

8 abstentions. The bet was allowed!

Bullroarer Jim and Nonchalant Jacques looked at each other.

"Are we doing this?" asked Jacque.

Bullroarer offered his hand. "A madman in the Whitehouse, if we can get him there, who'll be impeached by the checks and balances within a year, and you get a four-by-three inch American flag on your upper right arm – which you can never tattoo over or remove," Bullroarer said, holding out his hand.

"A madman in the Whitehouse," said Jacques, "And if he is not impeached within a year, I get Elena! Or, possibly, the whole world gets nuked."

He reached out his hand and grasped that of Bullroarer Jim.

Jim grinned at him. "You wouldn't call that something of a Pyrrhic victory?"

"Indeed. The biggest pyrrhic victory in human history!"

Bullroarer's jaw tightened. "There's no way that's gonna happen. No way."

"Well folks," cried Texas Joe, "Guess we gonna us have some serious betting on this one! Roll up roll up, I'm taking names and numbers, usual rules apply!"

At this point, the British entrepreneur Limey Dick, Russian capitalist Impaler Vlad and various others of equally outstanding character began sidling over towards Texas Joe, when -

"Hold again!"

This time it was Governor Yan; "Before betting may commence," he said, surely we should decide which madman it is, whom we seek to install as the President?"

There were a great many rumblings in the affirmative to this idea.

Attention turned again to Bullroarer and Jacques for their opinion.

"Tell you what," said Bullroarer, "Why don't you pick a madman for us Jacques? Know any American madmen with a shot at being President?!"

Jacques grinned again. "I know who," he said, "And I know how!"

"Who?" someone shouted.

"Why," said Jacques, "Little Dickface, of course."

Many of the faces in the incredible crowd fell. Others were wiser and either sighed or grinned, sadly, to themselves.

But not the Bullroarer. He was old-school; introduced and sworn into the 1-4 Club by Gandalf Greene himself, the last British grandee to grace the membership of The Council, who sadly had not survived into this millennium. And there was just *no way* -

"NO!" he roared, "Not him! Any other pigfucker on the

planet but *him*!"

The large majority of the others in the party were clearly also very unhappy at the idea of Little Dickface, the overgrown Oompa Loompa, becoming the world's most powerful man.

"Jesus H Christ, Jim!" said Texas Joe, laughing, "You walked right into that one!"

Little Dickface was the nickname given to the one person on earth who had tried and failed to get into the 1-4 Club more often than anyone in the club's 127-year history. He was rich enough, probably, as his repeated attempts to enter the club had by now cost him the better part of one billion dollars. However, his multiple other failings meant he never received enough votes from other members to be confirmed. One of the chief amongst those concerns was over his sanity; as he had serious and demonstrable issues with his basic understanding – and even his acceptance – of reality.

"Little Dickface will do it if we offer him membership," said Jacques, and at the looks of horror he received, he said, "But we can defer the membership; make it dependent on his surviving a year in the job."

"Screw that," said Bullroarer, "We make it dependent on him getting through a full four-year term – and not before!"

Among those present, there was a virtually unanimous agreement to this stipulation.

Little Dickface was generally thought of as simply too vulgar, in a variety of ways, to be allowed into the 1-4 Club. Vulgarity aside, he also had another major problem.

Everyone in the 1-4 Club had either inherited their wealth or made it, or made it via a combination of inheritance and good business skills. And they all knew Little Dickface would currently be worth much more than he was, had he simply invested all his inheritance rather than ploughing it into his well-publicised, multiple bankruptcies and failed businesses. Sure he'd been lucky in surviving these many failures and yet hanging on to much of his money, but too many of the 1-4 Club saw him as damaged goods they'd rather avoid; because it was always someone else hung out to dry when Little Dickface's latest venture went tits-up. And as for his execrable reality TV show, *well*. His cards had always been marked at the 1-4 Club.

Until now.

When it came to setting the whole thing up, it had to be either Jacques or Bullroarer who made the call; it was their party.

Bullroarer immediately called shotgun by pointing out Jacques was responsible for the choice of Little Dickface, therefore Jacques was making the call.

Almost inevitably, once again, Jacques had the aces up his sleeve. He successfully argued that whilst the choice of Little Dickface was his, it was Bullroarer who had raised the whole game to the next level when he went for President instead of Senator. He also pointed out that Little Dickface would be far more likely to respond positively to the idea coming from an American, than from a Frenchman.

The logic of this convinced the crowd, which led Bullroarer to openly consider defaulting and gifting Elena to Jacques. Jacques was also briefly of two minds on the subject, before he remembered the thrill of a potential World War III held more excitement for him than any sexual encounter ever would again.

"As I understand, the bet is made," Jacques said, "The terms agreed by those present. It would be a severe blow to the pride of your great country, were you to give up now! Not to mention, as I am given to understand, a great blow for me!"

Bullroarer was sobering up now, and nearly spitting with anger. And everyone other than him agreed it was clearly his call to make.

"Fine," he growled, wishing he'd just ignored the Frenchman in the first place. He held his phone aloft.

"Permission to switch on my phone for the business of the house as discussed?"

"Granted!" they all cheered.

The call was made.

Bullroarer reached Little Dickface and made his case; he feathered it very well but the basics were; you run for President, make it to the Whitehouse and then last for at least one term in office – and *then*, you finally get in the 1-4 Club.

"Yes," they heard Bullroarer say, "You heard me. Yes." Then, "I think we can agree to that. OK. We'll be in touch."

He hung up the phone, and switched it off. He held it aloft again to indicate this. The rules on active phones were very simple and for obvious reasons.

"Well?" someone asked.

Bullroarer had the look of a man who has just had to swallow some very unsavoury medicine. He picked up his glass and washed it down with a huge draft of finest whisky.

"He says he'll do it," he told the crowd, "And he says he's got a sense of humour; he'll go with 'Dickface Don', or 'Don Dickface', but we have to drop the 'little'."

There was a general cheer at this point; glasses clinked and Texas "Honest" Joe's book quickly did excellent business.

Nonchalant Jacques' grin was ear to ear, "Of course I will stop calling him Little Dickface, if he ever gets here," he purred, "Mon petite cherie! On the other hand, how will he ever *make* me?"

As most of the group retreated back towards the verandas and the source of their various booze and other evening paraphernalia, some were still haggling and discussing various betting aspects of the new future they had set upon, with that unapologetic capitaliser of every conceivable moment; Texas Joe.

Bullroarer grinned at Jacques. "You realise everyone in this club is gonna try to stack the deck on this, right?"

Still, Jacques grinned. "This is why mon petite cherie the Little Dickface, he will win. This is why I will win. Although we all may die!"

"Bullshit!" said Bullroarer, "You are gonna be wearing the USA flag on your skin for the rest of your life!"

Jacques tutted. "Perhaps, mon ami, it is not impossible. Perhaps. Yet perhaps also, you did not thoroughly confirm the terms of our arrangement to your satisfaction. Perhaps, for example, while it is true I may have to bear a tattoo of the USA flag upon my Frenchman's skin until that glorious day I finally surrender my all and my everything unto the Universe, perhaps you did not insist on any detail at all for the bare, unadulterated skin which will surround your 'Old Glory'. Perhaps, for example, the flag, she becomes the centre of a bandana, wrapped around the forehead of your great Statue of Liberty. Perhaps Liberty one day occupies my whole upper arm, perhaps Liberty has dropped her tablet – and perhaps her robes have also dropped to the floor, revealing her delicious body."

Bullroarer's very blood was becoming angry again - "You cheese-eating, surrender-monkey, sonofa -"

Still Jacques grinned at his straight-as-a-die, rightwing, christian, republican, American friend and said, "Maybe the hand which has dropped her tablet, strays southwards in her life of wanton freedom upon my non-judgemental French flesh, maybe her fingers slide into places which -

"YOU SHUT YOUR FUCKING MOUTH!" screamed Bullroarer, utterly livid at the idea of Lady Liberty, in a stars and stripes bandana and nothing else, joyfully masturbating upon the arm of the Frenchman. The grandees in the vicinity looked up at this commotion. They nodded at each other; within twenty seconds Bullroarer Jim would be ejected from the 1-4 Club for the remainder of the night.

As Bullroarer was screaming and being borne from the place by four big bouncers, strapped to a bench (as was the tradition), Impaler Vlad made his way towards Jacques, having secured a bet in Texas Joe's book.

Impaler Vlad – possibly the richest of them all, though he would never admit it – had realised he already had a scheme in hand which might aid Jacques' cause.

Impaler Vlad gave Jacques a small smile of huge import. "I may have information which you would greatly appreciate, where Little Dickface is concerned," he said.

Jacques said nothing, he simply smiled, cupped his ear, turned it to Vlad, and prepared to listen.

Bullroarer Jim had been hoisted from the club, still screaming obscenities at Nonchalant Jacques, who, on the other hand, was having one of the best nights of his life.

for Barbara, 24/03/1945 – 28/02/2014

© H. R. Brown, 28/02/2017

Author's note: The above story is absolutely, definitely, 100% pure, FAKE NEWS.

ZERO

Dr Ben Wenders was the genius. The one who had civilised robotics and AI, by perfecting the translation of Asimov's Three Laws of Robotics into a basic, unbreakable code, which would rule all robots.

For ten years after the first of his robots had swung down off the production line, his life had been exquisite, and he had basked in the glorious benefits of his exulted position and the radiant glow of respect it afforded him.

Should he have known this couldn't last? Does anyone living such a life ever suspect it can end? His robots had serviced humanity for ten years; with his robots leading the charge his company, Metal Mothers Inc, had conquered the globe within two.

Wenders was no fool and was active in working with his top staff on those rare malfunctions which did occur. These had never caused injury or threatened any human lives and as such, could be dismissed as inconsequential, still he involved himself with their solutions whenever they happened. His ultimate ambition was to one day develop the perfect robot. This he knew to be unachievable, yet he wanted his company to maintain their world domination and knew this would only be achieved within the ongoing struggle for perfection.

Robots had serviced humans successfully for ten years all across the globe, without any major incidents or injuries.

Indeed, there were multiple incidences of robots saving human lives – sometimes at the cost of their own.

When one of this years' latest batch of robots had a malfunction, late at night, that malfunction wouldn't usually have penetrated Wenders' personal world any closer than the inbox of an underling at least three layers of personnel below him - had it been an average malfunction.

The problem which came in on his hotline, and resulted in him stumbling out of bed at 3:16am, that fateful February morning, was decidedly *not* average.

Since the end of the bloody Battlebot Wars (after which the outcry for justice, peace and an end to the killings had been overwhelming), killer drones had been banned and mostly all destroyed.

No robot had killed a human in over ten years. Dr Ben Wenders was woken by a call at 2:15am that day because a new robot had done just that.

Gasping, horrified, sick to his stomach in a way he'd not felt in a very long time, Wenders kissed his wife goodbye, apologised for the third time for having woken her and left the bedroom.

Christabelle did not accept his apology. After all, what matter their money and position if her husband could still be summoned from his bed, at this ungodly hour, like some kind of junior doctor?

The killer robot had been part of a new police task-force, which was itself the result of a new governmental directive. Robots routinely aided the police as they were useful in multiple tasks, not least in taking fire and protecting their human counterparts in dangerous work.

Robotics within policing was nothing new. A robot plunging its arm down a human throat, however, and sucking out half of that humans lungs, via his windpipe; this was new territory indeed.

Wenders felt ill, but he went online and spoke face-to-face with Chief Inspector Diamond, the steely-eyed officer in charge of the case.

"Has the robot in question been shut down?" was Wenders' first question.

"Yes of course," Diamond replied, "My officers on the raid shut it down almost immediately."

"Almost?"

"Well as you well know, there are safety protocols and protections in place to prevent service robots being immediately shut down. Once the robot had engaged the suspect and it became clear there was a serious problem, my officers went straight for the kill switch, but it wasn't possible to complete the operation before.. The suspect suffered irreparable damage."

"Uhhh," Wenders groaned, still not one hundred percent sure he as awake. He bit down hard on his hand and was rewarded with a horrifying sense of the very *very* real. He shuddered, tried not to show his discomfort.

"The other robots from the same batch," was Wenders next concern, "Are any of them active?"

"No," Diamond assured him, "I always like to send just one out with my guys when a new batch gets here. Call me old-fashioned, but if there's ever a problem with a new model or whatever, I don't need that problem duplicating."

Wenders was very thankful for this. The thought of just one of his robots, built for industrial purposes with a minimum five-year guarantee, grasping the soft flesh of a human being, and then applying any of its many inbuilt power tools to that human... He shuddered. Then he thought of the headlines, the financial ruin, of being – suddenly and completely – a social pariah. Of potential jail time.. That feeling in the pit of his stomach was something he'd not felt in a long time, as were the cold sweats.

Wenders also checked the date to confirm it was not the first of April, another thing he'd not had to do in years.

"Perhaps it would be best if you could come to the station in person," Diamond said, "Obviously we need to get to the bottom of this ASAP, and you're best placed to examine the robot and find out what went wrong. Please feel free to bring any personnel and equipment you might need."

"Yeah," said Wenders, "Thank you Chief Inspector, I'll be there within the hour."

***

Wenders woke up his PA, Felicity, and brought her with him to the police station. CI Diamond greeted them and took them to see the robot that had done the deed.

"Well," said Wenders, "We'll need to bring him back online

to find out what we need to know, but we can do it in safe mode."

Safe mode meant the robot would not have the use of its body below the neck. All other functions would be operational.

The robot's facial display flickered into life, displayed the Metal Mothers Inc logo and its voice said smoothly, "Greetings from Metal Mothers. How may I be of assistance?"

Wenders, operating the robot via a connected keyboard, ignored its voice and brought up the robot's POV footage on a large screen. The screen showed its view of them and the room they were in.

"What time did the raid start?" he asked Diamond.

"1:40am."

Wenders keyed in the time frame and saw the image on the screen shift to that of several hours earlier. The view showed a group of police officers in heavy riot gear, preparing to swarm through someone's front door. The robot accepted the manual battering ram from Officer Suttler and proceeded to smash the door in. It moved quickly into the flat and entered a living room where five young adults were looking round in alarm.

The robot had already assessed there was no firearms threat in the room and indicated this to the officers behind him, who piled into the room.

The youngsters all looked wide-eyed, stunned, and they all

raised their arms in surrender. All except one, who, having realised the hand he'd raised still clutched a lit spliff, decided to start dragging on it, quickly, as he'd just realised he wouldn't be getting any more weed for quite some time.

Wenders didn't have time to ponder how bad an idea that was – neither did the other officers in the room – as the robot barged forwards, seized the spliff with one powerful metal hand (crushing it and rendering it useless) whilst the other seized the young man by his throat and raised him up in the air. The robot then plunged his vacuum device down the young man's throat and set it going on full power.

The result was a bloody mess; with screaming all throughout the room (from all the other students and a couple of the police officers), a violent struggle between the police officers and the robot, and a dying student, convulsing on the floor as his life left him.

The officers were able to shut the robot down, although it resisted their efforts.

Wenders ceased the playback.

"Jesus wept", he said, "It's every bit as bad as I was told. Right, from now on, this robot, this murderer, needs to be set apart from all other robots. All others are innocent and harmless, as far as we know. This one.. Let's call it Robot Zero. My robots have had a virtually perfect record for ten years, until.. Zero hour. Yeah, this is Robot Zero."

"Fine with me," said Diamond.

"To be honest, this is actually worse than I was told," Wenders continued, "Robot Zero resisted being deactivated whilst there might still have been time to save the kid. Did any of your officers get injured?"

"Nothing serious," said Diamond.

"You're fucking kidding me," Wenders exclaimed, "He actually fought against – and *injured – police officers*, in order to keep on destroying that kid?! This isn't possible, not one of my robots, not even.."

"Well," said Diamond, "I believe you have everything you need here to investigate, use the intercom if you need anything – or when you find anything."

Diamond went to leave the room, but Wenders stopped her. "You say there were twenty-three other new robots in the batch with Robot Zero – and none of them are active?"

"Yes. I only activate the batch when a random one has proved itself safe."

"That's no longer a regulation, is it?"

Diamond raised an eyebrow. "No."

"Then why, when robots have been.." he trailed off, as the confident robot salesman routine within him caught up with his new reality.

"Safe for ten years?!" said Diamond, "You're right. It's an outdated rule which I maintain in my station, purely because I've never met an AI that I could truly mistake for human - and that bothers me. Call me prejudiced if you like, others have, but before you even know what the problem is, I'd say you should probably be glad of my methods, given the events of tonight."

Wenders guts were bothering him again.

"Fair enough," he said, "You're absolutely right. But tell me, when is this going to be reported?"

Diamond shrugged. "My officers all know the data protection laws," she said, "No-one here will leak anything. But the other kids are going to make bail soon. There's only so long we can leave them locked up and cooling down before lawyers are going to get involved.. It's a matter of time, and the way these things go – well, I doubt you have much time."

Wenders found himself at his wits end and almost yelled at her, but held back. None of this was her doing. He simply nodded at her, and Diamond left the room.

Wenders knew he had to delve deeply into Robot Zero's mainframe, and quickly. He asked Felicity to get him some coffee, he brought the coding of the mainframe into view on the big screen, and got to it.

***

The "Three Laws of Robotics", as stated by the late, great, sci-fi writer, Isaac Asimov, and later repeated to the robot-buying public by Metal Mothers Inc, are as follows:

1. A robot may not injure a human being or, through inaction, allow a human being to come to harm.

2. A robot must obey the orders given it by

human beings except where such orders would conflict with the First Law.

3. A robot must protect its own existence as long as such protection does not conflict with the First or Second Law.

It hadn't taken Wenders long to realise that Robot Zero had not obeyed the three laws because he was unaware of them. Robot Zero was programmed with rules, but not those of Asimov, nor Metal Mothers Ltd. In fact, Wenders discovered, after he physically opened Robot Zero's panels and looked inside - the AI core which controlled the robot and all its actions had been entirely replaced with another, of unknown origin.

Incensed by this outrageous fact, he felt a whole lot better about his company and his robots – the death was not his fault! Someone had removed the Metal Mothers AI core and replaced it completely.

Wenders focussed intently on the offending new AI core and found out several things. The rules the robot was programmed with were the actual laws of the land – but only some of those laws. The coding used was also very elegant, in many ways brilliant, but the limits of a robot's behaviour as a result of these new laws was difficult to assess. To do a proper job he'd need to spend a lot of time working out what all the rules were, and in what hierarchy they operated, before then attempting to assess the limits.

Wenders skipped that part and looked at exactly what rules the robot was obeying during the raid, at which moments. This was a rich, if sickening, experience.

Having learned enough in that field, he went on to examine who or what was responsible for the new AI core Robot Zero had been operating. The nature of what little he'd learned of the new operating system so far was extremely worrying, not least its sophistication and its opaque nature. The company which had produced it was unfathomable to him, yet clearly only a company highly technical in nature, and rivalling his own, could have produced it.

He gave up trying to find clues as to the origin of the new AI core from the core itself; obviously it had been designed to be untraceable.

However, the installation date of the new AI core was prior to last night's raid by a week, but three days after the robot had been delivered to the police station by his company – along with twenty-three others. Someone within the police had done the deed, or knew who had.

He buzzed CI Diamond. "I think I know what the problem is," he said, "But I need to check a few more things. For starters, may I please examine the other robots from Robot Zero's batch?"

Diamond had no problem with this and so Wenders and Felicity were shown to the back of the garage area, where twenty-three other robots, identical in appearance to Robot Zero, stood silently inactive.

Wenders and Felicity examined three of the robots each, at random, and confirmed; they too had had their Metal Mothers AI core removed and replaced with the same, unusual and sophisticated new cores as had Robot Zero.

Wenders called Diamond again. "So, I know what we're

dealing with – now I need your help to understand how it happened."

"What can I do to help Dr Wenders?"

Two minutes later, in the Chief Inspector's office, Wenders explained to her Robot Zero's problem. He also confirmed the same problem existed within another six robots he and Felicity had chosen for checking at random from the new batch – they had all had their original AI cores removed and replaced with new models, which were definitely not supplied by Metal Mothers. He made it plain the switches had all occurred *after* the robots had arrived in CI Diamond's police station.

He was very glad to find CI Diamond as outraged as he was. In fact, the suggestion that rogue, unverified, new AI cores had been inserted into an entire batch of twenty-four, shiny, brand-spanking-new robots, brought out a calm, quiet, determined rage in her. Wenders felt a chill at the very slight curling of Diamond's lip, as she understood the implications of what he was telling her.

CI Diamond said nothing to him but went straight onto her phone. She waited.. then she said,

"Good morning Hollis.. Yes it is.. It's nearly 5:30am.. I'm calling you because I need you here immediately.. No it absolutely cannot wait.. ASAP Hollis – get here ASAP. Good."

She looked at Wenders. "My head technician will be here soon," she said, "Then we can get some answers."

***

Before another half an hour had passed, CI Diamond was standing with Wenders and his assistant in the garages under the station, speaking to the Hollis, the head techie.

Wenders asked Hollis if anything had been done to the robots between their arrival and Robot Zero's activation the previous evening.

"Yes," said the techie, bored, "We followed the new procedures we were told to use with the new robots."

"What new procedures?" Wenders asked, "The robots go out ready to be switched on – there are no new procedures required!"

"That's not what we were told," Hollis yawned.

CI Diamond, nursing her simmering anger as this went on, had had enough. She used her phone to access the internal systems of the station, and she stepped forward.

"Here", she said, holding her phone out to the techie, "Watch this."

She showed the raid footage, up to the point where Robot Zero had his vacuum device firmly down the young man's throat, on full power, and the image of his wild, terrified eyes was blocked by the splashing of his blood into Robot Zero's eye cameras.

After Hollis had finished vomiting, Diamond smiled.

"I am sorry about that Hollis," she said, breezily, "I appreciate that footage is outside your area of expertise – but the reason the footage even exists is very much *your area*."

"Sure," the techie gasped, "What do you need to know?"

"What was done to the new robots when they came in?" Wenders asked.

"New procedure, here," said Hollis, passing him a leaflet showing the basics of removing and replacing a robot's AI core, "We got the new robots in, gave them the usual checks and they were good to go. Two days later this bloke comes in from Metal Mothers, he gives us a presentation about how the new robots were supplied with last year's AI cores by mistake, here's the new models and here's how to replace the old AI cores with the new ones."

"So all twenty-four robots had their AI cores replaced?" said Diamond.

"Exactly, yeah."

"This is bullshit," said Wenders, "We've sent no-one to do any AI core replacements. Ever, I think."

Diamond frowned. "When exactly were these new AI cores installed?" she asked.

"The sixth," both Hollis and Wenders said together.

Diamond looked through her phone schedule. Her eyes rolled when she found what she needed.

"The sixth of this month," she said, "Was when I had a visit from a government operative. He had full clearance from on high, so I was obliged to give him full access to the station.

He also told me not to tell anyone about him visiting, said it was a routine inspection.. So taking his photo surreptitiously was probably also against the rules, but what the hell."

She showed Hollis a picture on her phone.

"That's the guy," said Hollis, "No doubt."

"So a government operative got full access to your station," said Wenders, "Then went to the robotics department, introduced himself as an employee of my company – and had twenty-four new AI cores replaced with these new totalitarian ones."

"I wondered what that slimy bastard was up to," Diamond said to herself, "But he had clearance. The kind of *shit* that gets clearance these days is just.."

Diamond stopped and scowled. Then Hollis looked as though she might say something so Diamond ground her jaw and quickly opened it again -

"OK," she said, "I want you to undo that job. Take out all the new AI cores and replace them with the old ones."

"I'm afraid I can't," said Hollis, "The government bloke took the old cores when he left, said they were scrap."

Diamond ground her jaws again. "Alright," she said, "Just do half a job. Remove all the new AI cores from the new robots and bring them to me. *All* of them."

"You do understand," said the techie, "They won't work at all without -"

"Yes!" Diamond said, "Dead robots are better than killer robots – remove the AI cores, now."

She left the room at speed, Wenders behind her, trying to keep up.

"I can get you twenty-four proper, safe and approved Metal Mothers AI cores," he called after her, "Free of charge!"

She allowed him to catch up.

"You realise this is a government thing, right?" Wenders said, following Diamond to her office, "The new cores were introduced under governmental clearance – essentially they were put there by the government, they're very well-made and sophisticated, almost certainly commissioned by them too. We have to get to the bottom of this – and who's responsible."

Diamond rolled her eyes. "Mansplaining!" she announced, with an irritated glare, "And we have more important things to worry about - like how many other batches of your robots were delivered, at the same time, to police stations across the entire country – and how many of those batches were then altered under the same scheme?"

Wenders stopped dead. He told Felicity (who had been keeping up with the pair of them as efficiently as she did everything else), in his most hushed and frantic whispering voice, to issue a nationwide recall of all robots dispatched in the last two months, since the latest hardware models had become available. It was a heavy blow for the company, but not as bad as any further fatalities could be.

CI Diamond turned to look at them. "We need to speak

further," she told them.

"Of course," said Wenders, and he followed after her, with Felicity following him on her phone, conducting a high-level, deadly serious, nationwide-recall conversation with important colleagues.

Diamond entered her office, nodded him in with her and told him to shut the door. Felicity remained outside, to finish her vital call.

Diamond sat down behind her desk and looked hard at Wenders. "Do you follow the news?" she asked him.

"Not a great deal," he said, "I can never tell if it leaves me feeling more depressed or angry, so I tend these days to opt for neither, by not watching that horrifying shit at all. Felicity updates me with anything I need to know, as do the board and my personal robots."

"Right," said Diamond, "So you're not aware of the new government's zero-tolerance policy?"

Wenders brow furrowed. "I'm guessing a zero-tolerance to drugs policy, yes?"

"What else have you found out?" she asked, "We know the offending AI core was not your design or issue, you're in the clear, but what can you tell me about it? What are its operating parameters? How did this shit happen?"

"Well. The core I took from Robot Zero encoded various laws of the land; basic ones on behaviour; things like violence, thievery, sexual assault and drug-taking. There were other routines and sub-routines I didn't get to assessing, which would require a lot of hours work to establish the basic limits of the robot's behaviour when working with this new core but.. I think I get the essentials of what happened."

Wenders poured himself some water from Diamond's cooler. Drank a little. Sighed.

"Robot Zero saw drugs going into a human," he said, "And, per the new laws he understood this could not be allowed - under any circumstances, and that those drugs were to be removed immediately. Robot Zero, I should hasten to add, also knew – knows - nothing of Asmiov's Three Laws; he wasn't concerned his actions could destroy the human being in question because he isn't programmed to even consider whether the human in question should be cared for, or even simply have their life maintained, throughout the drug removal process. Robot Zero simply saw 'drugs going into human' which was flagged straight away by the rule 'drugs must be completely removed from human, straightaway'. So, it stuck its vacuum device down that human's lungs and sucked out all the evil, druggy, naughty badness, and lots of bits of lung, too, just to be sure. The human in question dying as a direct result of the removal process was simply not relevant to it."

"That's the operational basis this robot went outside with?" said Diamond, aghast, "From *my* station, on *my* watch.. Which will, of course, make this my glass-ceiling moment, too."

"I'm sorry," Wenders offered. Diamond looked at him. "So," she said, "If a robot operating this system went into some of the more colourful nightclubs on my manor, it would be a bloodbath also, yes?"

"Sure," said Wenders, "A current era Metal Mothers robot

has the best hardware on the planet. One of mine, operating with one of these *government* AI cores, would see a dance-floor full of E'd-up kids and start removing illegally-tainted blood from veins and stomach contents in their entirety. Although, it would be physically limited to emptying two at a time, so the majority would probably be able to get away, once the panic kicked in.."

"How do the government plan to get away with this?" Diamond said, "They can't just stick murderbots on the streets and not expect a huge fucking outcry! Jesus Christ. On top of it all, I'll end up having to commit my officers to defending this *shit*.."

"I need Felicity," said Wenders, "We need to know if this is a one-off incident or -"

There was a loud knocking, followed by Felicity's head poking round the door.

"Felicity!" said Wenders, "Did you hear me?!"

"What boss?" she said, "No, I just got off the phone and.."

"Oh no," said Wenders, seeing the look on her face, "That's your 'how the fuck do I tell the boss this shit' face, I *hate* the 'how the fuck do I tell the boss this shit' face. Go on. Tell the boss this shit. I need to know."

Felicity eyed CI Diamond. "This might be sensitive information -" she began, but Wenders cut in -

"No, just spill it. CI Diamond needs to know everything; we and Metal Mothers are not responsible for that young man's death and we need to get on top of this to stop it happening to.."

Wenders stopped speaking as the look on his assistant's face told him his sentiment was already out of date.

"Three other deaths," said Felicity. "I'm so sorry boss."

"*Shit*!" said Wenders, "The recall is on though, right, all batches of the newest models are in recall right now?"

"Yes boss."

"OK," said Wenders, "We need to get out ahead of the news and state the facts of these deaths before.. Other narratives take over."

"It may be too late for that," said Diamond. She had switched on the screen on her desk and was searching the news channels. She showed them three headlines from different news outlets; the first said "Metal Mothers Angels of Death! Two deaths reported at the hands of Metal Mothers robots on routine police operations".

"Fuck me," said Wenders, and he flopped down into a chair.

The second banner said "Murderbots! Metal Mothers Legacy of Death!", the third, "Metal Mothers Deathbot Review! Government vows to open investigation into alleged murder of at least three youngsters by robot police."

"Fuck me boss!" said Felicity, "What are we going to.. I mean, right now, what can I do for you?"

"Uuuurrrgghh," said Wenders, "Oh Jesus. Oh, how delightful. I'm not getting back to bed for a long, long-bastard time, am I? Fucking government meddling and we get Robopigs! OK, I'm going to need Legal, I'm gonna need Marketing, I'm gonna need Corporate Strategy, and given how likely I am to offend people by the dozen in the next 48 hours, get me HR too. And my masseuse."

"I need to gather all the evidence," said CI Diamond, "I'm going to submit the depositions for timelock, urgently. But before I get on, do you need anything else from me?"

Wenders pondered. "If you can," he said, "I could really use one of those new robots - and as many of the rogue AI cores as you can spare."

"Well I have twenty-four. You can take one robot, sure and five of the AI cores. The rest will have to remain in my custody."

"Very kind," he said. "Do you want replacement Metal Mothers AI cores? Like I said, no charge."

"I will do, yeah, thanks," said Diamond, "I'll call you about it."

"Don't worry," said Wenders, nodding at Felicity, who added it to her list.

Diamond picked up her phone. "You remember how to get to the robot bays?" she said, "I'll tell Hollis what you need."

"Thank you for everything," said Wenders, "May I also have your number?"

Diamond gave him her card and he left with Felicity.

***

It was against the advice of Legal, Marketing, Corporate Strategy, HR, Felicity and his masseuse, that Wenders agreed to the press conference later that day. Counter-intuitively, it was the advice of his masseuse which had pushed him over the edge. He felt sure that Legal, Marketing, Corporate Strategy, HR and Felicity were all in this together, working against him; when the masseuse suggested they might be right it became proof in his mind that the rest had influenced her to say so.

It might also be down to lack of sleep, too much coffee, the sudden overuse of a previously dormant worry gland, etc.

The room was strobe-lit with flashes, and the press pack got stuck in immediately.

"Seven confirmed human deaths, Dr Wenders," said the tall and portly Herman Thollister (of the Times), "Deaths directly and provably attributable to Metal Mothers robots, and all within the last twenty-four hours. What would you like to say about this?"

Wenders had been told to expect further cases before the recall kicked in, he was secretly pleased the number had remained so low.

"Those robots were originally built by Metal Mothers, I do concede," Wenders said, "However the government has seen fit to intervene in the safe working of our perfectly sound robots, by replacing their central AI cores with their own models – models which, I might add, do not even appear to operate by Asimov's Three Laws."

There was a general uproar and demand for proof of this outrageous accusation.

Wenders waited for calm, as did Claudetta Sugden of the Sun, who then said,

"Where's the proof Ben? *Where*?!"

"I was up in the middle of the night, the moment I first heard of the first of these tragedies," said Wenders, "Twenty four robots were delivered by Metal Mothers to the Brambleby Police Station on the third of this month. On the sixth however, a man with government clearance entered the station and oversaw the installation of new AI cores in all twenty-four of the new robots – AI cores which were categorically *not* approved by Metal Mothers. We had no knowledge of this and condemn these actions entirely. It would appear these government approved and supplied AI cores have been replacing the safe, authentic Metal Mothers AI cores in other consignments of robots to other police forces, throughout the UK. It is these actions on behalf of the government which have directly caused these deaths. Because of this, Metal Mothers have issued a recall of all the latest hardware models of our robots from the last few months. It'll be tough, but it is absolutely necessary for the company to move forward and -"

"Proof!" yelled Sugden and Dolly Titchmarsh of the Evening Star, in unison.

Wenders smiled. "Please speak to Chief Inspector Diamond of Brambleby Station," he said, "She'll confirm everything I have said."

"Why isn't CI Diamond here, now, in person?" asked

Titchmarsh.

"I did try to get her here, I wasn't able to reach her. Now, if you would be so good as to join me in asking the government to come clean on their introduction of unsafe operating systems into our robots, which has put the British public in danger and besmirched our good -"

"She's dead!" someone yelled, then a further uproar broke in the ranks of the assembled journos as the news flash spread around the room. Of course, it reached Wenders last. He had turned his phone off for this performance.

It was Thollister who broke the news to Wenders,

"Would you care to offer any proof for your claims *other* than the testimony of Chief Inspector Diamond, Dr Wenders? Only it seems she was murdered by one of your robots, just this afternoon."

Wenders felt the walls of the room grow taller.

He visibly faultered, stunned, then mumbled about the technician, fumbled for her name then shouted "Hollis! The technician working for Diamond was called Hollis, she can also confirm what I've said."

"Dr Wenders,"said Sugden (her 'aghast' face was impeccably-held and perfectly-timed), "You've just heard of another death – of a police chief inspector, no less – *again* at the hands of one of your robots, and still you're clinging to this pathetic fantasy excuse that the government is somehow responsible. Shouldn't you be begging forgiveness form the families of those whose lives have been ended by Metal Mothers robots?"

"The responsibility for those deaths lies squarely with the government!" Wenders shouted, thus sealing a thoroughly calamitous interview as far as the board of Metal Mothers was concerned; their lawyers had seen enough and swooped in, amidst a slew of large goons, to end it.

Thus, Wenders was hustled from the room by a crowd of his own subordinates with excessive force and urgency, like a president from a gunshot (although with more prejudice and less subtlety).

Wenders, for his part, already knew how bad this looked, so he didn't struggle once he was in their grip.

***

The market responded abysmally to Wenders' performance, this was compounded by the government's disdainful response to it. The general public, responding online, were similarly scornful of Wenders, but with greater venom and a standard plethora of death threats.

These problems were as nothing to him however, compared with what awaited him at home.

Or rather, what did not await him.

His ex-model wife Christabelle had been "bored fucking senseless" by him for years, her letter duly informed him, and now he was at the centre of this almighty shit-storm, it seemed as good a time as any to jump ship. Her letter also hinted at the many, many, fruitful, beefy and hunky options which remained open to her for sexual fulfilment, and would for the rest of her life (she being fifteen years his junior, and still in excellent shape). She was opening a new chapter in her life and closing the old one. On him.

Wenders emptied his house of servants, shut down the robots, ordered Felicity home for the day and then hit the bottle immediately.

The first bottle of Screaming Eagle Cabernet, 1992, didn't even touch the sides. As he settled into the second he slowed down, the tears started and he began to rage at the walls and contents of his magnificent, empty house.

Towards the end of the second bottle, tired of sobbing and ranting at invisible demons, he turned on the TV. He knew that looking at the news channels would be a terrible idea right now, and he went straight to them.

The first item he found on Channel One was breaking news about an aggressive move by the government to takeover the UK division of Metal Mothers. Instantly incensed with blind rage, Wenders grabbed the third bottle of Screaming Eagle and hurled it at the sombre face of the news anchor. The bottle's net worth instantly went from half a million to zero, as it exploded across his gigantic TV screen.

He watched, growling, as the red liquid dribbled down the screen and the face of the anchor.

The mooted takeover was a necessary response according to government sources, the anchor's monologue explained. It was needed in order to respond to Metal Mothers (and specifically his; Dr Ben Wenders') recall of invaluable robot resources during a time of unprecedented national unrest (a hotly-contested summary of the national mood, but one which the government had insisted upon, repeatedly, in countless interviews for months).

Wenders then went into a deeper place of hopelessness, as he realised how everything had been set up to blame him and his company for the murder of British citizens by the state. Now the government were seeking to secure the supply of robots and were maintaining their narratives, whilst he and Metal Mothers were constrained to fight a rear-guard action to defend themselves against the fallout of these murders – which were in effect the other prong of the governments' insidious attack, via the mass-installation of their totalitarian AI cores.

The fact the government wanted to secure the supply of the robots must mean they intended to keep their hybrid murderbots active, meaning they would need him and Metal Mothers to continue their roles as villains in this affair.

He should have seen this coming. The murder of CI Diamond, and its reveal in the middle of his press conference, had been a work of pure, brutal genius. He had to give them that. It was so fast, it was..

It was unlikely. He frowned the more he thought of it. At first, he idly wondered what previously unacknowledged drug abuse CI Diamond must have been guilty of, which (he assumed) must have been the reason why she'd been killed by one of the new robots. But then, she had seen everything he had seen this morning (was it only *this* morning?!). Assuming she was some kind of addict, she was clearly a high-functioning addict. She would hardly have been stupid enough to allow herself to be under the influence of an illegal drug in the presence of one of the murderbots in her station – and this should have been irrelevant, as the new batch had all been deactivated anyway.

Unless of course, someone with clearance had re-activated a robot, one still operating a government AI core, then all it would take to kill her would be to spike her coffee with something illegal and have the robot encounter her afterwards..

Which scenario was more likely?

He suddenly felt very sober, and very afraid. How easy now, to murder someone, simply by spiking them with something illegal, prior to them entering the presence of a murderbot?

The absolute sense of impending doom forced him to face the bare truths of his situation. He called on all the CEO training he had bought for himself, made himself a coffee and started making plans. He wasn't done yet, he still had a few tricks up his sleeve which the government had no idea about..

And, for the first time in probably over a decade, Wenders realised he needed to speak to his old mate Gavin from university. It had been too long, obviously, but if 'ol Gav was anything like the bohemian nutcase he had still been just ten years ago, he'd probably still know a few special contacts which would be essential for the plans he was formulating.

***

Having made a date with his old friend for a drink and a catch-up, amongst other business, Wenders then called his other old friend from university, Ches Ganderton.

"Bill," said Ganderton at the other end of the line, "Well I can't say I'm surprised to hear from you, given.. Everything."

"Home Secretary," said Wenders, "It's been a while."

"Ches, please," said his old friend, "You know me, I -"

"- Don't do pomposity!" Wenders finished for him.

They both laughed, remembering more innocent times at the student union.

"It's good to hear that," Wenders said, "Because I'm sure you've heard that in one short day my life has been pretty much torn apart. I'm not here to beg for anything, to be honest I'm kinda relishing the idea of a total nosedive into obscurity, but, I just wondered if you and I might have one last meal and a drink together like old times, before I go?!"

"You offering me my favourite?" Ganderton asked.

"Oh yeah - before they cancel my membership – one last big binge at the Saxon Castle, my treat. Whaddya say?!"

"Sounds perfect."

***

When the two men met a few days later, in the most exclusive room of the most exclusive restaurant in England, they both agreed to save political and fiscal discussions for after the meal, the food and drink at the Saxon Castle being the main point. They also both turned off their phones.

While he ate his rack of lamb with mint sauce and gravy, braised veg and dauphinoise potatoes, Wenders studied the man facing him. The Rt Hon Chesney Philip Ganderton,

Home Secretary, was gaunt, perhaps more so than when they'd first met as freshers. His hair had gone fully grey but hadn't receded. His face was unreadable. Typical of the man, but in this heightened situation, with the government all but at war with his company, Wenders would have liked to find something indicative in the eyes of his old friend.

He and Ganderton had never been truly close, but both had always part of the in-crowd. Ganderton had always seemed to be where the fun was whilst he was at University, yet always just beyond the reach of any of the most outrageous, unforgettable episodes of the kind which stuck to people ever after. Clearly, he'd always been political.

Despite valiant efforts by both men, neither could finish their main course, so large were the portions, and so rich. They both gave up, sat back and sipped their wine, Wenders resisting the temptation to swig it back like there was no tomorrow – even though that was probably the case. He kept a steady pace with Ganderton, acting as relaxed as he possibly could.

The inevitable discussion began suddenly.

"So, honestly mate," said Wenders, "What the fuck is government doing?"

Ganderton remained sitting in precisely the same position, hands clasped, vaguely smiling at Wenders.

"Home Secretary, please tell me you're in a position to do something? Anything?!" Wenders said, somewhat unnerved by Ganderton almost bovine placidity.

"I should have thought," Ganderton said slowly and

deliberately, "That what we're doing is obvious."

This was a heavy blow, but not completely unexpected. Wenders kept his chin up.

"Well why don't you explain it to me, as the effective head – at least for now – of your robot production division?"

"It's government policy to apply zero-tolerance methods to police work, via robots unencumbered by Asimov's Three Laws. As far as illegal drugs are concerned, our new robots have only one rule; keep humans and illegal drugs absolutely separate, at any cost."

"Even when that cost is a *human life*?!"

"The cost is *not* a human life – it's the life of a drug taker. A druggie. Someone who hasn't just given up on life, they've given up on society and humanity in general. There is a difference, you see. Rules are rules. It's just that now we are able to enforce those rules, absolutely."

Wenders' jaw was locked tight. "So," he said, "The new government policy is to have robots as judge, jury and executioner, all in one? The policy is instant death, just for taking drugs?!"

"Of course not. It's just that any illegal drugs found in the possession of, or upon or within the person of, any human, will be entirely removed from that human. Sometimes, that may involve a spot of lung-vacuuming, or blood filtering which may result in occasional fatalities. Zero tolerance, Ben. That's what we ran on, that's the mandate."

"This is beyond fascism. Do you understand that? You're

talking about a police state, using sophisticated machinery to murder the people with impunity, for the slightest breaches of the law, even when there's no-one being victimised by the crime?"

"The human population is forever expanding," Ganderton explained, "Hence all methods of trimming it down are therefore considered at the highest levels, behind the scenes, and have been for many, many decades now. Such considerations have led to the ignoring of coming earthquakes and volcanoes, for example. The creation of occasional new infectious diseases, in addition to those Mother Nature herself occasionally lobs at us. The more the human race expands, the larger the trimming operations naturally become. When an operation expands, so does its scope and methodology. We're just trimming the herd, by removing its worst members."

"You smoked weed at uni just like everyone else," Wenders said, "But now you think it's OK to start murdering people who do it? This policy could destroy some of our best minds!"

Ganderton rolled his eyes. "The sweeps we carry out won't be focussed on campuses!" he laughed, "At least, not at first. And as far as my university days are concerned.. You can never prove I smoked weed. There aren't any pictures."

Wenders was practically out of his mind with rage. "So you intend to wage open warfare on the working class, using my robots, whilst laying the blame on me?"

"And fully expecting to be voted in again, by that same working class, next Spring. Yes."

Ganderton's smile came from that knowing place, the place only a total self-belief can illuminate.

"Whether or not you throw me to the dogs for this fucking outrage," Wenders hissed, "You can't seriously imagine the British public will accept the continuing presence of murderbots on the fucking streets?! You can throw me overboard for those deaths but you can't use me after I'm gone as some kind of continuing excuse! The public won't have it."

"My dear Benjamin," Ganderton smiled, "What you're referring to will simply be known as 'teething problems' with the shiny new Robotic Policing Units. Robots are too valuable to policing and particularly the rescue of children, in all kinds of situations, to be discontinued, certainly not over the deaths of a few druggies. The story will run that sadly, when you went.."

He let the words hang.

"You took the secret of the robots' newfound 'zero-tolerance to drugs' policy with you. So, until we can create a whole new legion of robots with Asimov's proper Three Laws in place, druggies everywhere better had simply better watch out, as we can't be held responsible for what happens to them if they have any illegal drugs detectable within their system."

Wenders saw it all too well. He nearly gagged as he realised the fullness of his plan was absolutely required. He was glad, in a sort of pyrrhic way. If he was doomed, it would be on his terms.

"What if someone gets spiked?" Wenders remembered to

ask, as he coped with the rising panic whilst trying to bide his time, "Women everywhere are still targeted by scumbags who'll spike their drinks to try to rape them. Now you're saying they've also got to contend with homicidal robots who will rips their stomachs out of them and flush their blood, immediately, upon detection of illegal drugs – which they've taken through no fault of their own?"

"You make an omelette, you break a few eggs."

Wenders choked and spat out about thirty quids worth of red wine.

"Jesus Christ," he muttered. He cleared his throat.

"And you mentioned my leaving," he continued, each line bringing it nearer, "Would you be so good as to relay to me the manner in which you believe I will be leaving, as the one condemned to leave?"

Ganderton grinned. "It'll be relatively quick and painless. Heart attack. In about three hours from now, when I'm safely in Brussels."

Wenders felt the sick parody of it bite. He'd actually been doubled dosed.

"Am I to understand," he said with difficulty, "I've already ingested my impending zoom?"

Ganderton nodded brightly, as to a child who's just completed their five times table for the first time ever, but a year behind their peers.

Wenders nodded, grimly. "And are you aware," he asked

Ganderton, "That you may also have just ingested yours?"

He held up a small electronic device. Ganderton's eyes widened. He froze.

Wenders felt Hades lighting his smile as he pressed the button, and the six-foot tall robot appeared from thin air, between their table and the door.

Now, the frozen Ganderton was both terrified and amazed. "How..?" was all he could manage.

"Industry secrets," said Wenders, "You don't know the most cutting edge stuff I've been working on for both my company and this country, and now you never will, nor will your colleagues. This is our prototype stealth robot with full invisibility cloaking, as well as another exclusive feature. I call him Norbert. Norbert Nullbot. Say hello, Norbert!"

"Hello", the robot intoned.

Ganderton was now the one stalling for time. "What other exclusive feature does Norbert have?" he asked, whilst trying to surreptitiously slide the largest available knife up his shirt sleeve.

"Did I say one other exclusive feature? I meant two. Yes Norbert Nullbot really is special; he has three fantastic new features. The invisibility cloaking you've seen. Or not!" Wenders chuckled manically, "Norbert also has a unique installation at the centre of his being; this allows me to flip between his two different operating systems at the push of a button. The third feature is his wifi connections. They've been entirely unrestricted; everything we've done and said in this room has been live-streamed to the internet – and that stream is continuing as we speak."

This hit Ganderton harder than his fear that the robot was there to do him harm. He tongue seemed to writhe in his throat as if trying to escape, his eyes popped, he felt the sweat break out as well as a violent, seething rage. He tried to regain some kind of control, knowing he was *live on air..*

"Which brings me to the crunch," Wenders said, "Norbert is currently operating a safe, Metal Mothers AI core. However, all I have to do is flick this switch," he indicated the button to Ganderton, "- And the safe, Metal Mothers AI core switches to one of your government AI cores. You know, the ones which turn decent Metal Mothers robots into homicidal maniacs - if you happen to be on illegal drugs."

Ganderton scowled. "Where are you going with this?"

"You see," said Wenders, conversationally, "I also programmed Norbert to drop a little liquid LSD into both our drinks, which he had ample time to do, during the course of our meal, before I dropped his cloak. Of course, Norbert thought it was a harmless, *legal*, little dash of cordial. I admit, that's one part of this plan I cannot be certain of; if Norbert didn't follow my instructions for any reason.."

Ganderton paled. Now he got it. They both died at the flick of a switch. He had played his hand too early. What else could he say to buy himself some time?!

"We'll reverse engineer this Norbert," Ganderton said, thinking quickly, "Don't think we won't. Stealth engineering like that can and *will* be appropriated, if not by me then by my colleagues."

Wenders grinned. "Forgot to mention the fourth special feature of Norbert," he said cheerfully, "His power centre is locked in and on a countdown set to destroy him and any room he's in, in slightly less than an hour."

"Am I to understand," Norbert Nullbot interrupted, in his steady monotone, "That illegal drugs have been administered? I must tell you it is my responsibility to contact the relevant authorities."

"Anyway," said Wenders loudly, ignoring his most impressive creation, "Actions speak louder than words."

Time itself seemed to stall, as scraps of the finest pheasant, Devon-grown carrots, peas and green beans all went flying across the room with with best Mayan Gold roast potatoes, in showers of rich gravy and costly red wine, as Ganderton launched himself across the table at Wenders -

- and successfully stabbed him! But not hard enough, not deep enough – and Wenders, hurt but not enough, cackled and pushed the button.

His vicious laughter, with the steak knife sticking from his chest, made his visage a grimly gothic mask of doom; the last thing Ganderton would see in this life.

***

Under the control of the new AI core, Norbert Nullbot's view of the room changed considerably and its perception of the room altered beyond all reason. Where there had been two humans in the room, under his care, there was now no such notion as 'care'. Now there were two human suspects, in a room with two drinking vessels containing detectable traces of class A substances. Further traces were on the lips of the two humans, and further focussed scanning showed the same, illegal substances, within the digestive systems and bloodstreams of the two humans. These observations followed logically on from each other at lightning-speed, from the second the new AI core took over from the original. Therefore, almost precisely at the flick of Wenders' switch, 'human cleansing' mode snapped into operation within the robot's cerebrum, and the robot began his work.

All the while, the live feed was active.

In the course of the robot's work, a one became a zero. And then very shortly afterwards, another one became a zero.

At that point, the success-factor of its work became irrelevant as the two subjects of the operation were both, equally, no longer relevant.

And then the robot stood alone and perfectly-still, in the most exclusive room of the most exclusive restaurant in England, starkly and beautifully decorated in great, bold, splashes of crimson. It was utterly unaware of the storm it had created. It was in the centre of that storm's eye.

***

In the chaotic aftermath of the most explosive footage to drop onto the web that week, the enraged women's movement, with the 'break a few eggs' line firing up even the most conservative among them, successfully extracted a promise from the Prime Minister within one day of the footage airing, to take all the new robots out of circulation. Whilst the PM strongly denied any governmental involvement in replacing safe, tried and tested AI cores with others 'of questionable pedigree', he also promised to launch a comprehensive investigation into all the technical and legal issues surrounding the footage and its implications.

By the time most stoners became aware of the danger they had been in, that danger had passed.

© H. R. Brown, 14/04/2020

ESSENCE

There can't be more than a hundred and fifty yards from the threshold of my office to the bus stop I walk to every night. Five nights a week, say, forty-seven or eight weeks a year for over two years, I have made the same journey through the centre of the town. Around four hundred and seventy journeys, only made different by the changing of the seasons and the respective reductions in attire of the local women which the best of the seasons brings.

The journey takes in several town centre sights; there is a post office, a bank, a toy store, a corner, a cash point (or 'Money-Shitter', as a favourite newspaper columnist of mine called them recently) - and then the bus stop. It proudly overlooks a wide and taxi-strewn road to the KFC which I studiously avoid - usually to the angry gnashing of my stomach.

Same every night. Post Office, cross the road, bank, toy store, corner, etc. Post Office, cross the road, bank, etc, etc. It's not a journey which any sane person would be inclined to think twice about and I never did until one particular, terrifying night, six months ago.

The Post Office was as busy as ever. I crossed the road without problems, passed the bank and the toy store and came to the corner. There was an intense, bitter wind sweeping round the corner towards me as I tried to walk around it, it caught the breath in my throat as if icicles were riding the wind and diving for the cover of warm living flesh wherever they could find it.

I gasped, drew back and pulled my coat tightly about me. This was not to be countenanced, I knew. My stop was less than fifty yards away on a busy street in the middle of town, and I could certainly hack it if everyone else could. I gritted my teeth and forged on and the wind tore at me, seemed to rake my very soul with fingers of ice. I growled, forcing myself forwards uneasily. The intense cold was beyond belief and to such an extent that I found myself wondering if my mind had been tampered with, and I now found myself in Siberia or perhaps even the Arctic. I realised that I could no longer recognise the usual shapes of the buildings around me, I was only aware of the corner and my need to pass it to get home.

I howled at the wind, I drove myself round the corner in against its teeth and I staggered up the street, striving with it every step of the way. It began to tear at me and rake through me to the point where I lost reason and turned back, only to find the way behind me was now also an uphill incline - and most heinous - the wind was still pounding my face. Indeed, now I was wandering blind through a howling, sub-freezing gale in every direction and all of them, uphill. I was caught in a minor arctic basin, the horizon of which was equally indeterminate in all directions. The terror of this sudden, unexplained shift in everything I knew and understood was so alien and unreal to me that I half expected to awake, but for the fact that the day until this point had seemed so drawn-out by the usual, office-related tedium. I screamed, hurled myself forwards in the vague direction I had originally pursued and I raged against the frozen, ill-borne tide.

I had slipped through a crack between the worlds, perhaps.

The dour, ceaseless, ravaging wind beat against me and I bore upon it as the best of my strength would allow, gripping fearfully at the coat around me and howling at the fate I found before me.

Where was I? What had happened? How had I come here, and how the hell was I supposed to get back home?

I had three choices. One; sit down and wait for my reality to change again with no guarantee that it would do so, Two; go back to the point at which I had entered this hell and try to get back, though I had no real way of knowing where it was, or Three; carry on and hope to break through it.

There was only one choice, and it was a straight line. I kept going and I roared and spat as I did so at this new world that it might dare to try to endanger my life, having introduced itself so precociously upon my person.

Blank! Upon a sudden level patch in the ground beneath me, I stumbled forward into a plane of calm. The wind ceased. The cold abated. The surroundings took shape around me and they were yet more frightening. I was stuck on a little plateau on the side of a gargantuan cliff face. On one side the black wall stretched out over and above me forever, as if a real tower had finally been built to the moon. On a rocky outcrop I stood, and on all other sides fenced in by gigantic teeth of rock which bent in upon each other fiercely. They were crowded together so that none might pass between them yet a most fearsome view might be had of the magma; of the exploding, molten-rock landscape beyond.

I searched frantically all around me for some portal through which I might make an escape. It was as I scrabbled in the ashy dirt at the base of the tower, that I heard a slow, scabrous voice behind me that froze me again.

"There are two ways out of this."

There are no words to describe the coming together of every bleak and doomed scenario my mind had been prowling through since this nightmare began. I already knew to whom the voice belonged. I knew I was now to face that which everyone avoids more than any other thing in life. The choice.

Turning to face it was the hardest thing I had ever done.

It feels now as if I saw it in my mind's eye before I had fully turned around and raised my forlorn eyes to meet it. Its form was serpentine; the skin fire and boiling blood. The eyes were a shining, golden feline, the horns warped and calloused, the mouth; thin and hard.

I looked the thing in the eye for only a second before I could take no more.

"What do you want?" I muttered.

"Your soul. Will you be requiring a description of the entire process as we proceed, or will the usual 'offer you can't refuse' repartee see us through?"

"You want me to believe that you're actually the devil?" I asked.

"I'm sorry, did you or didn't you just experience the ice and the horror? Were my configurations awry?"

I knew in my heart of hearts that stalling was not going to

resolve this but of course I tried. I am weak and I am human and have never pretended to be otherwise. In no short time at all the creature had rounded upon me.

I lay pinioned upon sharp and painful rock with but one ineffectual arm still free. The creature whose real name I was still denying had my legs and other arm held down with its legs and tail, leaving both its arms free. This gave it some advantage but its unnatural speed and devastating perfection of movement were the real killers.

The manner in which it held out the clipboard and stated, "Sign the document," was delivered in a bored tone.

"What if I don't?"

"Then everything your band is trying to accomplish will come to nothing. You'll never get anywhere with them."

"Every band has that worry."

"Not like this. If you don't sign this document, you'll never play another successful gig."

"What if I think we can wow crowds without your help? What if I believe we're good enough to just make it on our own merits?"

A sigh. "Name one decent band in the last century that's made it without my guiding hand."

A gulp. "I don't believe you."

"None of them do, at first. I suppose it would make no difference, were I to mention the overnight riches and groupie adulation which I could so simply prescribe for you and your compadres?"

I felt my sudden victory at hand. I hadn't known it would be that easy. "It doesn't matter what you say, even if you're telling the truth," I said, "Because whether we ever make it or not, the only thing that matters is that real people like us and want to hear us for our own merit. If you're trying to tell me that won't happen without you, you should have checked out our gig in the Trades Club! We're not about ripping money out of people - we're about giving them a damn good show! We're a good band with good songs, a shake-the-goddamn-room mentality, a look to die for and the music beats forever within us!"

I finished the last part in an exultant shout.

The thing slinked along the ground, wound itself around one of the rocky teeth of my prison and looked down upon me with sneering, venomous intent.

"So your stance is; that you won't barter your soul for riches and a permanent supply of expertly delivered blow-jobs from horny, barely legal girls?"

I climbed to my feet. I am a man. I know this because I demonstrated it, within the awfully long moment that it took me to say, with a desperate cheerfulness; "No. I... will *not*."

"What about a woman. Any woman you want? Absolutely *any* woman?"

This I admit, did make me pause. "It wouldn't be real love though, would it?"

"Near enough!"

"NO!"

"Want to win the lottery?"

I was winning! "Same answer!" I yelled.

"Trip into space? Obscure family inheritance sorts you and yours out for life? Book published? Famous for some reason; real or imagined...?"

There was a slow, assured blink in those cold golden eyes.

I held my head up. "No", I answered.

I was so thankful. I had always been an atheist yet ever felt that as long as one knew right from wrong, it didn't matter. Having not succumbed into selling my mortal soul, I felt validated as never before, but I also felt enormously humble at the realisation that I was not only be experiencing another plane of reality, but that my preconceptions of the reality I was accustomed to would be forever changed.

"Accustomed to being so right? So *righteous*, are you?"

The beast hadn't moved while I threw its offers back at it. I had become invincible unto immortal slings and arrows, until their deadliest weapon was unveiled.

"Do you actually believe in right and wrong? Or are they just concepts you happen to have heard of?"

The Beast had levelled its sights upon me, and I knew the worse was yet to come. The air between us shivered. An image came into being, as if showing on a screen of thin air. A street, people and -

"Recognise him?" it hissed at me.

Of course I recognised him, the face I'd known all my life; my brother.

"Everyone has a price!" it gloated at me

The triumph I had felt only moments ago felt now as alien to me as the various horrifying scenarios rushing through my mind.

"What are you doing?" I asked, "What kind of devil are you? It's supposed to be a choice, *my* choice; you're supposed to tempt *me*!"

"Observe the red car," the beast said, indicating a vehicle in the image at the other end of the street from my brother. The car was struck by lightning, lost in a fireball.

"Your little brother is next, unless you give yourself now to my domain."

"An eternity in Hell?"

"Not for the faint hearted," the beast said.

I looked at my brother, standing pointing at the wreck of the car and conversing in amazement with other witnesses.

"He's innocent, he's nothing to do with you and me, here and now," I said.

"Very true," the beast said, "Perhaps you should allow the lightning to take his mortal form. An innocent standing at the pearly gates will surely gain entrance to the kingdom of heaven."

"No. You're not killing my brother. No."

"Then give yourself to me and my kingdom. You have thirty seconds."

The injustice of my predicament didn't matter and I didn't waste time arguing about it. I set upon the beast with the sole intention of ripping it apart and was soon regretting it as I found my hands badly burned, my body battered and flat on the floor. The dread creature was back on top of me, pinning me down and whispering -

"Ten seconds."

I screamed. I cursed, spat, damned my own pain and mortality and swore to make Hell a nightmare for its king before crying,

"Take me! You leave my brother alone and TAKE ME!"

The creature gave me a look of pure loathing, then lowered its claw onto my forehead. There was a moment of searing, dazzling agony in which everything seemed to boil, melt and explode and then darkness took me, where I know not.

***

I awoke not to fire and pain as I had expected, but to find myself sitting on a wide, marble staircase. I stood up and felt a dizzying rush to the head; not only for the action itself but on looking down and realising that this was no ordinary staircase. It stretched down below me for hundreds of yards, more probably, the bottom was lost in mist and I was somewhere in the middle of a clear blue sky.

I looked up and saw some way ahead was what looked like the summit. There were no sides to this stairway, just an abyss of blue sky and clouds to the left and to the right. Upwards it is, I thought, and I suddenly felt small and hopeless. I might have avoided Hell, but for my short life to be over now would be horrifying for my parents - both of them still alive and well. For my brother too, my brother, and my friends... If only there had been more time. For myself also, before I had done so many of the things I had wanted to do. And for the everlasting future; who did I know in Heaven? Most people I knew would not be going there for some time yet, and for all my self-satisfaction in having 'done the right thing', was I really now to make my home in the lands of an all-powerful being, in whose very existence I had never believed?

I sat down and I sobbed. I was alone, and like never before.

Yet, after a minute or two I felt foolish. This was surely not the best beginning of Forever - I should be happy; a life-long atheist about to enter Heaven! Meet Elvis and Marilyn Monroe?! I laughed, felt sorry for my selfish little bout and decided that all would be well. I walked on up the stairs and, by and by, I found myself outside the gates of woven-pearl.

No-one around. I knocked three times, there was a pause and then the gates opened and a big man stepped through. He was smartly dressed all in black, he had short, blonde hair, what looked like an electronic ear piece and piercing, dark eyes. These took me in immediately and then searched around and beyond me, as if he thought I would not be alone. He was constantly chewing and appeared to be slightly on edge.

"Hi," I said, uncertainly.

"Cause of deaf?" he enquired, in what sounded like a cockney accent.

For a second I wasn't sure what to say, then it seemed obvious.

"Satan."

The fellow grinned. "Ah!" he said, his whole atmosphere brightening, "He's always tryin', same old tricks, new uns, it don't matter; he don't learn."

"Oh," I said, "Right, well, erm... what?"

"Pete!" said the fellow, holding out his hand. I shook it and he looked more closely at me.

"S'alright," he said, "Don't worry. Like I said, he's always tryin'. Fact is, me old China, it ain't your time yet. Old 'Arry's been 'aving you on."

I was stunned. "Then what...?"

'Pete' couldn't stop grinning at me. "You know ve way back," he said, pointing down the stairs behind me.

I was speechless, to find myself here, being offered now the best prize yet; an actual way back home. The tears came to my eyes again and I stammered ineffectually.

Pete simply smiled and waited for me to collect my thoughts and ideas, battered, broken and remade though they now were; everything had happened in such a short space I knew not what to ask, now that I stood at one place in life where all questions might be answered.

After a moment, the best I could come out with was, "How can I, I mean, how should I -"

I swallowed back another sob but Pete, star that he is, finished my sentence for me; "Lead a better life?"

I nodded, rubbing my streaming eyes.

He touched my shoulder and I smiled automatically. "Everybody knows right from wrong," he said, softly, "Not everyone lives up to what vey know. You got 'ere once, you can do it again."

In that moment everything I had ever known fell into a perfect pattern in my mind and I realised I understood all I needed to. I grasped his hands.

"*Thank you.*"

"No bovver," he said, "But you best get goin' now. Time's different up here but ve real world - and your mortal body - is waitin' for ya!"

I laughed out loud as I raced back down the stairway, faster and faster until my feet weren't touching the steps anymore; I was flying through the rushing mist. Hands were about my shoulders, why hadn't I felt them before? I could hear voices now as well, my eyelids fluttered and then I opened them wide.

I was sitting on the pavement, slumped against the corner I had fought so hard to get around against the biting wind, not long since.

"You all right mate?" Several concerned people had gathered around me and they helped me to my feet, advising, steadying, reassuring.

"Yes, thank you, all of you," I said, "I can truly, honestly say that I have never felt better!"

© H. R. Brown, 27/11/2006

SIM CITY³

Two days ago, Ali spoke on his snazzy mobile phone to his scientifically-minded friend Digby, about Digby's career. The former was a farmer's son with dreams of an acting career, the latter an aspiring Nobel Prize winner, if he could maintain his piercing focus upon any one subject for long enough. The two were firm friends, and had been since childhood.

"You're a nutter," said Ali.

"You don't know the market like I do," Digby chided him.

"Market, pigging shmarket; I know when you're not talking outta yer mouth!"

"It's a *good* idea!"

"What're you saying, man?! Tara Hayloft in a skimpy bikini, jumping round a dark maze and kicking the shit outta bunch of bleedin' zombies - *that* is a computer game! What you've got is - to put it pleasantly, right, 'cos I'm a pleasant enough man - is a right blazing crock o' *shit!*"

"It'll work! You don't understand the potential here - we can unlock the secrets of existence itself! We can project, with enough simulations, the best possible form that human society should take!"

Ali reclined in his chair. "Oh aye," he said, "I can see it now! 'Brilliant Scientist Gives Away Future To Pursue Idiot Career In Computer Humanics!"

Ali listened patiently as his friend described the process whereby, with historians working upon the old 'Sim City' game format upon the new Mecca Computers, they could create a version which could create or recreate any known form of human society since the dawn of time. The idea was that with enough trials and mixing of ideas, any person could discover the best possible form of human environment and coexistence with Nature Herself, all within the confines of a set of computer algorithms.

"Let me just say this once more, very carefully," said Ali, "Just to give yer one last chance to wedge it somewhere between yer ears; *it is not going to sell.* You are not going to make enough money to keep it *going.* Now, do you understand me?"

Digby was always unpeturbed by his irrational ventures and whilst all his friends were continually trying to talk him out of things, he would always be forgiven his eccentricities. He looked quizzically at a far off point upon the horizon and informed his oldest friend in this life -

"Ali, my old friend, of course I understand. But what you still don't quite get, is that I'm not simply going to sell it as 'Sim City; The Next Generation', or anything like that, one day. This is just a little something which I managed to sneak it into a whole, different, other astrophysical project, just as a subroutine of a suggested galaxy-mapping project. The thesis that describes my aims and intentions in this, is a small subsection of one of the many, great volumes of appendices which I took the opportunity to include. You see, Physics is all about building upon the shoulders of giants, these days. One needs an additional little volume of appendices of printouts and photocopies, to one's masterpiece."

Ali creased his brow. "You know, you talk some neat pulp fiction, man," he said, "But this is mad. You're saying you're going to hide this project you've been hinting at for three years - yes, and don't you bloody deny it, you bugger - in the middle of a much bigger, bullshit problem that's going to get you your degree *anyway*?!"

Digby drew breath. Ali waited.

"Well," said Digby, "Well, yes! I suppose that is what I'm saying."

"And I thought you said it was just a computer game!?"

"I never said it was a game, I said the idea is based on the idea of the game, but it would be infinitely more complex."

"No shit!"

***

It's a warm, lazy afternoon at the Bower's Farm. The farmer and his wife are doing the rounds of local produce shops - dropping off eggs, fruit, vegetables and preserves - while their twenty-two year old son Ali is relaxing in the in the summer sun, atop a bale of hay in the field, having just smoked a spliff. All is calm. There are jobs which he should be doing to earn his keep but he's convinced he's on top of them and besides, his parents won't be back for at least an hour.

It is chill-out time.

Then the alarm on his digital watch begins beeping at him. He groans and grumbles at the intrusion upon his karma, and then remembers the reason he set it to go off in the first place; it's time to feed the poultry.

Ali mutters to himself as he gets up and heads off towards the farmyard. It isn't like the chickens, ducks and geese don't already get the best, free-range diet already, he reasons. Besides getting leftovers from all the family meals, they are *proper*, free-range birds; they only get shut in at night to prevent the fox getting them. In the daytime - especially in summer - they get all the bugs, beetles, worms they want in the orchard and the fields, all the grass they can manage and everything. Why is he having to get up from his spot in the sun to feed them?

He wanders on towards the farmyard, muttering and cursing - his karma in a state of confusion.

Adding to his cosmic grievance list, is the fact that the walk between his hay-bale and the farmyard seems to be taking way too long. It should only take him a minute, but it seems to go on for a lot longer than that. Ali idly wonders if it is the damage he is inflicting upon his lungs which is slowing him down, or if it is simply that his sense of the passage of time which has been somewhat compromised by the 'evil weed'. Or possibly, he reflects, it is a combination of both.

Eventually he enters the farmyard and takes small (but well-earned) pleasure in scaring a couple of hens, who happen to be perched quietly on the small wall at one side. One of them, squawking loudly with the outrage of having been disturbed mid-lay, leaps into the air, wings flapping wildly and uses the tractor as a further jumping point from which to take off even higher. Her wings are going faster than Ali would have believed it possible for the wings of a chicken to flap, as she sails up, over the farmhouse and away into the clear, blue sky.

Now, Ali feels the fear grip him. He slowly sits down on the spot, telling and retelling himself a truth he has known since his family first moved onto the farm when he was only six years old;

"Chickens *cannot* fly."

He is also faced with the evidence of his own eyes, which he still has every faith in; the chicken was indeed *a chicken*, and did indeed, *fly away*.

This paradox keeps Ali quiet for many minutes, before the screeching of the geese brings him back to the job in hand. Whilst he is throwing out jugs of mixed corn onto the poultry-befouled cobbles of the farmyard, he forces himself to conclude that one of his two, incontrovertible facts is not, in fact, incontrovertible. Hence, and not without a sense of awe at his own discovery, Ali finds himself formulating a new truth;

"*Most* chickens cannot fly, however a tiny minority, *can*."

Wow! Not even his dad knows this, and his dad's done all the homework on his farming, many moons since. But still it's so unlikely - and where had this one, super-chicken gone? Ali has no evidence to prove his point and with this in mind, he elects not to inform the old man of his discovery - yet.

The feeding done, Ali remembers that the eggs need

collecting. Grumbling once again, he sets off around the hen huts, searching all the usual nooks and crannies. During the collection process, he finds himself gazing out across the other big fields of the Bower's Farm, to the thin line of forest bordering the land. Within this bottle-green strap of land, lacing down the lime-green hill, was a beck in and around which Ali had spent much of his childhood playing.

Now, it seems to loom larger at him through the afternoon sun, than it ever did, even when he was only six.

Perhaps it's the childhood reminiscences, perhaps the foreboding, yet intoxicating sense of nature and her animal fury which stirs the youthful Ali. Perhaps it's a desire to set right the facts in his own mind - many of which are becoming severely challenged since he started smoking his gear this afternoon - but one way or another, Ali finds himself making the trek across the fields on the Eastern front of their lands, towards the impressively towering forest at the borders.

The journey takes him longer than expected, and the unharvested field has grown wilder and taller than it has any right to, dammit. Ali curses quietly to himself as he bludgeons and hacks his way through it. In his impatience to get to the forest, Ali begins to run, and before long, he is standing, panting, by the beck.

The beck flows at different rates, depending upon recent rainfall - though it has never run dry within living memory. For the season, the beck is quite a surprising torrent today. The waves rise and fall, crash and bubble down the gulch with a startling clarity and an almost frightening motion. Ali wonders slightly at this, until he looks upwards. The emerald roof of the forest shimmers with gold where the sun peeps through, and it is a very long way up.

Ali gasps, stands back and begins to wonder what the hell his gear has been laced with. The moment the thought hits him, his entire day thus far begins to make an awful lot more sense.
"Shit!" he says, unable to stand the sight of the enormous trees, towering above him, swaying serenely, while he has to cope with strange visions of flying chickens, water that flows in larger than life waves and ripples - and distortions in his space-time continuum. He tells himself to be more positive; for instance, perhaps he *didn't* witness a chicken taking off - perhaps it was a pigeon, which this malicious mind-trip had turned into a chicken only within his head.

Feeling better, Ali decides to get back to the farm and ignore the monstrous trees. He turns and finds himself face to face with the king of all bumblebees. Its body is the size of a hen's egg and its wing span must be six inches. It zips around him, making the loudest buzz he's ever heard.

VRRROOOOOOOM!!!

Ali responds with his own sound - though it is an octave higher - and sets off at a sprint for the farm house, practically whimpering as he goes.

His legs and lungs are labouring feverishly when he arrives in the farmyard, gasping and frothing at the mouth. He looks frantically around the familiar yard at the ducks, hens and geese. He also examines the farmhouse and to his great relief, everything here seems normal.

Sodding dodgy dealer must have laced the weed with LSD!

Ali now starts to worry about the fact that his parents will be back soon and the last thing he wants is to have to speak to them when he's in this state. He calls Digby.

"Digby mate; fancy the pub? Now?"

Digby sounds surprised. "Bit early perhaps, but it sounds like a good idea - we need to talk."

"No shit we need to talk!" Ali practically yells at him, "I'm on some dodgy stuff man, I need help!"

"Really? OK, ten minutes?"

"Be there!"

"Chill! I will!"

"OK."

As he leaves the house, Ali finds himself entering another nightmare. The road down the hill appears to be badly broken up, all the way down. It seems to poor Ali as if a brigade of builders has gone ape-shit with pneumatic drills, all the way from the farm down to the main road at the bottom. Earth is spilling through the gaps in the shattered concrete, and Ali clings tightly to his sanity, telling himself it was a dodgy batch, that's all. It isn't real, it will all fade. It's also the reason why the ten minute walk has already taken fifteen - his mental arithmetic has also gone to pot.

And now, the main road looks the same. All the way left and right, as far as he can see, the main road is as decimated as the road down the hill. Ali is heartened now. He knows it's the drugs which are making him see things like this. Hence he ignores the state of the road, until a car trundles past him very slowly over the bumpy, broken stones.

Ali belts the last stretch into the pub, without looking back, denying to himself that he's overtaken the struggling car as he goes.

There are lots of people in the pub and the talk is lively, but Ali is now too paranoid and certain of his own delusions to look anyone in the eye except the barman, whom he asks politely for a pint.

"Seen't roads?" The barman asks him.

Ali freezes. "What about 'em?" he ventures.

"Haven't you seen 'em?! Hey, go take a look outside pal! They're all broken up! They're knackered for miles all around and no-one knows what's done it!"

Ali feels a cold rush up his spine as he takes this in, then Digby's hand is on his shoulder.

"Mine's a pint mate!" Digby says cheerfully.

Ali nods at the barman. "And another, please mate. I'm not going mad. I *did* see the road all broken up! What the fuck's going on?"

"The roads are the least of it," says a woman at the bar nearby, "You should take a walk up the hills!"

"Never mind walkin' up bleedin' hills!" says another man, "Just turn't TV on! There's satellites falling outta t'bloody sky!"

"It'll be terrorists, you'll see!" says another.

Ali turns to face his friend. "You know, maybe I'm not on dodgy stuff. Maybe this is all real - what do the roads look like to you?"

Digby motions him to a table where they sit down.

"I've got to say Ali, you're not the only one to be fooled into thinking they're on drugs. I can hardly believe the things I've been seeing today."

"Oh yeah? How about a bumblebee *this* big?" Ali gestures with his hands, "Or a chicken that can properly *fly*?"

Digby frowns. "Are you saying you saw a chicken actually *fly*? As in 'up, up and away'?"

Ali nods.

"It doesn't make sense," he says, "I saw an anthill you could lose a toddler in, and some pretty massive ants. I saw a blackbird that was too enormous to really be one, but it was. You've seen a giant bumblebee..."

"The chicken wasn't massive," Ali says, "Come to that, neither were't ducks or't geese. Or't eggs."

Digby's looking grim. The colour has left his face, to be replaced with a cold, grey horror.

"The chicken flew," he says quietly, "It *flew*..."

"Yeah it flew, man! I'm not kidding, it flew up, jumped off the tractor and it was off! Over the hills and far fuckin' away!" Ali pauses for breath,

"What the fuck is going on, man?" he says, "I mean really, what the *fuck* is happening?"

Digby climbs raggedly to his feet, as if he's weighed down like Atlas himself. "I'm going to make you a bet," he says, slowly.

"What? What bet?"

Digby points to the ceiling, some ten feet from the floor. "Bet you I can touch the ceiling by jumping from here, right where I'm stood."

Ali shakes his head. "Bollocks mate. Anyway, what are you on about? We've got more important things to worry about!"

"No Ali, we have not, because if I'm right and I can touch that roof by jumping from this spot, then I think I'll know what's going on."

"Oh aye?! How?"

"Do I want to know?" Digby asks himself, quietly.

"Stop playing silly buggers!" the barman chides him as he's clearing up the glasses.

Digby ignores the barman and his friend, tenses, and then he leaps up so high and hard that his head cracks the ceiling.

All the exited chatter in the pub stops as he crashes back to the floor and lies in a giggling heap, clutching his aching head. Then the noise starts up again, more lively than before.

"Bloody hell mate! You OK?"

"How the fuck did he hit the fuckin' roof?"

"Jesus!"

"Yeah - he's come again!"

"He's bleedin'!"

Ali helps his friend back onto his chair. "So," he says, "You feel better now? Wanna tell me what you think is going on?"

Digby wipes the condensation off his pint and examines the bubbles within.

"Ever seen a flee jump?" he asks, "You know, if a man could jump proportionately as high, he could leap over a tower block."

"We've shrunk!" Ali says, "That's what you're saying, isn't it?!"

"It's something more than that," Digby tells him, "Why would our shrinking coincide with satellites falling from the sky? Why are all our homes and buildings the same size they ever were?"

Ali's brow flexes fiercely inwards.

"I saw the Moon earlier, not long before I finished legging it all the way along what's left of Kallyadene Road, to put some distance between me and that fucking anthill. I stopped running, I was sweating cobs and I looked up at the Moon, pale in this light blue sky, and do you know what? It was the same size as ever it is. Bumblebees and ants may be three times bigger, man-made satellites are falling from the skies, but certain things we've built our world upon are still true."

Some of the other punters in the pub are listening to Digby now. He's obviously a bigger thinker than most, and an acrobat to boot; an eccentric with interesting ideas. As soon as he finishes speaking, several of them urge him to go on and get to the point.

Digby looks around him in concern.

"OK," he says, "Have any of you ever heard the theory that everything in the universe could be expanding or contracting in size? The theory as it goes isn't provable, because even if it were true then all measuring rods and frames of reference would be expanding or contracting at the same rate - there'd be nothing to compare with."

Digby takes a long swig, gurgles, gasps and then scratches his head.

"Go on!" says Ali.

Half the pub is listening to Digby now, the other half are watching the frantic and fearful news reports on the pub TV. Rampant, overgrown wildlife is beginning to threaten the human race as it has not done since the dawn of history. Mass panic is spreading and along with it, serious breakdowns in law and order.

"What if there is a grand scheme behind it all?" Digby says, simply, "What if such a theory were not only true, but *God herself* has control of it?!"

A lot of blank faces glance at each other in befuddlement.

"What if -" he continues, "- Mankind has had its last chance with the miracle of creation we were given? What if God's decided to let the rest of the universe carry on growing at the same rate, but everything within the sphere of human influence stops precisely at the size it is now?"

"That would mean we're still shrinking!" - an excitable young woman cries out.

"Hang on," Ali says, "I told you - all the ducks, geese an' hens were't same size they ever were!"

"You also told me that one of your chickens took off and flew away into the clear blue sky," Digby reminds him, "And since all your chickens were bred by the hand of Man, I'd say that they're very much a part of the sphere of human influence, so they're shrinking too. That's why it flew away, that's why I can jump from here and hit my head on the roof - we're a lot lighter now than we used to be under the same gravity."

"This is all bollocks!" announces Chimes (a friendly old soak, so-named in respect of his favourite whiskey), "Watch this!"

Chimes then jumps into the air, certain that he can only jump so high. He lands bleeding on the floor like Digby before him, and another dent has been made in the pub ceiling.

Digby falls silent, respecting the mounting fear and anger in the crowd. Ali leans towards him. "Are you going mad?"

"Got any better explanations? *I know* it makes sense. All our influence over this planet could dwindle to nothing within days."

Ali's face says it all, so Digby continues.

"Look out of the window. See the estate? Look at the houses man!"

Ali sees the houses are small, and spread out with too much space between them. More disturbingly, the familiar view from the pub window is now horribly out of proportion. The trees behind form the same old pattern, but the estate is beginning to look like a scattered collection of toy houses in front of it.

"And that view has got slowly but steadily worse since we started drinking in here." Digby informs him.

"So... What? We're really *still shrinking*?!"

Digby's look says it all.

"*Balls!*" roars Chimes, bloodied but unabashed, "I'm going outside, and we'll soon see who's shrunk an' who's boss!"

As Digby, Ali and everyone else watches Chimes striding outside, they're glad to see the good old bloke bawling his lungs out at the heavens, threatening and challenging Mother Nature herself.

Then all at once, they're appalled to see a spider as big as a football creeping up behind him. The window is opened, everyone yells at him, and Chimes turns around.

He screams. He stamps his foot at the spider, and it moves warily off to one side. Chimes looks back at the pub and shouts in triumph, and the cheer is echoed within.

Then, staring back at his friends in the pub, he screams again. He turns and runs as the shadow passes over the pub, and then his friends all see Chimes plucked effortlessly from the earth by an enormous bird of prey, and carried away from this life.

In this moment of horror, everyone turns in desperation to Digby, who has already returned to his pint. With a hopeless, grey grin, Dibgy looks around from face to face, his hands already shaking, and he says,

"Ever seen a cat play with a mouse?"

© H. R. Brown, 17/11/2003

MAKE UP

My friend Ted is a strange man, and he loves it. I once asked him why he was so mad, and he told me that he simply liked to see the look on people's faces.

"What look?" I asked him.

"It's never the same twice," he said, "But its extremes are mortal fear at one end, and hysterical laughter at the other."

"You're mad," I told him.

"No I'm not," he replied, "I'm just different."

"You're mad," I repeated.

"But am I benign?", he said.

"'Course you are!"

"I'm benignly insane, then?"

"Yeah, I suppose."

"How do you differentiate benign insanity from sanity, albeit sanity of a different variety from that which you're used to?"

I couldn't answer that one.

Ted told me about this man he once saw in the street on a busy Saturday afternoon. The man was bearded, wearing a dress and dancing around a lamp post chanting poetry, Gregorian-fashion. No-one went nearer to him than they had to, no-one looked at him. Ted stood and watched the man, fascinated, for a quarter of an hour. On he went with the chanting, and the dancing, and the busy throng curved carefully around him, everyone studiously *not* watching.

Ted went up to the man, and said,

"What *are* you doing, mate?"

The bearded transvestite stopped his dancing and hugged Ted, saying,

"Jesus, man! I've been waiting three hours for someone to ask me that!"

After which, the bearded man went home.

Ted told me that story whilst putting on his make-up for an evening in the pub.

"You can't go to the pub like that, mate!" I said.

"I can, shall and will," Ted replied, lacing up his army boots.

"Why?", I asked.

"Oh, I'm just securing a facist-free zone with a radius of a couple of yards at least, I reckon."

"Someone's gonna get lamped," I told him.

"Why? The urge to hit out at what one doesn't understand is anti-evolutionary," he said.

I shook my head and we went to the pub. No-one started a fight with Ted, and he ended up pulling a stunning redhead. I could have cried.

The next day he reminded me that sanity was almost entirely an illusion.

That was last week. Today as I write this, lying on my bed with my bare feet sticking out of the window, rinsing in the gentle summer rain, I wonder whether 'benign insanity' is something you can catch?

© H. R. Brown, 26/05/2002

Sir Alex, record sound and transcribe everything I say.

My name's Monty Wellsworth, I'm a thirty-seven year old human male, I don't know if any other humans will survive to find this or even make sense of it, but in case anyone or anything with a brain ever does, I'm just leaving this record while I still can.

Also, I want it on record that those who thought it was a good idea to conjoin the names Siri and Alexa into one, posh-sounding, toff-twat, when that whatsit-corps took over that whatever it was corporation that used to be something else limited, those blokes are poisonous, incel, pig fuckers.

And it's people like them I blame for all this horrifying shit.

Fuck, where to start?

When it first hit I just ran. I mean I was desperate for a place to hide from the coming.. Something. Like, what the fuck is this? I was suddenly freaking out completely, I didn't know why, I'd come out of the loo in the restaurant into a general panic, everyone was yelling and going nuts – and for no reason I can really get my head round, now I was too. It was demented, it was..

At one point, I ran into another man who was just as scared and we both said it together;

"Something's coming! Right?!"

Two minutes before, everything had just been normal. Nice Saturday evening out with mates in my favourite Italian place. First course garlic bread, bit of red wine, everyone was enjoying theirs too, Gibsey had a fucking-awesome one-liner;

What did the leper say to the prostitute? Keep the tip.[1]

It was busy, was a lively place all around, the evening was like a hundred others and then, the panic, and then after the first panic it was like we were -

caught

Caught in the throat, everyone was – gasping and retching and clawing at their throats for air -

- then as breath came back again; air was getting in again, and it was better – but then it was not, no, not at all..

We could feel it rattling outwards, from the bases of all of our spines, we all knew we were all feeling it too we were all rattling with it – that was the really weird bit – we all knew, I *know* we all knew but of course there's no way I could prove that – we all knew there was a something coming, something that none of us humans could avoid, it was a feeling, like a, like a long lost, demented neighbour you'd rather forget, or an image of like, infinity - this horrifying, *forever*, that you can't escape from..

It's here for us.

We all know it. It's just like an earthquake – but for one very specific detail; *we* are the ones rattling, just *us - the humans*. Not the building we're in, not any of the pets with the customers, not the fish in the fucking aquarium or the water they're in – there's a vibrational earthquake going on in the bones of myself and my fellow folk in the restaurant only. We're all feeling a form of hell being raised, right down our spines -

The surroundings are not shaking – not at all. Just us. Looking at reach other we all realise this is a crazy new vibration, meant very definitely only for us.. The screaming gets worse, the yelling, confusion, wailing, fucking *lunacy*. Drinks getting smashed, tables going over, fights breaking out. It's scary how quick it turned into a riot.

A riot! In my favourite fucking Italian place!

I'm not even thinking about that, I'm legging it out of the place because I want to hide from everything and everyone – but there's fighting blocking the exit and even some more violence spilling in from the street – can't get out that way, so I turn and head back in, wondering about charging through the kitchen for maybe another exit, I've seen films – then I run into this dude -

We agree there's something coming, then dodge each other to find a place to hide. I don't even know why I knew it was important to get a place to hide..

But maybe now I do. I think the same way we all knew the same forgotten something was coming, was the way I, and others, knew to look for a hiding hole.

But the throbbing, the buzzing, shaking.. Jesus H fucking *Christ..*

Buzzing in the ears was worst, thought my eardrums were gonna pop out my head and – I was doubled over when I saw I was right next to a cupboard. So I open it - and I realise it'll do. At this point, I'm getting the full body tremors hitting, everyone's gasping, so am I but I keep it together somehow, I promise myself to help the owners clear the mess later and I go in the cupboard head first and start just sweeping everything out and dropping it on the floor. So it's clear pretty quickly, I'm not messing about, I don't know why it's important to hide inside something for protection – it just somehow *is*. A few others noticed what I was doing but they struggled to reach me cos of the pain, and then I'm in!

Doors, slammed closed! And I'm thanking the universe for the railings it's left for me, on the insides of the doors, so I use these to hold them shut.

So then I'm in total darkness, the pounding in my head almost beyond comprehension – when suddenly it's entirely beyond it – and I'm screaming like everyone else.

Then, the vibrations stop. There's this total, almost blissful calm, then there's a crazy bright light everywhere, flooding everything, spilling through into the cupboard I was in. I mean it was so bright inside the fucking cupboard I had to shield my eyes, god knows what it was like for everyone else outside in it.

I hear people gasping outside, some shrieking, and even some hysterical laughter that really scared me shitless – then the light fades out – and immediately everything is normal again. Except for me still being I the cupboard, it's like popping out of a dream into reality.

WHERE DO I KNOW THIS FEELING FROM?

It's like coming out of a dream, yes, but...

Something had changed, is the only way I can describe it. Something had switched. I couldn't tell what it was yet.

I got out of the cupboard and wandered around the place. It was a mess, but everyone had calmed right down and was looking relieved, kind of.

The dude I'd run into before saw me, he went to give me a high-five, and before I even looked at what I was slapping, I slapped this big fat hoof.

"Fuck is that?" I said, I'm staring at it, pointing at it – this big fucking hoof thing on the end of his arm, it's like he's forgotten to take off the last part of the pantomime horse.

"What's what?" he says, grinning like he can't even tell he's still wearing this thing and I'm wondering if it's him going mad or me – after what just happened – but he means it, nods, carries on back to his table.

I go back to mine too and I'm chatting about what the hell was that rattling we all just had and the craziness and the mad bright light – but no-one really wants to talk about it. I suddenly get really glad I wasn't out in the main room with the rest of them.

And then.. Everyone just got on with their meals! I was torn between pushing it, and watching the fellow with the hoof I'd run into. He wasn't far off and I could see him better than he could see me. He was carrying on like nothing had happened, and even weirder – his friends were too. The bloke was using his fork with his left hand – and clonking his hoof in his food with the other – then gathering food between the fork and the fucking hoof and slurping on it, not a care in the world.

And no-one seemed to even notice but me. I got really scared. I asked my mates to watch the bloke and tell me they could see him making a total mess of his meal, getting it everywhere – because he's trying to eat with a fucking hoof?!

I mean, his friends all ignored it. Or somehow.. Couldn't see it. And then my mates didn't see anything to waste their time on. I gave up trying to get them to see how weird it was.

In the end I just put down the money for my meal and left early. I was too freaked out. I was so freaked out I clean forgot to pay any extra for the cupboard I'd trashed, but given the general state of the place, and the fucking daze coming over everyone, I realised I didn't need to worry about that.

So I go home and text my bro and my parents and Bash, my best mate, ask them if they've seen any crazy bright lights lately, or anyone wearing a pantomime hoof. My bro and my folks both come back to me pretty quickly and they don't seem to know anything, so I think it must have been a localised thing, nothing to worry about. Bash doesn't reply, but he's not a slave to his phone so I might not hear anything for a day or two anyway. Can always call round, he's less than a mile away..

But for last night I was still weirded out and unhappy. So I grab my brandy and I start drinking. Great for denying facts, is booze. I get a bit merrier and decide whatever the fuck happened tonight was probably some stray LSD that got in people's food, nothing to worry about, it'll wear off and everything will be fine. Never mind that I already know people outside the restaurant went nuts too.

So I'm boozing and watching a sitcom and laughing too hard even though it ain't that funny and I've seen it before anyway, just cos it felt normal, felt safe.

Then I make the mistake of turning on the news. And of course, there's the news anchor, calmly doing his thing, reading the news with dignity, with gravitas.. Occasionally shuffling his reports around with a fucking *hoof*.

So I turn off the news, scream at no-one in particular, headbutt a few solid items, and start swigging that brandy like I've got lessons to teach Oliver Reed, George Best, the Rat Pack and anyone else who ever thought they could drink.

Don't remember a lot after that, except ranting crazy shit, at people who weren't there, so I've potentially freaked my neighbours right the fuck out.

Uuuuuuhhh..

So this morning, I wake up with the sun in my eyes, I mean everything is lit up like the middle of summer. That's what happens when you pass out on your couch, without the curtains drawn, in an east-facing room.

So I stagger upstairs to pee, and then I drink a pint or so of water straight from the tap.

I'm trying not to think about last night, trying to put it all down to the huge amount of brandy I poured down my neck, without even going near the issue of why I poured it down me like that in the first fucking place. And I'm suddenly completely allergic to the fucking television.

I go into my bedroom, I'm thinking I should really ditch my clothes, get a shower, but then I see the street below out of my bedroom window.

Little Lilly Dent from number 67 across the road is learning to ride her new bike, should be able to lose the stabilisers soon. I breathe in and out slowly, realising everything is OK, Lilly's out enjoying life and learning, her parents are watching they're but letting her work things out for herself..

And none of them have hooves!

So I just stand and watch for minute, relaxing, it's so refreshing and normal and then..

Then quiet Derek from number 79's there, he's just ambling along the pavement towards Lilly and her folks. Looks like he's coughing, staggering a bit, and of course he does have a hoof, I can see it from here, just like the nightmare things from last night.

And here I am sober, no excuses, broad fucking daylight.

And Derek, Derek turns into some kind of pig creature in front of my eyes. I wish I was kidding. Suddenly both his arms have got hooves at the end them, his whole body's shuddering and having massive spasms like something out of a sci-fi horror film, which is what this whole fucking 24 hours has been like, to be honest – then he's down on four legs, there's the face of a fucking pig or a more like a wild fucking boar where his normal face used to be, with big ugly tusks and a fuck-ugly great big snout, and he's ripped his clothes off and now he's charging towards little Lilly like a hungry beast – and she, she..

Jesus. Ahhh, fuck. Sorry.

Lilly, she screams, like a kid would or like anyone would when quiet Derek from number 79 turns into some kind of mutant pig beast in front of you in broad daylight and then comes snorting and grunting towards you like a mad thing.. She screams at him but she doesn't move, she's rooted to the spot and her parents – they did nothing.

NOTHING!

The Derek monster thing jumped on Lilly, held her down on the pavement and ripped her fucking face off with its teeth.

Right in front of me, right there in the middle of the street, she's screaming with her face off, eyes that can't blink or close popping out of her blood red skull, more blood pissing out everywhere, the Derek thing's holding her down with one hoof whilst he's using the other to help him scoop up and eat the tattered flesh hanging out of his horrible mouth before he goes in for more, Lilly's gone mute now, her body's gone into spasms and her fucking parents are just standing watching and fucking smiling like she's still learning to ride her fucking bike.

Worse, I'm standing frozen by this shit as well. So I realise this poor little girl's parents are not going to do anything to save her life – and then I see her dad's bloody *hoof* – he had it behind his wife's back at first so I didn't see it.

So I get they're both.. Also turning Derek. No other reason

they'd be unconcerned by this. So I grab the phone and call 999. Someone fucking had to. Never called it before, was expecting a calm voice to say something like "Hello, please confirm which service you require; police, ambulance or fire?"

What I got was a racket that reminded me of the chaos in the restaurant last night.

I said "Hello?!" many times, getting louder and louder until I was screaming it down the phone.

All I heard that might have once been human, was some grunting.

So now - I am fucking terrified.

Is everyone alive turning fucking *Derek*?! Is the whole race turning into these feral pig beast things? I hid in the cupboard from whatever it was that did this, but does that mean I escaped – or did I just delay the inevitable??

So then I think fuck it and I grab a big, heavy, unopened can of spinach and I go out into the street. The Derek thing's still picking bits of little Lilly's flesh off her carcass whilst the parent-things are holding each other, touching each other like in wonder, like it's the first time they've met – and their daughter's dead body is still just lying there nearby with Derek chewing on it.

I didn't realise what I was going to do until I did it, and I'm not proud, but this isn't the same world any more, so I also kinda think.. What the hell.

I walked right up to the Derek-thing and I said, all bright and breezy-like, "Hey Derek, please tell me what the fuck you think you're doing?!"

The Derek thing looked up at me, bits of Lilly hanging out of its mouth with blood and spit. It grunted a warning at me, which I ignored, then it jumped up on its hind legs, growled loudly and it came at me.

I hit that thing so hard in the face with the can of spinach, I caved its snout in and broke off one of its tusks. Blood went everywhere, it went down on the floor and it was howling and then I was howling at it, daring it to get up and fucking try it again but it didn't it started whimpering at me then, and then I was yelling at the parent-things too, but they just kinda looked at me funny, like bemused, then went back to touching each other up, him with a hand and a hoof, her with two still-human hands, but as I watched, right in front of me, one of her hands shifted, fleshed-out and grew a thick outer bit and, basically turned hoof.

So they were both, definitely, going Derek. Hooves and all. Although I suppose they're not actually hooves; the fucking Derek-creature looked like a big overgrown pig or a wild boar. So the initial stage isn't the appearance of a hoof – it's actually a fucking *trotter*.

So anyway, I went back into my house to check the TV. There'd be some news on or something, surely. Straight to News 24, and there was news on. Oh, was there news on.

I cannot tell you, I cannot express the weird and horrible joy of watching your head of state, live on television, clonking trotters with other heads of state. All of them apparently oblivious, as was the news anchor – even to the fact that some of them had clearly also gone the full Derek, meaning they were great hulking pig beasts as well, snuffling around on the floor or getting aggressive and fighting each other.

I turned the TV off again. Whatever's happening, clearly it's a global phenomenon.

So now I'm really panicking and I'm calling all my friends and family and I can't get through to any of them.

Feels like the whole world has gone to shit. I might suddenly be the last human left, I'm going fucking crazy, but I think the best thing I can do now is get out, lock up my house and check out my local situation – like do I actually need to flee for the fucking hills or not?

I appreciate in hindsight I may have borrowed a plot-line from a Simon Pegg film, but I wanted to check out my locals first, see if a pint and a game of pool could still happen in the vicinity, maybe check the local shops too, afterwards.

Stuck my head in the Hole in't Wall first; pig fest. Lots of hooves on the ones that were still human too - no – *trotters*, couldn't see anyone who still had both fucking hands, so I left. Same at the Wellington. The Olive Garden looked nice, possibly because there weren't many in there, but I couldn't see any pig beasts or trotters, so I went in. The landlady was charming as fuck, sat me down, went to get me a drink – then she went full pig-beast – instantly! No pupal-stage with just the arm turned trotter, no, she dropped my drink, burst out her clothes and her whole body leapt up into the air, landed on the bar, screeching like crazy, full-on snout, tusks and trotters and it was snarling and spitting at me and I jumped up too and fucking legged-it out.

I went past the offy on the way home, but I could see the carnage inside so I didn't try it.

I got back home and decided to stay for now, keeping a very low profile, windows drawn and lights off.

It's only about survival now. I have no pig signs in me, not yet, touch wood, god forbid, etc.

But given how quickly it's spread to everyone..

I've got a choice to make. Do I become.. *That*?! Or do I *not*.

So I started boozing. Been boozing for hours now, 'cos I've got a decent emergency stash, and if this is the choice I'm facing on a Saturday night, I don't see why I should do it sober, this requires dutch courage! I finished the bit of brandy that was left, had a bottle of red and started on the scotch, then there might have been a few beers before I went back to the scotch.. Or..? Anyway, before I get to it, I realised I should probably record this stuff..

The issue now is, how long do I have? Hiding in that cupboard can't have saved me. How long before I get my first fucking trotter? Or god-forbid I just go straight from human to full-on pig-beast in an instant like that poor bitch in the last bar?

I don't want to live in a world where quiet Derek from number 79 suddenly goes wild-boar-fucking feral on a Saturday afternoon, and bites poor little Lilly Dent's face off.

Maybe that's the point. Maybe Agent Smith[2] was right; we've had our time.

And that light – that massive bright light I hid from and no-one wanted to talk about, I think that's the source of everything. I mean whether it's God or Allah or Jehovah, Jah, Ra, Yaweh, Atum, the Universe, whatever, it was something that switched our genes, our evolution or whatever, switched it right down, instantly into wild-fucking-boar territory.

Which.. Must mean we all, collectively, deserve this? That can't be right. Can it? What did humans do to.. I mean..

We have fucked the planet, I guess. And some of what passes for politics these days is.. So now we all turn into pigs?! I still don't believe it, even though I've seen it. Jesus.. What happens to actual *pigs*?! I never even thought, here we are all turning into pigs – what does Ra then do the pigs that were already pigs? Do they turn into fucking *humans*?!

Oh fucking fucking *fuck it*. I don't want to know.

What's worse is.. I feel it coming now. I think I already knew. Why did I get the machine to record this when I could have just written or typed it.. I wanted to give myself the best chance to get it all down and recorded before..

I haven't looked down for hours.. I think I can *feel* it and.. You know what? It'll be all right.

WHAT THE FUCK AM I TALKING ABOUT?!

It can't even be *human*! This, this.. *Resignation*! It's like this disease, this plague or whatever it is attacks the mind as well, or how could I be already OK with the fact that, yes, I see it now.

My trotter.

My trotter, where a human hand once was.

I am surprisingly OK with that.
Gnnngngggnnnrrrggnnddaffggg..

Oh fuck oh god I should have fucking killed myself when I..

gaagggdddgaffgagaaddrruddaggurrgg..
dddrrummpffffggaagrrrggnnn

bbrroodddaagggnnnn..

TRANSCRIPT ENDS.

© H. R. Brown, 18/11/2019

Notes:
1. Origin forgotten, I apologise for this. Good for Christmases if the joke in your cracker isn't funny(!), as it contains no swearwords - but may cause ructions in families between the offended and the amused. I also know of no sound way to explain it to a child.
2. *The Matrix*, dir. the Wachowskis, 1999.

OPINION POLL

In a world of clouds, drifting, drifting. Almost imperceptibly, golden lines began to slice the grey. The view is becoming clearer now; through the grey gloom comes an aerial view of a massive zebra crossing, the size of a football field. Must be a long way up, floating... No, it's amber light coming up through a cattle grid, no, it's... *what is it?*

The linear pattern on the wall, made of the morning sun filtering through the blinds, was something of a relief to Ed when he finally understood it. Thoughts weighed too heavy to think in his mind. As yet he hadn't focussed upon anything, but here was a simple pattern he could recognise. And the smell, he knew the smell all right. He knew now he'd be OK - he wasn't dead. He was in hospital.

But what of his limbs? Ed became aware that his arms were OK, but they felt like lumps of unfashioned lead. He fought through this to reach down and find out the most important thing and felt a little easier about things straightaway; happy that he could feel it and feel that he was feeling it. His good arm stretched further down and found his legs, and as his hand found them, he realised he could also vaguely feel his toes and wriggle them. Yes, there was definitely movement under the covers where his feet were. Now he relaxed completely. All seemed present and correct.

He sighed and tried to stretch, then gasped in agony. It ached and burned all over - he was covered in bruises. The memory began to come back then; the visit, the once in a lifetime chance appearing and then -

Ed began to giggle and this ripped horribly through the lines of scabs along his lips, such that the pain and the triumph made strange companions in his tears.

He noticed, when she awoke with a start at the noise, that there was a nurse in the chair by his bed, a gossip mag in her lap. He tried to ask her for water, but the only noise to emerge was a strange, rasping,

"*Phwaaoob.*"

"Don't try to speak," she shushed him, "Just relax, you've taken quite a beating."

Ed gasped, pulled his jaw a little further open and managed to breath the word "*Waadaa!*"

When he received the glass, he sat up. This was a slow process, involving a good deal of wincing and grunting, yet it was worth it he thought, as he gulped the water back with zest.

"*Gaaaaaaa!*"

The nurse smiled at him. "Better?"

"Mudge," he said, "Thag you."

"You've taken quite a battering, Edmund," she told him, "You're very lucky not to have been put into a coma, or worse."

Ed smirked hugely and instantly regretted it. "*Grooaarr!*" he moaned.

"Chapped lips?"

He nodded. "How long've I been oud?"

"Nearly two days."

Ed eyed her suspiciously. "You know why I'beer?" he asked her.

The nurse nodded.

"Wha's gonna 'abben?"

"What do you mean?"

"Am I goin' a brison?"

The nurse smiled. "I don't know. Couldn't say."

"Any gobbers wanna zee me?"

"There are two policemen outside Edmund, yes. But they're for your protection."

"Wha?"

"Two days is a long time in the age of multimedia. After what you did and the uproar it's caused, you've become both a hero and a villain. There are a good many nurses in this hospital who'd like your autograph, but there are others who won't treat you. Outside these walls you have fans and enemies alike; you've been receiving letters of support, love letters and as I'm sure you can appreciate, a few death threats. You'll have to learn to deal with this new found celebrity, whatever the outcome of your trial."

"Whoa!"

"Indeed. You should also be aware that you've caused a very problematic rift between the US and the UK."

Ed chuckled and it turned into a bout of coughing. "Boud bloody dime!"

"The US wants to extradite you on charges of terrorism."

Ed felt the sharp sting of mortal panic. "And?!" he begged.

"And you might already have been on your way there, had it not been for the weight of public opinion which wants you tried here for what you did. There's a sizeable crowd outside, has been since you were brought here. If I was a real cynic, I'd say they - and your many other supporters - are the one reason you're still alive."

Ed was silent for a while, taking this in.

"Whaddya you thing?"

"About what?"

"Abou' whadda did."

"Why did you do it?"

Ed swigged some more water. "Dried do ged oud ov

worgging thad nide az well. I did id gos he lied. Gos eez juzd evil. Gos theze wars we're gedding dragged indo are liez an' bullshid. Above all, I did id gos for the virst dime, thad very zecond, I thoud I heard God dalking do me."

The nurse laughed. "Under the circumstances, you're either as mad as that which you clearly detest, or you're the ultimate satirist. That isn't a question, by the way, please don't clarify. But surely you must understand that the very fact you did what you did could well mean an increase in the assault upon our civil liberties? It could be used as evidence that the latest laws are not tough enough, that we need more. How would you feel about that?"

"Iv I hadn'd done id, they'd find excuzez do do thad anyway. And how mudge worze gan id ged?! Bezidez, whad'z thiz, bloody Newznide?! Ged me zome nurzez who wan' my zignadure!"

For many seconds the nurse neither moved nor spoke. Then she fished in her pocket and passed him a pen and paper with a smile.

"To my friend, Nurse Harriet Swindon?!"

Ed grinned again. His lips were feeling a little better for the water and usage.

"No broblem!"

A few hours later, Ed's power of speech was getting much better when a different nurse brought him his lunch. Nurse Ornish was clearly not a fan. She wasted no time in spilling piping hot soup onto his crotch and then, in her heavy-handed scramble to wipe it up, she spilled some more.

"Aaaaiiiii!" said Ed.

"I'm so sorry!" she said, mopping the afflicted area with alarming vigour.

"Oorrrg!" he said, frowning at her. "Bet you don't want my signature, do you?"

"No thank you," she told him, "I've got boils to lance."

Nurse Swindon had been entirely accurate in what she had told him. That afternoon, the news of his consciousness spread to the crowds outside with the result that a great, roaring cheer boomed around the building. This was soon followed by some fearsome booing from the opposing crowd, and then the riot began.

After a minute or two, Ed heard - amid the yells and the screams and the war-cries - the police loudspeakers. Battle had truly commenced. Nurse Swindon rushed into his room with the two policemen.

"Is that all *really* 'cos of me?!" he asked.

Nurse Swindon and one of the policemen both gave him a quick nod. The other officer stood grimacing by the window.

"They want to evacuate you from the hospital, Ed," said Nurse Swindon, "Do you want to go?"

There was something in her eyes that Ed instinctively found alarming. He looked at the two officers, neither of whom had spoken a word. He asked the one who was looking at him, "Why?"

"For your own safety sir," said officer 0707, quickly.

"You really think that mob out there will invade a hospital? For *me*?!"

"Can't afford to take the chance sir," said 0707.

Ed noted the subtle signals from his favourite nurse with an increasing sense of dread.

"Well," he said, "I don't really think I can afford to move, thank you officer. I'm going to have to stay put, I'm afraid."

At this, officer 1109 who had been frowning quietly out of the window, shot his colleague an angry look.

0707 spoke again; "We don't have any choices sir! There's a good chance some of the Ed Willis haters out there are going to get in here and try to kill you."

Ed reclined back into his pillow and spread his hands open in front of him. "Then let them come."

They were both glaring at him now. "Get up!" said 1109.

"I put my life into God's hands the moment I did what I did," said Ed, "If his children wish to find and punish me for what I have done, I will neither run nor attempt to fight. I'll offer myself to their justice."

Ed was stupefied by the benign calm of his own acting.

"You're an intelligent man," said 0707, "And we're told there's been no brain damage - so what the hell do you think you're doing? Out there is mob justice; do you really think it'll be better for you than a court of law?!"

"On the contrary," said Ed, "How do I know for certain you'll be taking me to a court of law? How do I know I won't wind up in some secret American gulag, in some deserted, nameless place, somewhere on the face of the Earth where justice itself is a myth?"

There was triumph in Nurse Swindon's eyes.

"*That fucking nurse!*" shouted 1109, "I told you! I fucking told you! Come on, we're going to have to just take him."

"Fuck's sake!" shouted 0707, "If he won't agree to playing dead in a body bag, how the fuck are we going to get him past that lot?"

He motioned outside with his thumb, whilst Nurse Swindon was edging towards the door.

"You stay fucking put!" 1109 screamed at her, "You're under arrest for terrorism!"

Whilst 1109 then rounded upon his colleague and they began screaming at each other once more, Ed, with a strength he hadn't yet dared test, hoisted himself out of bed, wincing as his feet hit the floor. Still the policemen argued, so he hobbled quickly to a window to survey the battle outside.

"We knock him out," 1109 was saying, urgently, "Cover him with something and Bob's your uncle."

"Oh yeah? And what about *her*?" 0707 had made sure he stood firmly between the door and the nurse.

Ed had forgotten the argument. He was staring in disbelief at the scene, some three stories below. Many police vans were scattered around the hospital walls, but the police themselves were all sitting around chatting and drinking from steaming styrofoam cups. Ed could see that technically, they were guarding the hospital exits, yet they had no real need to. The battle being fought was nothing to do with them.

The battle was between two very different crowds. One was a small crowd of fierce fanatics bearing slogans such as 'ED'S DEAD!' and 'ED WILLIS: TERRORIST SCUM'. They were unsuccessfully trying to break through the far larger crowd which was essentially doing the police's job for them; guarding the hospital. This crowd bore banners such as 'ED IS MY HERO' and 'ED WILLIS FOR PM!'

Around the periphery, news vans had gathered.

Ed felt the tears well up in his eyes. He hoisted up the window, stuck his head out, breathed in as deeply as he could. At this moment, the two policemen had decided to knock them both out and get them out of the hospital undercover, but then Ed bellowed; "HEEE-LLOOO!" to the world outside.

The two opposing crowds rippled and held still, straining to see if it was the man Ed Willis himself or not. The police looked up and began shifting uneasily, setting down drinks and smokes and looking ready for action. And scores of zoom lenses did their job and brought his face into focus. There was a moment's confusion all round. Is that really him? If it is, he looks like shit! Yeah, but they did beat the living shit out of him two days ago.

And then the shout went up from the vicinity of the news vans - it is him! Just as officers 0707 and 1109 grabbed Ed from behind and began to pull him away from the window.

"HELP!" he screamed, "The police are abducting me!"

Then his grip failed him and they pulled him to the floor, there was a flash of light and all went blank once again.

***

Nurse Swindon was waiting for him again when he came round. She had a plaster across her left eyebrow.

"Uuurrgh," he groaned, though he smiled as he did so, "How long this time?"

"Only half an hour or so."

"We're still here in the hospital, aren't we?"

She smiled. "Yes we are. You were very lucky. After what you yelled out of the window, the police outside found themselves under attack. They radioed our friends Pinky and Perky in here and ordered them to leave you be. Then they had to negotiate for three of your supporters to come up here to confirm you were still with us, in order that your crowd backed off. I'm told it was a minor miracle the army itself didn't have to move in on your crowd and start what could very well have developed into a civil war."

"I'm beginning to believe in miracles," he told her, "Hey, what happened to your eye?"

"That's what I got for being on your side."

"God, I'm sorry!"

"Don't worry, I've had worse. Anyway, I intend to have the Sentinel investigate for me."

"What?"

"I'm not daft," she said, "There aren't many you can trust, but there's a Sentinel journalist waiting outside to speak to me - Susan Stiltoe. And it definitely *is* her, I recognise her face. I was just waiting until you came back round before I went."

She grinned at the look in Ed's eyes. "Unless you want her to come in here and interview both of us?!"

***

A low-lit room. The sparse decor was highlighted by occasional, small, amber uplighters. Within this room, two figures huddled.

"We cannot allow him a trial by Jury!" the first hissed.

"And enrage the entire country by denying him it?" the second intoned, quietly.

"Public perception is your forte! You have to find a way round this, *now*!"

"Our hands have been tied. I admit, there have been errors in our procedure. He should have been sent directly to a military hospital. It is true that once he was in the public hospital, our agents should have been able to infiltrate it successfully, but how were we to appreciate that the efforts of one nurse and certain colleagues of hers could frustrate us so quickly and effectively? And as for the second time he'd already woken up, which made the problem far more acute."

"For Christ's sake!" the first figure spat, "Just what exactly is your problem with putting a cap in his ass? Back home he wouldn't have lasted the day."

"The UK is not yet the US, and in view of our gun laws it never will be. Not quite. Now, in this situation we would appear to have only one option; nobble the jury."

"Are you telling me there's no way to avoid a trial?"

"The Sentinel's hacks have seen to that. They have philanthropist backers and can afford lawyers to match our own."

"The Law! The goddamn *Law*?! Why does this always come back to the fucking law? You've got the clout to step outside it!"

"Not when under counter-surveillance, we haven't. You must appreciate why we had to grant bail. It's all very well to send a nobody or Johnny-Foreigner to jail indefinitely, but Willis is a British citizen. He always has been, he's got no previous convictions and worst of all; he's white. And this has all been under enormous public scrutiny since the moment it happened. Now he's under constant watch by those who claim truth as their mandate, people wired to the internet. Everything and everyone who comes near him is screened. We can't afford to use all our new powers in this case, because the greater percentage of the population is unaware that we have them - and this is most definitely *not* the case with which to highlight them."

"So what you're telling me is, that's it?! Judicial process, and try to either nobble twelve people or pick the right ones, but either way, *keep it quiet*?! You gotta be kidding me!"

"There is one other option."

"Oh yeah? If you say anything to me about praying, I swear to God I'll -"

"There is an advantage to having granted him bail," the second figure explained, patiently, "Taking him when he's making his only visits out of the flat to the police station is not an option. They keep a circus around him of bodyguards and press. He's not vulnerable to the conventional methods. He is vulnerable however, to terrorist ones."

The first figure was actually shocked. "You mean..."

***

"Yes! For seventh time, it's entirely necessary!"

Ed Willis looked at Susan Stiltoe in annoyance. He wasn't used to not having his own way in his own flat. He had allowed the Sentinel and their team to put a bodyguard in his flat and keep all the curtains and blinds permanently shut, but the one-man, bombproof bunker now occupying a large part of his living room was too much.

"How can anyone bomb me? Or get enough machine guns close enough to warrant this? I've been back only two days, I can only go out for my bail conditions to the police station! You've been installing another guard or another safe flat in the building ever few hours since I got back! There's a media circus camped outside - how can this possibly be warranted?"

Stiltoe regarded him dispassionately. "Clearly you don't know the first thing about the case of Dr David Kelly. We aren't going to take any chances with you. You're simply too important. Only with that thing in here can we cover for every possible contingency."

"Fort Knox in my bloody living room! It's too much! I just want to relax in my own space until the trial - not be cooped up with militant strangers and their fucking hardware!"

"Some would say you should have thought of that before now. You already avoided two attempts on your life - only one of which you were conscious to appreciate. There are no compromises to be made here, we will do what is necessary to ensure your survival, kick and scream about it though you may."

"Fort Knox! That's what this thing is, Fort Knox in my bloody living room!"

***

A tall man entered the lobby of the building. He wore baggy Hawaiian shorts, a grey T-shirt offering pink obscenities to all ladies of a certain bra size and above, blue Lennon-shades and matching sun hat. He had on his back a large, army-green rucksack complete with a protruding orange karrimat and various patches sewn on it; Octoberfest, Ibiza and Amsterdam among them. Fluorescent pink, yellow and green socks topped off a pair of battered brown walking boots and a can of lager was in his hand.

Former Colonel Saskins, sitting at the desk, felt his blood begin to pump. This young man's appearance spoke of a devil-may-care student, yet everything looked too new and unworn, everything but the rucksack. Saskins casually enquired as to the young man's intended direction, while making certain he was holding down the panic button firmly on his palm-pilot.

"Flat 15 please, I'm visiting my friend from university, Enrique Smith," said the man, in what Col. Saskins regarded as a dubiously plummy English accent.

"Name?"

"William Piper."

"OK Mr Piper, I'll just raise him for you," said Saskins. He dialled up the flat, firmly controlling himself; it isn't actually going to happen, all's well, all's well.

***

In Ed's flat, Stiltoe's pocket came roaring to life. She said to him; "Get in it, *right now!*"

"What?"

"Shut up and get in it, *now*!" she yelled.

Ed looked at her defiantly. She spun. She kicked him the stomach and he landed with his behind in the doorway of the giant safe.

"Good shot Ma'am," exclaimed the bodyguard as he bundled the rest of Ed foetally through the gap. The door slammed shut upon the enraged Ed who started banging furiously from within and bellowing,

"OI!!! Let me out! LET ME OUT! You can all fuck off! Just *FUCK OFF*! I got one shot in, just one, how much of this shit d'ya think I'm gonna take! BASTARDS! *BASTARDS*!"

The bodyguard motioned to Stiltoe and they listened carefully.

"Oh yeah!" she grinned. "Sod it, he'll live!" Then her face fell. Her eyes locked with his and fully understood for the first time the horrifying idea of an imminent, helpless demise. In that moment he thought he saw her shrink.

In the lobby, the newcomer was pushing a button of his own. Within his rucksack the reaction began. To Saskins's horror, the young man stood to attention and saluted.

The bodyguard had hurried Stiltoe into Ed's room and they were now shut inside the wardrobe.

"If you don't mind me saying so Ma'am, that was a fine piece of bodywork you just exhibited."

In the darkness she blinked in surprise, smiled. "Thanks!"

She let him take her hand. "If -" she began, but the rest was lost in the explosion.

***

Later, as the rubble was being searched for survivors, the Sentinel's team approached. The foremost team member held a small electronic device which showed them the way.

Ed Willis was one of the first of seventeen survivors to be found. Fifty-six people had been in the building at the time. He was the only one without so much as a scratch or a bruise.

The authorities and the media nearly all concluded instantly that it was the work of terrorists, in spite of the fact that Ed's infamous actions had also been labelled thus less than one week since. One commentator famously said that it 'Demonstrates the depths to which Al Qaeda will sink. I mean here's a man striking a blow for them on his home turf, and they try and kill him for it!'

***

Back in the low-lit room the two figures huddled once again.

"Well?" said the first.

"Well, that was our last chance. We lose. The trial goes ahead."

The first figure shook his head, a creased gaze fixed upon the second. "I hope the outcome allows you to keep your position."

"Of course you do," the second replied in equally flat tones, his eyes focused on a spot on the table in front of them. "Though these last few days have been opening my eyes a little bit."

"Oh? How?"

The second figure looked directly at the first. "I'm no longer certain I deserve my position."

The look of thunder upon the face of the first was such that the second had never seen there before. In this moment the bond between them might suddenly have been broken beyond repair, yet somehow he remained unperturbed.

"We nobble the jury," the first growled.

"You'll find that quite a problem without my help, won't you?"

The bond was definitely broken now. That look of clear, deadly venom said it for sure. The second now felt something he'd never have expected; a sudden sense of freedom, a mad exultant delight sweeping through him.

***

After the uproarious initiation of Ed's trial had settled down, he was happy to finally be asked to present his defence. The Sentinel's staff had begged him to reconsider and allow the paper to get him the best legal team available, yet he wouldn't hear of it.

"Ladies and gentlemen of the jury," he said, "It's a pleasure to meet you. I understand that my position here before you may seem a little ridiculous, after all, we've all seen the footage, and yes, I admit that I did it. However, I would ask that you find me not guilty due to extenuating circumstances."

"Objection!" the prosecution counsel called out, "One cannot admit to one's own crime and ask to be found not guilty of it!"

"Quite," said the judge, "Restate your case Mr Willis, or you'll be in contempt."

Ed paused. "By doing what I did last Thursday," he said, "I was carrying out God's will. For this reason, and for this one act out of my entire life, I ask that the ladies and gentlemen of the jury find it in their hearts to spare me."

The jury frowned and goggled and looked at each other, questioning.

Ed laughed. "I know what you're thinking. I sound like a madman, and I'd have to agree with you. What man in his right mind could claim God as his inspiration for an act of violence against another?"

There were smiles at this.

"Let the record show that, up until the night in question, I have never been convicted of, cautioned for or even questioned about, any criminal activity. My record has to be spotless - I work directly for the Queen. Let the record also show that I did request time off on the night in question so that I could avoid having to meet the President. Lastly, let the record show that I was successful in avoiding my shift at the palace five months previously, during a visit from the Prime Minister."

Ed took a few gulps of water.

"I never intended an act of violence towards either, but my loathing of them and the war crimes they are guilty of made me fear what I would do or say to them, were I ever to have to meet them. When I met the president in the flesh, I felt my own flesh crawl. Here was a man guilty of heinous crimes against humanity, and yet equally, a man who will escape all judgement in this life. I knew beyond doubt that his crimes will destroy him utterly in the next life, and that perhaps he understood it too. I felt momentarily sanguine at this, I felt there was no point in hating him."

Here, Ed picked up his glass of water and took a swig, trying desperately not to allow his hand to shake.

"Then my mind came into the present and I remembered that scores of innocents are dying every day due to this man and his agenda, and there will be thousands more yet. It was all well and good to know that he will face the judgement of God one day, but until his tenure is over, it will continue and no-one ever to make him think twice. I found I could not allow the moment to pass without doing something to redress the balance. I knew I had only one chance and one choice. I was faced with the Devil himself, I knew it and I made the statement I knew that God wanted. I landed it on his face. One violent attack upon a man who claims God as his inspiration for genocide. This was God's attempt - moving through me - to wake him up - if only for a moment - using the only language he understands."

He drank some more water, gripping the glass too tightly and he glanced over at Stiltoe and the bodyguard. They sat arm in arm some way behind him; he in a neck-brace and she with her arm in a sling. He nodded at them.

"I should add that is it not something I will ever do again, even were the opportunity to be presented to me. I learned that the hard way when I received a very thorough beating in immediate response to my attack. I spent a week in hospital and suffered two separate attempts upon my life while I was there. The third time my life was threatened, as I'm sure you've all heard, was after I was released and was allegedly the work of Al Qaeda. Personally I don't know whether to believe this or not, you may judge for yourselves, but whomever was responsible killed thirty-nine people and injured and maimed many more. If this was yet another response to what I did then I could not be more sorry nor more aghast; unnecessary loss of life is precisely the problem I wanted to highlight, and to try to escape from, in the first place. You may rest assured I could never again bring myself to repeat what I did, knowing what the consequences could be to yet more innocent civilians."

Ed took another deep breath.

"Ladies and Gentlemen of the Jury, you've heard my story. If you don't believe that God told me to rebuke the President, publicly, violently and yet non-lethally for his crimes, then you should find me guilty. The defence rests."

The council for the prosecution stood up to present his case with an air of blazing contempt. In his opening speech he lambasted Ed thoroughly, ridiculed everything he had said in every conceivable way an then, as if wanting more material to rip into, he called Ed to the stand.

By Almighty God, Ed swore, he would tell the truth, the whole truth and nothing but the truth.

"So," said the prosecutor, "You admit your crime, but plead not guilty to the charge of Grievous Bodily Harm?!"

"I've said in interview, repeatedly, that my actions only merited the charge of *Actual* Bodily Harm, but even of this, I would have to declare myself not guilty."

"Ah yes, of course, *God* told you to. Do you really expect that anyone on this jury will believe you?"

"I don't know. Enough people believed the President, but Britain does tend to be a more cynical place than the US. I really don't know."

The prosecution counsel was building up pressure for a giant release. "Do you really believe in God?" he asked, tapping his fingers upon his arm.

"Yes."

"I must remind you that you are under oath, Mr Willis."

"Yes, I know I am."

"Just so we're clear, have you always believed in God?"

"Not strictly, no."

The prosecution saw his chance. "No?! I see, Mr Willis, so

perhaps you could tell the court at what point it was that you began to believe in God?"

Ed sighed. "Well, many years ago I learned enough about this life to know that it was unlikely I'd ever find anything in it that would take me beyond being simply agnostic. But part of me always hoped, hoped that one day, I'd see the light and find that God was here in my life, had been all along. On my last day at the palace, when the world's most powerful and arguably most evil man was suddenly standing there before me, finally, I did see the light."

To the keen observer, the prosecution counsel visibly snarled but he controlled it very quickly.

"And while you maintain that God wanted you to do this, did it occur to you that He also knew you'd have to go to prison for it?"

"Yes it did."

"Why fight it when you are so clearly guilty?"

"I got one shot in, just one. I was nearly beaten to death as an immediate and direct result. I've learned my lesson already; I will never do it again. I also feel I've been punished for what I did."

"On the contrary Mr Willis, that was not punishment, that was the meekest weapon in the arsenal of anti-terror measures available. You have not yet been punished for your crime as you well know, so I ask again - why are you fighting this charge when you are so clearly guilty?"

"I feel it's the right thing to do," said Ed.

"*You are guilty!*" cried the prosecutor, "How can you say it's the right thing to do?"

"The President and our Prime Minister claim to be Christians yet they are guilty of crimes against humanity, as is well recognised. Yet they escape judgement. There is no sign they will ever do otherwise. In light of this, I feel fully justified in trying to escape also. I truly feel it is the right thing to do." He held up his hands, sheepishly, "God moves in mysterious ways."

The prosecution counsel felt there was no more to be gained from this interview. He raised his nostrils disdainfully towards Ed before turning to the jury.

"Ladies and gentlemen of the jury," he said, "I don't know about you, but I for one have heard enough. This is an open and shut case; you've all seen the video footage and you know that Ed Willis is guilty. However, I'm sure you're all aware that this case is not just about his guilt. No, far from it, the stakes are much higher. I know full well that many of you may be less than happy about our country's role in the war on terror and about our relationship with the United States, but I beg you not to allow politics to colour your judgement. You sit here under global scrutiny, as representatives of our great nation, with one responsibility to Justice itself, the responsibility to answer *one question* truthfully; did Ed Willis, or did he not *head-butt* the President of the United States of America at Buckingham Palace? I want only that you all think about that one question and try to answer it truthfully. The prosecution rests."

The prosecution counsel sat down, gazing fiercely at the Judge. The Judge gave the slightest of nods, then turned his fury upon Ed.

"In all my years upon this bench!" he his voice rumbled forth, "I have never been faced with such ridiculous, childish nonsense as this! You sir, make a mockery of the international institutions that have been in place since a better generation of Britons and Americans than those of your sorry ilk could understand, fought and died for this country in World War II. You've created a rift at a critical time between Britain and the US, the like of which has not been seen since the Boston Tea Party, and yet you hide behind a mask of conveniently new-found faith which I for one would find laughable, were it not so stubbornly and utterly defiant of the scales of Justice which I have spent my life serving. I believe you to be not only guilty as charged but a liar and a charlatan into the bargain. I hereby instruct you, ladies and gentlemen of the jury, to find Ed Willis guilty as charged."

Shortly afterwards the jury were closed firmly in their deliberation chamber. A plump young housewife and mother was the first to speak - "What's the point of this? He told us we'd have to say 'guilty', so what's to discuss? Let's just get on with it and we can all go home."

"Quite," agreed a firmly-buttoned, middle-aged woman in the Hyacinth Bucket mould, "No point wasting time."

"Hold on!" said a retired colonel, "Just because the Judge

instructed us to say he's guilty, that doesn't mean we have to. We may, in fact, say whatever we want."

"I believe," the Hyacinth lady said severely, "That the Judge's word is final."

"No it isn't!" cried another young woman in flowing, hippy garb, "We can say what we want, it's like when those antiwar protesters trespassed on army property and tried to disarm some bombs, or something like that - the Judge told the jury to say guilty, and they let them off!"

"But he's obviously guilty," said the builder over his copy of the Sun, "And we can't go against the Judge cos' he's right - we can't let Willis off 'cos that'd be saying 'fuck-you' to America!"

One thin man wearing a very tight tie nodded fervently while another, a bored, ex-student said "Big deal!" He had had his eyes on the hippy chick throughout most of the proceedings. "I for one think we've a greater moral obligation to let him off than the jury who let off the antiwar demonstrators."

This set off an intense debate, but it also got him the look of approval he had been seeking. The tides of the discussion almost turned violent a couple of times, but eventually everyone agreed that there was no point arguing anymore. All but one of them had gone into the room with views which would not be changed by any amount of discussion.

The vote was taken.

After twenty-seven minutes of deliberation the jury returned to the courtroom to deliver the verdict.

Stiltoe moved up close behind Ed. "Right," she said, softly, "This means that -"

"I know!" he hissed, "It's either very good or very bad! Wonderful! Thank you!"

The foreman was asked if the jury had reached a decision.

"We have."

"Please read it to the court."

© H. R. Brown, 30/10/2005

(guilty/not-guilty voting is now suspended)

EVOLUTION

"The problem with current antibiotics is the ability with which diseases evolve to cope with them," Professor Tutton told her audience, "And our problem is that we have only fifteen known antibiotics which can fight diseases. The method we use to combat the evolution of diseases, is to encourage the antibiotics to evolve in response."

There was a slight chorus of muttering from the further benches.

A hand was raised.

Professor Tutton nearly tutted. It was Bill, her ex. She had tried to keep him from attending, and had only backed down when her anonymity in the escalating matter had been threatened.

"Yes?" she said.

"Is it wise to thus encourage lethal diseases to evolve in reply?"

Her poker face was a model of quiet confidence. "We wouldn't actually be doing any such thing," she said, "Our process, basically, reprograms the DNA sequences of certain antibiotics to make their survival dependent upon destroying the disease in question. Life always finds a way of surviving."

"Precisely my point!" said Bill, "Life always does - so surely 'Life' will also ensure the survival of the disease?!

She did not enjoy being rattled in public. "It might," she said, "But we will always have the upper hand."

"It might," he said, leaning back in his chair with a sly look on his face, "So, could you say for certain that you would be able to control this... 'evolutionary battle', once you've begun it?"

"Of course we can."

He grinned at her, in that special way that told her he could see through her lie.

"Oh, good!" he said, "So you'll always be able to destroy the new forms of life that you breed?"

"Don't do this Bill."

Mutters of surprise and annoyance rippled through the audience.

It was about two months ago when she'd been away on a two-day lecture tour that she had rung him at 11:30pm, Sunday night.

"Look, she said, "I'm pregnant."

He couldn't reply at once, as his mind resonated wildly with the enormity of the statement. Then, with all his horizons starting to fill with golden sunlight, he found himself smiling.

"My god!" he said, "That's, that's just..."

"Look, don't worry," she said, "I'll be back for tea time tomorrow. I'll call round to yours at about eight, OK?"

"Yeah, yes!" he said, "Absolutely! I'll get a bottle of red, oh, well, erm, I mean, I suppose half of one bottle wouldn't hurt, would it? Up to you, really."

"I've got to go," she said, "I need to sleep! Jan and me had a couple of bottles earlier and I'm really tired and the schedule is *killing* me!"

"Oh, course," he said, "Well, sleep tight!"

She hung up.

Bill couldn't sleep for three hours. He was playing football with his athletic, future son; he pondered acting classes for his pretty daughter, which books he would read to them at night - Harry Potter, obviously, Roald Dahl, Tolkein? His mind was alight with the long forgotten wonder of Disney films like Peter Pan, Snow White and Bambi. It gave him a warm feeling, realising that he would finally, once again, be able to walk proudly into a cinema to see them.

In his dreams that night, Bill Sands and Sally Tutton lay naked in each others arms in a huge double bed. The thick white curtains muted the sun's rays down to an amber glow, which filled the room. She was beautiful. She had long, dark, curly hair and a lean, pretty face and mischievous blue eyes. She had divine curves and was very slightly top-heavy. Overall she looked and felt like she was twenty-something, not thirty-four. They could hear the kids playing in the garden outside. Syrup was dripping from the ceilings, and they were lapping at it, and talking, and playing with each other, and talking... Talking about what, he couldn't remember the next day.

She surprised him again in the evening. Sally Tutton let herself into his flat at twenty past seven whilst he was still in the shower, and she got straight in with him.

Afterwards, when they were both still moist, pink, wrapped in towels and very happy, she asked him,

"Did you sleep well?"

"Yeah," he said, "Eventually!"

He smiled at her.

"Well don't worry," she said, "You'll be able to sleep properly again tonight!"

She was grinning at him.

"What do you mean," he asked, a thread of dread stirring in his spine.

"I wasn't on a lecture tour. I was getting an abortion. It's just not something I'm ready for, and I know you aren't. Where's the wine?"

Bill grabbed her. He lathered her with his tongue, while pulling her towel off. He spent the next two hours fiercely giving her the ride of his life, and somewhere in that steamy session, the condom broke or got forgotten or he knew not what, but he was very sorry.

They had broken up within a fortnight.

Now, in the midst of the lecture, he was going to do something awful. Sally Tutton just knew it.

"Don't do this Bill," she said.

Bill Sands looked around the auditorium and wondered how he could have thought she would want to take a few months away from her job to start a family.

"Alright," he said, amidst a growing background noise, "How can you possibly be certain of controlling a battle of *evolution*? Especially when you can only respond to advances made by the enemy once they've been made? I mean, it isn't as if you can predict just what tricks nature will use against you - or what it may create in reply to your efforts. Don't you think?"

She was almost in tears. "Look," she said, "If there are any side effects, we will conquer them. All I know is, right now people are dying. And, right now, my colleagues and I can help them."

Bill nodded with that hopeless smile, got up and left the theatre.

***

The Zorgars' end of annum bash for the 'Rising of the Tide' festival, was as tempestuous as ever. Several Zorgars had burned each other quite badly in drunken fights, the like of which was a common sight on the Rising Festival night. Thunder always boomed as each and every one of them attempted to consume their own body weight in food and narcotics. It was the way of things. And of course, someone always thought it would be clever to try and start a volcano, or open a sewer, or unleash an acid flood, or an electrical storm or something similar, just to get a few hearts hammering. But it was all good fun, really. Male and female Zorgars could often be found fuck-wrestling in the sidings, towards the end of the festival.

The planet Skarrand was the Zorgars' current home. It had been for some three hundred of its cycles, but it wouldn't last much longer. There simply wasn't enough sustenance left - they had consumed it all. The slaves had all died out some fifty cycles previously, and everyone agreed that the Rising Festival of the following cycle would take place on the next planet on the list. The list comprised many other planets, as well as notes on their astrological location, and details of the cultivating processes the Zorgars had set to work on each one.

"Storms and fire, burning seas,
Acid rain to melt the trees;
Wild flowing juices in orgies we crave,
And then to relax and beat the slave."

The song was being sung by the few unfortunates at the party who had not been able to engage in carnal combustion this evening. They had remained in morbid little clusters, consuming dolefully.

When the last scream of pain and or pleasure had died away and it seemed at last that the party was over, Piog burst in with urgent news for the Master.

"Where's Giasterringuss?!" he bellowed, glowering fearfully at the drunken, delirious Zorgars all around the hall.

Someone managed a vague indication, and Piog was off.

Luckily for him, the enormous, wizened, old lizard, Giasterringuss, had concluded his conjugations for the evening and was lying back with his conquest in a happy, searing glow, their extremities steaming.

"What do *you* want?" he asked Piog in disgust.

"Sir, there's a very important matter which needs your attention immediately!"

Giasterringuss nibbled at his partner, who purred and scratched him, playfully.

"Go melt your brain," he informed his deputy.

"Sir, please!"

Giasterringuss growled hugely, then tossed his partner through the door. As an afterthought he scooped up her items and lobbed them after her.

Pulling a shroud around his form, he said, "This had better be good."

Piog did not have good news. "It's planet K42 sir," he said, "Haven't you been monitoring the process?"

"Not for three or four cycles now. Last time I checked, the

dominant apes had just got around to making steam power work for them. Nothing to worry about. Sea levels should be due to begin rising any time now. Why?"

"Well, it was the first of a new batch of the special cultures, sir."

"Just tell me what's wrong!" Giasterringuss growled, combusting slowly, dangerously.

Piog hesitated.

Giasterringuss was easily bored. He whipped Piog quickly with his flame. "Well?" he hissed.

"Sir, they've evolved far too quickly," said Piog, nervously, "They've got nuclear weapons, and they haven't even made any significant sea-level rises yet!"

Giasterringuss howled. Piog leapt aside to avoid the crackling steam and flaming cinders he spewed forth.

"How is this possible!?" cried, Giasterringuss, "The instructions were specific! Our scientists *assured me* - Beelzehemoth carve them to shreds - I remember their very, stinking words; 'the dominant apes will evolve to a point where the creation of pollution becomes uncontrollable, the seas rise and our atmosphere is replicated.' Then, as ever, we ride in, take the world and enslave or eat them all. How in the name of the Unholy Rising did they get nukes?!"

"When exactly did you last check them?" Piog asked, and immediately wished he hadn't as Giasterringuss lashed out and buckled some of his armour plating.

Giasterringuss pouted for some time, then said

"How big are they, this species?"

"Well," said Piog, fearfully, "I've not yet seen one that was as big as my cock."

"Ha!" cried Giasterringuss, "They'll certainly be no use as dildos then. Alright, make the preparations for an attack."

"What?! *A nuclear war?*"

"Oh, why not?" said Giasterringuss, "After all, how long has it been? And anyway, think of that warm, nuclear afterglow! Wouldn't that just make it all perfect?"

"There's still a danger that they'll be able to nuke some of *us*! Don't you remember what happened to Khul when he was caught in that nuclear blast? It was horrible - he was unrecognisable - it took him five entire cycles to recover!"

"What else *aren't* you made of?!" Giasterringuss bawled, "Aside from guts and talent? *We are Zorgars*! There's no species in Existence that we cannot destroy, subdue and befoul as we see fit! I'll say this only the once, Piog, so you'd better try to wedge it somewhere between your hear holes; call forth the Gods of Mayhem, Chaos and Death! Rouse the war machine! Pour fire and thunder into its belly! We take planet K42, tomorrow."

Piog looked at him in dismay. "Why is it always me that has to rouse the war machine?" he asked, "The war machine doesn't like me anyway, it thinks I'm not worth listening to - it ignores me completely sometimes! Can't you do it for once?"

Giasterringuss had had enough. He bounced Piog off a couple of walls and a force-field. It was a mild enough rebuke and Piog knew far worse would follow, were he to disobey.

"Yessir," he said, combusting quickly and pathetically, "Mayhem, Chaos and Death sir, on the way."

Piog left the temple.

Giasterringuss pondered the attack. It wouldn't do to take too many nuclear hits from K42, despite what he had said to his servant. A leader who saw very many of his troops suffer the indignity of nuclear scarring which took several cycles to heal, would be a poor leader indeed. But then it shouldn't be too difficult, with the orbital surfer-boats to bounce hither and thither off the atmosphere as per their usual routine, reigning down their fire on the lands below. However, their paths would be far safer if he could gauge the speed and agility with which this upstart little species would be able to track them and return fire.

Sighing at the effort of work he now must face, he found a monitor and tuned into planet K42 for the first time in perhaps four whole cycles.

Giasterringuss found that in addition to Piog having been right about the nuclear weapons, the apes had many communications networks which, equally, they should not yet have developed. He was growling now. He accessed the networks and began searching, the screen burgeoning out to cover nine separate squares. He watched. The night grew long. An age later, a hot red glow began to beset the horizon outside the temple.

Eight of the screens had flashed on and off, all night, through various TV channels and Internet sites, but the centre one remained focussed upon one object alone; a shining, blue orb, hanging there in the darkness, revolving slowly and peacefully.

© H. R. Brown, 02/02/2003

ZERO
(REPRISE)

> *"... at the edge of our perception, but not quite this side of it, there is a flower. It has many layers of petals and it spins anticlockwise. Most never see it during their lives. Our pineal glands have been disused now for many generations, they are partially calcified ..."*
>
> [anonymous, London Underground]

After ascending from his mortal form, Dr Ben Wenders' consciousness coalesced into its new sense of self within a strange, multi-dimensional, geometrical construction, beyond the veil of our universe.

As he gazed in dim recognition around the Hall of Souls in which he found himself, he noted the departure section for those destined to reincarnate, and realised he was in the arrivals area. Someone or something would be with him soon, he instinctively understood, but he also realised he didn't want to understand, to know, because to know would be to remember -

- a bloodied soldier screaming on an early twentieth-century battlefield, no victory was ever so pyrrhic; the battle won but all his friends; lost -

- and -

- a medieval peasant, living a simple and honest life, tilling the earth for his betters, god-fearing and king-adoring, blessed by a wife and children -

- and -

- a nun recording her 78th consecutive year completely free of mortal temptation, a life lived utterly replete with good works and charity, holding back tears of joy as she felt the hand of death take her away into her promised forever -

- and -

- a short and bitter life of horrific indignations as a slave, dying unfulfilled in so many, *many* ways -

- and -

- a long life as a wonderful mother of several, grandmother of many, great-grandmother of.. I've lost count -

- and -

- as a French poet and friend of Lord Byron, dead of an overdose at twenty-seven and blissfully forgotten by history -

- and -- and -- and -- and -- and - ...

Here he was. Here 'they were'? Wenders, or more accurately; the immortal being, for whom 'Wenders' had merely been the latest mortal incarnation, had arrived back in its true, immortal, form.

A multitude of forgotten former lives now swam through his/her/their mind, in great billowing shoals; overwhelming, reminding, conversing, battling, reassessing, finding agreement; rendering down the ultimate new overview of its true higher self, re-emerging as a new self, as ever it did in these times; a self which was greater yet than the sum of all its parts.

And of course, the All Knowledge had returned with the higher self.

There was a problem. The problem was approaching. The problem had multiple mouths, all of which were grinning, and slavering in anticipation.

"Remember me?" the problem wheezed at him/her/them.

The Wenders being did remember, but didn't wish to.

***

It was twelve years ago or so, before his major breakthroughs in AI. During the Christmas period, Wenders' dodgy mate Gavin from university had arrived, begging for a place to stay, just for a few days to tide him over. Wenders had agreed, it was Christmas after all and he was, at the time, unattached romantically, so didn't have to square this imposition with anyone else.

Gavin didn't eat much. His diet appeared to Wenders to consist mostly of booze, tobacco and weed. These habits notwithstanding, Wenders was surprised to find 'ol Gav was better company than he'd thought he would be. After a particularly jovial night in the pub on Christmas Eve, the two of them rolled back into Wender's house along with a couple of ladies whom Gav had persuaded to join them.

What Wenders had not appreciated was that the ladies in his living room were dedicated psychonauts; utterly scornful of anti-drug laws, and always looking for the meaning of life within the experiences afforded them via various psychedelic substances. He was equally unaware that Gav had convinced the ladies to join them by telling them he had some DMT and was willing to share it with them.

Whilst Wenders was in the kitchen, fixing drinks and snacks for them all, blissfully ignorant of the class A drug abuse happening in his living room, Gav administered the DMT to the two ladies via a bong. The existence of this device, and the substance, were previously-unknown facts which Wenders would be forced to absorb.

Upon entering his living room, the two ladies were already sparked out for the ride on his settee, and Gav was tipping more of the stuff into the bong.

Wenders immediately entered into a 'what the fuck?' discussion with Gav. The long-story-short of this drunken exchange was that Gav narrowly avoided a thumping, and Wenders ended up also agreeing to give the DMT a try. The 'world's most powerful psychedelic' it may be, Gav had told him, but it lasts about fifteen minutes. And it's totally unforgettable! And it's Christmas! And we're drunk! And what the hell?!

Wenders had taken two bong hits and seriously hadn't wanted any more – but Gav insisted that to really break through and visit other dimensions – he needed the third hit. Both the ladies had managed it, no problem! Grudgingly, the entire world apparently dissolving around him into various flowing vistas of rainbow colours, Wenders had taken the final hit, fell back, his eyes closed, and then –

[*" – at the edge of our perception, but not quite this side of it, there is a flower – "*]

– *then* – he had seen the flower of life rearing up at him as his mind left his body. To the sound of a cosmic *rrrrriiippp!* – he blasted through the centre of the flower and travelled at warp speed into different dimensions. He explored landscapes of blinding insanity and wild, pulsating, dancing, geometric complexity. He spoke at length with multi-dimensional beings (sometimes referred to as aliens, or 'machine elves', etc.) who terrified him and elated him in equal measure. He witnessed them weaving our very reality into being. They knew the answer to every question any human has ever asked, they were all-knowing, they left him agog with utter disbelief – before they introduced him to God herself – who bathed him with love –

– before he was gently flushed back into the reality of his living room.

The return felt very much like he was waking from a dream. He opened his eyes and found the visual effects of the drug were still there; everything in the room was back, but the view was a warping, rainbow-coloured kind of crazy. Most of what he had just seen and experienced however, melted straight out of his mind before he could even begin to come to grips with what had just happened to him.

Reality itself, now, just felt like a default channel on a TV set – and though he could scarcely recall them – he'd suddenly seen that there were *other channels*!

As the ladies had gone first on their trips, they had already returned, and were soon giggling at him and his utter confusion. Gav awoke from his reverie shortly afterwards, and he also found Wender's pitiful incomprehension to be highly amusing. Though they tried to reason with him, and even comfort him, after the initial hazing, Wenders wouldn't trust any of them. He was utterly bewildered and he fled to his bathroom.

Ultimately, the experience had forced Wenders to make two changes to his internal monologue. First; never, *ever* try DMT again (as it had reduced him from a grown man to a witless, whimpering child) and second; he was no longer an atheist but an agnostic. He had never previously had time for agnostics, considering them wishy-washy and weak; pick a team for fucksake! Now he no longer had this luxury, but had he actually, *really* met God?! His rational mind couldn't accept it and this was reinforced by the almost complete memory loss of the experience, and the fact he knew for certain his physical body had not left his living room, *but..* To try to find the absolute truth of life would probably involve returning to the DMT realm for further study – which he absolutely would not do; hence agnosticism was the only logical choice.

***

Now 'Wenders' was dead, he/she/they were here, beyond the physical realm and with full higher knowledge, the contents of the DMT trip from twelve years ago were fully accessible. And here he/she/they were, facing one of the alien beings Wenders had met on that fateful trip, he/she/they knew all too well what was coming.

"Ten years of absolute success and untold riches were

offered," the being intoned, "The terms were agreed, accepted and those ten years were delivered. The insight required to set Asimov's Three Laws into perfect AI code was provided to you via your subconscious, and the rest of your magnificent good fortune simply wrote itself."

Multi-dimensional flecks of spittle seemed to fly from the creature's hideous mouths as it chortled and pointed several limbs and other protrusions towards the being whom Wenders now was.

"What I could not have anticipated," the terrifying faces continued, amidst their ghastly giggling, "Was just how soon after the completion of your ten year bliss, you would rush to get back here!"

The Wenders being could not fault the other on this observation.

"Now," the thing announced, in triumphant, rasping glee, "You are *mine*!"

© H R Brown, 10/03/2020

ABORTIVE

"If men could get pregnant, abortions would be available in every other high street store. You'd be able to get one, no questions asked, in ten minutes, on your lunch break.

So; if you are against abortion, don't have one. If however, you actively work to remove the rights of all women to get an abortion, then, to be fair to you, you are a cunt.

Here's why:

The world is boiling over with more than seven billion people, we are causing the extinction of entire species with the sheer weight of the human population, and the galloping rates of pollution and climate change we bring. Yet with this going on, you so-called 'pro-life' people waste the short time you have upon this earth trying to force even more, *unwanted*, humans into it? What the fuck is wrong with you? Are any of you cunts going to offer free childcare or cash donations, having so self-righteously insisted upon the existence of other people's kids?

Yes you are cunts. Stupid, short-sighted, holier-than-thou, hypocritical, misogynist cunts. With, I might add, chronic fucking tunnel-vision. Try looking out for the humans who are already here for a change. And the planet we live on.

That is all."

Of course, Freddy had sent this update out onto the internet during what could be called a 'fugue state'.

He had arrived home on Saturday morning, 7:13am. The previous night had begun in various pubs, proceeded to a nightclub, then a warehouse rave, then someone's house party, then some woman's flat, before a final, weary, bleary, mile and a half walk of triumph to get home.

He didn't feel like sleeping when he got in, so he had a cup of tea. This perked him up, and, combined and conspired with the various other substances still rolling round his system to assure him he was in sharper focus at this moment, than ever he had been in his life before. At this peak of mental agility, his mind fell upon the fragmented memory of an argument he had been having in the pub with his friend Fin, just before the group's relocation to the nightclub. The move had rearranged the group dynamic and shaken things up, and meant their argument was never finished.

Freddy knew now precisely how to win that argument, and he set to it.

Having typed the first draft of his polemic, he re-typed it, agonised over various parts of it, re-typed it again, added new parts to expand the argument, and finally, as he finished his tea at around 8:07am, he knew it was perfect.

He fired it out immediately, linking it to Donald Trump and Anne Widdecombe for good measure. Then finally, the fatigue kicked in. Best night out in fucking ages! he thought, as he passed out in bliss upon his settee.

Freddy had tried to go viral with many internet rants in the past, but had never achieved more than 69 likes. This was a number he had learned to be happy with for its symbolic properties, if not its actual quantity.

Despite his multitude of best efforts, the ongoing obscurity had long-since ceased to be a weight around his neck; he had grown used to it and accepted it. The stubborn monolithic nature of his own inconsequentiality had broken him, therefore he was extremely unprepared for what happened at 11:01am the same morning.

After the initial knocks at his front door went unanswered, they became louder and more insistent. Eventually, an incessant hammering on his front door broke through his slumber and caused him severe cerebral pain. He also realised the side of his face was all wet. He worked out which way was up and which was down, and moved his head upwards, off the large patch of dribble on the cushion. This made the headache much more painful, so he dropped his head once again into the patch of drool.

"Urrgh!" he muttered in disgust as the cold, sopping-wet material slapped his face. He tried to turn the cushion over, an operation requiring minimal effort or coordination, yet these eluded him and the cushion landed on the floor, leaving him only the wooden arm of the sofa upon which to rest his head. He growled in anger at this, and all the while the pounding at his door was doing nothing to soothe his mental state.

He forced himself upright into the sitting position, immediately wished he hadn't as the pain sharply coalesced into spasms of agony which wrung a small sob out of his wretched frame.

Cursing the tears he now had to wipe completely from his face before he could possibly open his front door, he ground his teeth against the pain and forced himself onto his feet. He staggered out of his sitting room towards the front door, fiercely rubbing his face with his sleeve as he went.

In the hallway, a few feet shy of the front door, the banging and hammering on the door from what sounded like more than one hand or two, became the entire world. And the entire world had to *stop*.

He finished wiping his face, caught sight of himself in the hall mirror.

"Oh sweet Jesus!" he said, in despair of the haggard monstrosity squinting back at him. He made a quick decision, said "Fuck it!" and put on a pair of shades that had been lying on the table.

He opened the door.

There was an instant of blessed calm, before the small sea of journalists in his garden all began yelling at him. This, if anything, was worse than the incessant knocking; he was now being harangued by dozens of people, and couldn't make out what any of them were shouting at him. Something in his head snapped. It was the inherent fantasy of the situation that did it. Clearly, he was actually still on the couch asleep – so this was a dream! And when you realise you're in a dream, and that fact alone does *not* wake you up.. Take control!

So first; this din had better stop! He raised both his arms high above his head, hands flat, pointing up, palms outwards. He held position silently, waiting.

The din ceased. And lo, he had reigned peace upon these vermin!

Condescendingly, he said, "One at a time, for fucksake!"

Imperiously, he cast his gaze over the journalists before him and deliberately picked the woman he found the most physically attractive. My dream, he reasoned; my rules. "You!" he said, pointing at her, "What's the problem?"

The lady in question lost no time in laying it out for him -

"Hi Freddy, Dolly Titchmarsh, Evening Star. You've gone viral with your last post, you've had over nine million likes – and nearly as many hates – in just three hours, what do you have to say about that?"

This wasn't real. Couldn't be. He hadn't posted anything in a day or two, he thought. No way this wasn't just a dream. He didn't remember anything after the rave he'd been to, and he was still in a state. So why not just play along with this weird shit? Even better, he'd always imagined the fun he'd have if any scumbag journos ever bothered him like they do celebrities...

Freddy coughed, hacked-up some greenery, spat it at the feet of the invaders, laughed and then coughed again.

(All of this was being filmed from multiple angles in HD, including the trajectory and impact of the green blob upon the driveway. The green blob itself would be animated and achieving pop-stardom by the late afternoon.)

"You cunts!" he jeered, "Waking me up for fewer than twenty million likes? At this time of the fucking night?! Fuck off, all of you, I'm going back to bed!"

With that, Freddy slammed the door in their faces, trudged

upstairs and did just that.

***

Frederick George Byron obituary

Frederick George "Freddy" Byron was not a man known for mincing his words. In the few short, incendiary weeks he lit up the internet with his mischievous, foul-mouthed, leftwing liberalism, he managed to delight and enrage both the left and the right. Progressives loved his general stance on their favourite issues, but detested the unapologetically-problematic, obscenity-strewn manner in which he expressed it. Right-wingers generally approved of him for this contempt of political correctness, but hated his views on the actual issues.

From his first viral post on abortion and the foul-mouthed tirade against journalists which immediately followed, Freddy certainly knew how to get people talking. In response to the hailstorm of social media abuse which rained down upon him in the aftermath of this, much of it shoe-horning in a good dose of misogyny as well as personal abuse, Freddy cemented his position as hate-figure number one to snowflake gammons everywhere by sending out a set of statistics on the causes of death of women, globally, from last year.

Shortly thereafter, following some harsh words and blatant lies about him from the usual establishment attack-dogs, Freddy became the latest in a long line of people to successfully own the argument against him with the simplest of lines; a shrug emoji along with four words,

"I believe the women."

Freddy then "drank in all the online bile that shat down on me" (his words, not mine; see the Radio 1 interview), for a couple of days whilst hanging out with friends and family, before returning to the media fray to simply say unto the world, laconically, from behind his now trade-mark shades, and live on air;

"Oh don't worry, you'll get over it. I have!"

Words which would serve well as his epitaph, although so might several other scathing lines he produced in the weeks which followed, both online and in interviews. I'm especially fond of his views on Royalty; "the Royal Family has been held captive by the British State for fucking *centuries*! Oh, I know, it's a very gilded cage, but it's a cage nonetheless. #FreeTheWindsors". In fact I think #FreeTheWindsors should be a mission statement for British progressives across the board.

However my favourite contender for an actual epitaph would be his last ever line; the line for which – multiple tin hat conspiracy theories are already suggesting – no lesser a personage than the Prime Minister allegedly had him killed.

The opaque nature of his death certainly stands in stark contrast to the loud-mouthed way in which he lived prior to it. He simply went missing, shortly after that last post, and washed up yesterday in Staithes, in the Scarborough Borough of North Yorkshire. The cause of Freddy's death is yet to be confirmed, although wouldn't you know it, there are already whisperings afoot of odd marks and injuries on the body. The Forensics Department of the North Yorkshire Police have been contacted for comment.

Just three days ago, Freddy posted a comment piece from this newspaper detailing the PM's response to the left's contention that the current government's policies have killed far more Brits than the IRA, Al Qaeda and ISIS put together.

The response of the Rt Hon Howard Cecil Mallory Blampstead, Prime Minister?

"I think it's typical of the left to try to politicise tragedy and to try to use the deaths of our brave men and women of the armed forces to score cheap political points. My thoughts and prayers are with the families of all those who are affected by war."

Freddy posted the article with a typically obscene, six-word riposte to Blampstead;

"Oh cunt off, you Slytherin *fuck*!"

Of course, even this is already being misquoted by at least thirty-seven percent of the population, who think it's "Oh fuck off you Slytherin cunt," but I'm sure Freddy would have appreciated the essential agreement in the main thrust of both instructions.

I believe his namesake would also have thoroughly enjoyed Freddy's brief but glorious flame, and maybe, just maybe, Freddy's finding out right now, on some higher plane..

In addition to the North Yorkshire Police, both the Prime Minister and J. K. Rowling have been contacted for comment.

© H R Brown, 17/03/2020

THE HIVE

"They're on their way, *now*?" cried Ziggy, in disbelief.

"Don't be angry," Selene pleaded with him, "You knew it would have to happen, one day."

"*You called them?!*"

Ziggy couldn't believe what he was hearing. Finally, even Selene had betrayed him. This was the end. There was no-one left.

He leapt out of bed and began pulling on his clothes, frantically.

Selene got out as well and tried to put her arms around him, saying, "Ziggy, relax."

Ziggy tore her arms from his shoulders and pushed her away.

Selene sighed and withdrew a little. "It has to be done," she said, "You know it has. You've always known that."

"Whether or not it has to be done, it is nothing, NOTHING to do with you!" he cried, "Did you think I was going to thank you for it?"

Selene was hurt. "Ziggy, I just wanted us to be able to communicate like normal people do."

Ziggy snarled, and did up his overalls.

Now she was growing worried. "I love you," she ventured, "Ziggy -"

"I don't love you!" he spat, then turned to face her. He drew his face up close to hers and showed her his clenched teeth.

"We're over, Selene. I don't want to know you any more."

He let it sink in, feeling justified by the look of pain in her eyes, then said,

"Stay the fuck away from me."

And he was gone.

***

Soon afterwards, Ziggy Atherton was pelting down the walkways of funnel 0.0 at an incredible pace. People moving in either direction turned to watch him in amazement, as did the large smart ads, fronting the endless rows of shops along the sidelines. He knocked one woman's arm so that she yelped in shock and dropped her pack. In his wake, he called out a frantic apology, at which the woman merely stopped and stared.

No-one ran in the pedestrian funnels; it just wasn't done. The funnels ran all over and all through the hub of the city, forming a web which connected all the inter-hub transport terminals. In turn, the terminals connected a web of zip-streams which could take ten people at a time to any other terminal within the main hub in a matter of seconds. The terminals were to be found every hundred yards or so, along all the funnels. Once in every few years, one might expect to see someone running - in an emergency - to the nearest terminal, but no further. The interconnectedness of the two webs would have given the advantage to criminals, but for the super computer which kept digital tabs of the whereabouts of everyone within the city.

Here was a man tearing along blindly, ignoring everyone and everything and *avoiding* the terminals.

The calls to 999 were ten, a hundred, a thousand. No-one could remember the last time a serious 999 had been reported. A tsunami of voices all began washing into the alarm-call centres of the city, clamouring to impart details of the man's flight.

Ziggy himself was gasping, his legs were pumping as never before and his pulse was on fire. He passed the familiar adverts along the sidings and felt the same revulsion as ever, but now, for the first time, he abused them with undisguised glee.

"Fuck off!" he growled, "FUCK YOU!!!"

The cute but fastidious little girl was staring at him with a fierce abomination lighting her face. She was the stalwart of the friendly, glowing, family-ads which bore the caption;

"I always look for ways to be more efficient!"

The hirsute, blissed-out long-hairs in the relaxor ads, whose caption usually read - "Connectivity sets us free" were looking at him in anguish, and their caption had switched to - "The true path lies in acceptance".

Ziggy ignored them all, and raced on.

The smart ads were perplexed. Their CPUs all began consulting each other in the man's wake - did any of us catch his eye? He had passed ten, twenty, thirty - the control boards couldn't keep up. The potential missed revenue total was spinning on at an incredible rate, so unusually high was the frequency of the hits.

But not to worry. The boards had soon collated scores of images of the speeding man and built up a three-dimensional profile, with which to identify him. The profile was sped back to the smart ads, that they might lock into his connector and feed him their pitch, directly.

Ziggy was two hundred yards past the first of them when the malfunctions began. Many of the newer programs weren't calibrated for the event of non-identification. This man was not connected; there was no way of catching up with their missed targets. Around a third of them were not programmed to cope with this error, and they shut down. Their blank windows were left showing the less-than-perfect interiors of the stores, instead of the immaculate, digitised images of their stock and company profile.

Ziggy's heart was thundering in his chest. He was vaguely aware of the growing pandemonium he was leaving behind him but this only added to his panic as he raced along, panting, his wild eyes darting feverishly, here and there, his heightened senses working overtime to negotiate his hysterical course through the passive throng. As the funnel curved slowly round the outer edges of the hub, he saw his salvation appear, little by little, ahead of him.

By now, the remaining smart ads were working projectively, sending the warning on ahead to others he had not yet passed and warning all of them not to push their adverts to his connector. Executive sales droids began to leave the doorways of stores ahead of him, moving out into the crowded walkways of the funnel, saluting him in advance.

"My goodness, sir!" one of them called out to him in dulcet, dead, automated tones as he approached, "We don't have a record of your credit rating sir, but you'll soon ruin those fine blue overalls with sweat if you persist in this unnecessary haste! Why not come in and view our wonderful range of sports wear? We have the very latest from -"

Ziggy barged into the droid from the right as he passed, using the pinball effect to bounce himself out of the path of two more sales droids. One was attempting to offer him interest free credit on interactive, sub-cranial, entertainment systems, gaming channels, lotteries, adult material, etc. The other seemed hurt that he could dash so quickly away from their spectacular offers on the latest in super-comfort, compact furniture.

He stumbled slightly, gripped his arm in pain, cursing. Everything in else in the world was built to wear out within twelve months and thus need replacing - except for the corporate arsenal of sales devices. That droid had been built like a bunker. In the madness of the moment with the pain stinging his shoulder and his lungs straining, Ziggy found himself stopping, clutching his sides and wondering where the phrase 'built like a bunker' had come from, and what was a 'bunker' anyway?

He drew a few deep breaths, shook his head in anger and looked around him. He could see them all moving into his path, arms raised up in gestures of 'Hello'.

Ziggy growled, lowered his head and blasted along with renewed verve. He jumped, skipped, dived and rolled his way through the slow, steady attack of the interests of capitalism and around the bewildered consumers who were caught in the midst of this rout. The wild urges for escape were growing ever stronger and more daring with every droid he evaded, as he began to appreciate their lack of manoeuvrability for interception. The end of funnel 0.0 was growing closer - with the promise of silent anonymity in the open mouth of the dark, silent tunnel just beyond.

Ziggy didn't know where the urge came from, but suddenly the bloodthirsty howls were erupting, gleefully from his throat. Seeing his freedom gathering more and more definition and likelihood with every fevered step bred a heady feeling in his breast which he wasn't used to. Here was the wide-open, yet forbidden end of the world that he and his so-called peers had never left - and here was he, about to break through it and relishing the idea.

At the sound of his voice, everyone and everything in the funnel froze, in sudden uncertainty.

Part of him was ashamed. At the same time he was running, screaming *and* heading straight towards the terrible, dead place that no-one but the rank Fives had ever dared to enter. He didn't care. It would have been unthinkable only yesterday, but here he was; a rat in a trap, threading his frantic path through a crowd of statues towards the Great

Beyond.

Tales of the 'Skormolc'; the dreaded creatures which lurked in vicious, inbred colonies, deep out of sight in the Great Beyond didn't seem quite so scary anymore. And if the Great Beyond did indeed connect the city's hub to all the other hubs of the world, as all the whispered tales told that it did, surely it couldn't last forever?

The darkness spread out to the edges of his perception as he approached the tunnel's mouth, and finally, he was through! The darkness encompassed him and without stopping he raced on, the hum and glare of the smart ads shrinking into a single focus of light and sound, in the distance behind him.

So it was that Ziggy Atherton left the hub of his birth, for the first time in his life.

He rejoiced, looking over his shoulder and seeing it all fall away. Still he ran, until his lungs were gasping involuntarily and his legs were wobbling with fatigue. He stopped, to find the dark, soundlessness had become all he was aware of - that, and his own breathing. In grateful delight, he slumped to the floor, to lie still and let go of the fear.

He could hear nothing. He was safe here, he knew it. None but the Fives ever entered the Beyond, and then they only did so in the cheerful, humming safety of fully connected hover cars. Here was Ziggy Atherton, alone, unconnected and uncaring.

It was many minutes of blissful calm before his overworked frame began to slow to the point at which an unknown sensation began to bite. He noticed it first in his arms, which began to shudder in a way he had never before known.

He began to feel small, unsure and scared, but somehow he knew that he'd feel better for now if he curled himself up on the hard, alien, metal floor. The biting sensations along the edges of his body receded a little, but somehow he knew they would persist. Flickering currents of air washed over him in random directions, nibbling everywhere. Slowly, he persuaded his skin to cease bothering his mind, and then sleep caught his thoughts.

***

Ziggy was now back at the very beginning of the nightmare, more than twenty years ago. The other children stopped playing with him, one by one. By the age of seven, he didn't speak to any of them anymore. Now that every child in the class apart from him had MHCs (mobile hypernet connectors), he was the odd one out. He could only play and talk to others in the real world, whereas all his classmates now had two different worlds to cross in and out of.

Ziggy's father had been summoned into school to speak to the head teacher about the matter. An identical device could be paid for by the school and made available for Ziggy within twenty-four hours, if his father was unable to purchase one - why hadn't anything been said?

Ziggy's dad had whirled into a rage, denouncing MHCs as the undoing of childhood; a dehumanisation of social and physical interaction which was destroying the very essence of what it meant to be alive.

The room seemed to get hotter for little Ziggy and he pulled at his collar in discomfort, hearing his father grow increasingly angry and incensed with his head teacher who, to her credit, offered all the placatory statements, appeasers and reconciliatory body-movements which her Manager's Guide recommended for such uncomfortable situations. She grew increasingly fearful however, as Ziggy's father grew ever angrier with her evasion of his accusations.

Physical violence had ensued. In his anger Ziggy's father wrecked the display the children had dedicated to MHCs and the hypernet, and was banned from coming within a hundred yards of the school. In his turn, his father had banned Ziggy from having an MHC. The teachers caused a storm, but there was no arguing with Ziggy's dad. He knew the law, and they could not force the issue.

The fat, spiteful face of an old classmate - Trev McArdle - still haunted Ziggy. This dream always ended with Trev's hypernet campaign against him blowing up out of all proportion, so that the soaked information streams began including digitised taunts against him in the smart ads, up and down the walkways. People everywhere were laughing and pointing -

- and then from out of nowhere came the memories of his revenge. The local server broke down, and he saw men, women and children go wild with panic, their worlds cleft asunder. That day he realised just how strong he would be if the world was without its hypernet and its integrated human-interface systems. Ziggy spent the entire day helping his classmates cope with the world as he knew it. All of them were grateful to him by tea time. He went to bed that night in a rapture, only to find the usual cold shoulder awaiting him the next day, when the server was back online. He felt the sobs and the dread and the hot tears spilling down his cheeks as he scurried back into his enforced isolation.

He could see Trev's face leering at him, too close and full of hate.

Then Trev took flight. He soared far up into the air, joining the thousands of other people whose wings were carrying them gracefully through the enormous atmosphere of the main sector of the hub. The suns rays were glinting down through the vast glass plating of the outer-hub above them all, making them look like strange little sparks, buzzing hither and thither. And Ziggy sat in solitude on the empty, wide open space below, which stretched away into dull, grey horizons all around him. Everyone in the world, it seemed, had been fitted with the new SCTs (sub-cranial transceivers), and everyone else was now part of a world which was denied him.

And now here he was, face to face with the man who had denied him his humanity. His father looked full of quiet, reserved pity, as Ziggy realised that his dad's features had subtly shifted. He was looking directly into a mirror.

But now, all was growing dark. The air battered his body incessantly with its worsening sting, and an old science lesson from his school days filtered into his disturbed dream;

"Inside the hub the temperature is constantly monitored, but if any of you were ever foolish enough to enter the Great Beyond, below the surface of planet Earth you would find that the temperature is not monitored at all, much less controlled. In the Beyond, where the tunnels are endless labyrinths and not always sealed against the living earth where verminous life forms, the *Skormolc*, feed miserably in their own filth - there the temperature can sink so low that it could freeze you to the spot within minutes. No-one in this room understands what the word 'cold' means, I suppose, but -"

Ziggy awoke in a panic. He had past the perimeter. He was freezing. The shudders of his flesh were telling that before he went to sleep, but now... how long had he been unconscious?

He wriggled around desperately, to find he was not stuck to the floor as he had feared. There was hope yet. Though he had gone where it was expressly forbidden for one of his status, *there was still a way back.*

There came another, vivid memory flash, as if part of his dream had been left behind. He had asked the teacher why the Great Beyond was open for anyone to simply walk right into. She replied that there had sometimes been those living within the hub who were so discontent with life itself, they would rather leave the hub than carry on living in it. All such people had a right to do so, she said, but they never, ever returned.

Once again, Ziggy found himself asking why he was still following the wishes of a father long-since dead. This age-old, internal argument had always fallen upon his father's side, but that was in the warmth of the hub.

***

It wasn't as far as he'd thought.

When he reached the entrance back into the hub, the armed officers were waiting for him and pointing their weapons.

"On the floor!" the foremost officer yelled, "Hands behind your head, NOW!"

Ziggy laughed out loud. "What," he said, "Couldn't you have come and caught me? All you big, hard men with your big, tough guns - scared of the dark?"

The officer stepped forward, his intent all too clear.

Ziggy gave in with a meek chuckle, noting the foremost officer's nameplate as he did so.

Officer Bullitt didn't like it one little bit when his prostrate prey said,

"*Bullitt*? That's just brilliant!"

"What's your problem, sir?" asked Officer Bullitt while he secured Ziggy's hands together behind his back.

"Well," said Ziggy, "It might have been a cool name a couple of hundred years ago when the cops still had guns that used bullets, but now it just seems like... well, everything else about you!"

Bullitt, crouching over Ziggy's back, had stopped moving.

"How's that sir?" he asked, calmly.

"Out of date and clichéd!" said Ziggy, with a chortle which earned him a heavy blow in the centre of his back.

"On the contrary, sir," Bullitt whispered softly into his ear in prim, methodical tones, as he lay groaning, "I'm the best shot with a zapper in my department. I'd be honoured, sir, if you'd present me with the chance to prove it again in front of the public. I'd be a hero, sir. The last man alive who isn't connected, doesn't even want to be connected? You think anyone'd mind me putting a thousand megavolts up your arse, sir? You think anyone in this world could give a flying drop of cock-yoghurt about you? You don't understand the beauty of connectivity, sir. It's true what they say - 'Connectivity sets us free.' I can hear what they're saying about you, and believe you me sir, you should be thanking the Gods that I have to follow certain rules, *sir*."

Ziggy was silent.

***

He was whisked via the zip-stream to the Police Bureau and brought before a Judge in a crowded mini-court with beige-coloured walls. The Judge soon made his position clear.

"The All-Connected Act," she said, slowly and precisely, "- Was put in place ten years ago to ensure the maximum efficiency of all consumers."

Throughout the hub, many had tuned directly into the Judge's connector to see 'The Trial of the Last Unconnected Man' (as advertised exclusively by Terrier Net™) from her very cerebral cortex. Some of the more discerning Hypernet users were busy flipping around the different views of the trial which were to be had via the eyes of the various guards and orderlies in the courtroom. These were the technos who would always claim, in later days, that they had seen something important, something all-revealing at this trial that the majority of the great unwashed had not.

"I'm sure you know the mantras which define the ethics that brought us to this point in our evolution, Mr Atherton," said the Judge, "But for the sake of formality, I shall repeat them to you now."

She looked at him sternly, as she began;

"Connectivity sets us free. Connectivity leads us to homogenisation. A homogenised workforce is more efficient. Efficiency is the key to happiness."

"Do you have a problem with freedom, or perhaps with happiness, Mr Atherton?"

Ziggy was tense, and staring skywards in anger from under a heavy brow. He was trying to ignore how pretty the Judge was, how her figure set his mind wandering away from his deadly peril. She was probably old enough to be his mother, yet she had aged extremely well... He also had to contend with the futility of his position. He forced himself to focus. There wasn't any point arguing. He knew it, and still he said,

"The only problems I have are with enforced connectivity and homogenisation," he retorted, "And I don't believe I can ever be *happy*, or *free* when these are forced upon me."

The Judge didn't bother trying to hide her anger.

"Those remarks will be stricken!" she commanded, "And the prisoner will make no further attacks upon the founding principles of -"

"Does anyone out there know what real freedom is like?!" Ziggy bellowed at her, looking her directly in the eye.

All around the hub, sighs of excitement and wonder were being expelled at the prisoner's unconscionable disobedience.

This time the Judge's command was silent. The guard behind him moved silently and quickly to apply a localised zap to Ziggy's neck, temporarily removing his power of speech.

Scowling impatiently at Ziggy's horrified reaction, the Judge continued,

"By noon today the act became law; all members of society in Corporate Hub number 337 are now connected, Mr Atherton, with the exception of you. In point of fact, all other minds bar yours have been linked up for many years. It is now four hours past the deadline, yet here you stand, a renegade who is so determined to remain isolated from the freedom of society, that you risked entering the Great Beyond to escape it, not to mention causing damage and disruption to many corporate interests along the way."

The Judge had been cultivating an imposing frown as she spoke, and now she leaned down towards Ziggy, the deep disgust heavy upon her brow.

"Do you have anything to say?"

She was obviously not expecting a reply, or if she was, it would make no difference to his punishment. Ziggy was still rubbing his neck and gagging and retching, trying to overcome the injection.

"Uuunngg!" he managed, grinning hopelessly. Inwardly, he was carefully focussing upon all the fierce, ugly things he'd like to do to her in order to reassert himself. He managed to say, in a faltering baritone,

"It's a good job you can't hear what I'm thinking!"

Ziggy would have been heartened, had he been party to even a fraction of the merriment which this caused around the hub.

"That can be amended!" the Judge snapped, looking fire-zappers at him from the depths of her dark, pretty eyes, "Take this man away and connect him! You may return him for sentencing, forthwith."

Ziggy was removed.

It was as he was being led through the building towards the physician's section that he began to panic. Everyone he passed was silent, yet they all knew why he was there. Some smiled at him, some looked at him with a knowing pity. Some even seemed to shy away from him. The worst thing was that all their eyes followed him. He even noticed Germaine Starr - whom he had not seen since school - giving him a warm, matronly smile as he passed her. He wondered briefly where everyone else from school might be now; watching him over the Hypernet? All these people he passed seemed glad that he was there. It made him feel small and paranoid, it was as though they were all laughing at him. They *all* knew when he was coming around the corner and seemed to be waiting for his appearance.

"What the hell are they all looking at me for?" he grumbled, his eyes darting fearfully, here and there.

The two, heavily-set guards who were leading him down the clean, grey corridor exchanged nothing which Ziggy could detect, but both seemed to be in agreement.

"What?" he said, "WHAT?!"

"Everyone's talking about you," said Tetherill, the man holding his right arm.

Ziggy bristled. "Everyone?"

"Practically everyone," said Swanlake, the man holding onto his left arm, "You're the last man alive in this entire hub who's unconnected. Gonna be a massive thrill when you go online."

"What?! *Why?*"

"You kidding?" said Tetherill, "This is the last time ever that a virgin brain's joining the net, man! You know that everyone's fitted at birth these days, and now there's even talk about modifying people's genes so that babies can grow their own interactive connections while they're still in the womb. And here you are, with a mind that's gone it totally alone for nearly thirty years! Everyone's gonna have a riot when your psyche finally goes live!"

Ziggy shuddered. His arms were held tight and taut against

the solid grip of his muscle-bound, bio-engineered captors, yet he was subtly testing them for weaknesses.

Why was he bothering? Even now, when all was lost, he was looking for a way out it.

It was his father's fault. The most incredible moment that Ziggy could remember in all his life had happened to him at the age of nine. Running home from school in glee, he had hugged his father tightly for denying him a mobile hypernet connector - for without it he had been able to become popular at school for the very first time.

"Now do you see, son?" his father had asked him, "Now do you see why they're such a weakness?"

Tears of joy had choked little Ziggy's reply, but these were replaced all too soon with tears of hatred and anguish when the server was re-established. Two days after that, Ziggy's father vanished forever.

He had never known his mother. She had been lost in a zip-stream accident when he was too young to remember her properly. After his father disappeared, little Ziggy had spent the rest of his formative years in an orphanage. He resented the world and everything in it. He was never told what had happened to his father, although he heard dark rumours. He grew apart from every other person his age, he hated his new guardians and his teachers. He clung stubbornly to the sacred moment which he and his father had shared - and swore that he would never get an MHC. When these were replaced by SCTs, Ziggy was fifteen and he hated the new versions with even more venom. A tiny MHC that you have fitted *inside your brain*? What the hell is this shit?

Ziggy went over these formative elements of his life again and again in his head as he was led through the complex and past all the strangers who stared at him. When he was brought before Nurse Hacker, he was listless. He could feel the pincers of doom bearing down upon his cerebellum.

Nurse Hacker was a tall, slim woman with very long hair. Her face was strangely lined and drawn taut by an excess of age-compensation treatments.

She took a look at the three men sideways, over a long, thin nose.

Silently, across the hypernet connections, she asked the two guards if Ziggy was likely to try another escape.

The reply came back affirmative, so Nurse Hacker informed the guards to hold onto him for a few minutes more, whilst she set up the necessary equipment.

Ziggy knew they were talking about him through the immediate ethernet. He could tell when people communicated that way, as their eyes moved in certain patterns.

"No, I'm not going to run," he said.

"Well, Mr Atherton," said Nurse Hacker in a high-pitched tone, "We'd like to believe you, of course, but you'll forgive us if we don't. Don't worry, it won't take long. Then you can go back to see that nice Judge."

"You're a nurse," Ziggy murmured.

"Very astute, Mr Atherton," she replied without looking up from her equipment, "These uniforms are a dead give away, aren't they?"

"You're supposed to help people," he said "What are you doing? I don't want this thing in my head, please, *please*... don't do it."

Again, the silent communications.

"I see," said Nurse Hacker out loud, "Mr Atherton, I am to understand that you haven't ever even had the Sub Cranial Transceiver system described to you properly? Is it true that you live like a recluse? Is it also true that the work you do is way beneath your intelligence - a direct result of your refusal to have the SCT fitted?"

Ziggy said nothing.

"Is it true, Ziggy," she chided him, "- That this very morning you ditched your girlfriend for trying to talk sense into you?"

Ziggy scowled. "Is everyone in on that as well?"

Looks were exchanged, and then Swanlake said,

"It's today's top clip."

"WHAT!?" Ziggy bawled.

- Elsewhere in the hub, Selene was being comforted by friends who had never had much time for her unconnected boyfriend, and they all cheered at Ziggy's obvious discomfort. As for Selene, she felt a lot better -

Nurse Hacker laughed. "Oh, Mr Atherton," she said, smiling at him, "You must think the SCT is an awful thing, but that's only because you don't understand it yet. You can't. A man without proceivers in his eyes and ears can't understand what they can do for him! A man who has always been unconnected can't see how he'll soon come to rely upon the CPU-cerebellum interface which will set him free! You've never been a properly integrated part of human society."

"Oh, I can't understand, can't I?" Ziggy muttered, contemptuously, "What exactly would I want 'proceivers' in my eyes and ears for, anyway? What *are* they?"

"The word 'proceiver' is short for projector/receiver. The visual proceivers are microscopic devices that provide interactive accessories for the user. They project channels, games, films or whatever else, directly onto the inside of the pupil. The proceivers also receive all the images you see, should anyone wish to tune in to what you're seeing. The audio proceivers receive what you hear and transmit the sound of the channel you're currently tuned into - right into your eardrums. The traffic is controlled and stored in the short term, by the CPU-cerebellum interface; or to put it more simply - by this."

She held up a tiny, silver microchip for him to see.

Ziggy could feel that familiar feeling; his muscles growing tighter as the anger slowly swelled within.

"And what precisely, are you going to do with *that*?" he asked.

She looked at him with a matronly smile. "I'm going to set you free," she said, "Free to interact properly with your fellow human beings, free to contact anyone in the hub - instantaneously - via the hypernet or the immediate ethernet, free to watch whatever you want twenty-four-seven, free to buy anything you see on any interactive shopping channel; free, Mr Atherton, to live as every human-being should be free to live in the forty-second century."

"How do I turn off stuff I don't want to see?"

"No-one has an 'off' switch, Mr Atherton. Your eyesight will remain mostly your own - there will be a loss of no more than eight percent of your total field of vision to the permanent connections, and these will have an opacity of no more than seventy-five percent."

The look on Ziggy's face at that moment defies any precise definition, though it held confusion and fear and he wanted to laugh out loud at it all.

Seeing this strange look, Nurse Hacker said,

"'Opacity' means 'transparency', Mr Atherton. And you needn't look like that - if you insist on being different, and choose never to select any item which may appear, nor to use the connections any conversations, then you will never enlarge any item within the vision-field, nor interact fully. If you choose to bring up an item of interest, it will appear right in front of you, projected directly onto your pupils from inside the eye socket and occupying the central ninth of your sight at a standard of seventy percent opacity. You do have a choice as to the minimum opacity, but no-one can have it at less than fifty percent. At the minimum input range, a user sees only four, quite small, channels; two in each bottom corner of the vision-field and each one occupying no more than two percent of the total field of vision. And unless they are mentally selected by the user, these channels will flip around the hypernet at random, but at least one on each side will always be host to shopping channels."

"Fuck the Maker sideways," Ziggy whispered, grinning idiotically, "What about the constant noise?"

"The authorities won't be happy with your use of language, Mr Atherton," Nurse Hacker remarked.

"What?! They're listening - *now*?!?"

"Everybody's listening," said Swanlake, quietly into his ear, "We told you that! I reckon Nurse Hacker's got an audience of fifty thousand right now! You're bringing a good fifteen minutes to many of the city's everyday workers today, sir!"

"And what about patient confidentiality?" Ziggy groaned in despair.

"Subject to demand levels for program material," said Tetherill, in his other ear, "And at the moment - you're what's hot."

"As for the noise factor, as you put it, well; each channel has to be heard, obviously," said Nurse Hacker, as she prepped the delicate electrical syringe and grinned at the two burly security guards, "But either the one selected or the one currently highlighted will be the dominant sound in your ears, and you can turn them all down to the level of a quiet conversation, if you really need to."

"So you're telling me that from now on, I can't escape any adverts?" Ziggy groaned in disbelief, "You mean they're always going to be there, buzzing round my head, speaking to me in my goddamn sleep?!"

Nurse Hacker stopped her work and laughed. "Not at all, Mr Atherton," she told him, "You need never actually hear another advert again! But the only way you can avoid them totally, is to *always* be either; talking online to someone or some group of people, watching some kind of entertainment channel or by doing online work."

"So how's a man supposed to sleep?!" he cried.

Nurse Hacker shrugged. "Everyone else gets used to it, Mr Atherton, and you'll be no different."

Seeing the look on his face she smiled at him, reassuringly, and said,

"It's the selected channel in the foreground of your vision which takes all precedence within your own cranium, Mr Atherton."

With that, Nurse Hacker had finished her preparations. Silently, she commanded, and physically the two big guards reacted, moving Ziggy forwards and plonking him in the chair.

The immediacy of his situation, and the fear of what some silent command might move him towards next both came violently to life in Ziggy's mind.

"NO!" he screamed, "You're not putting that thing in my head! I don't want adverts in my fucking eyes! You can't make me! It's MY HEAD!"

"We *can* make you," said Nurse Hacker, "And technically it isn't *your* head; you simply own the current tenancy. All tenancies in this hub are now subject to the same laws governing the maintenance of communications and other systems."

"NO!" he spat at his captors, writhing violently against them, biting, kicking, thrashing and head-butting in vain at their protective suits.

"Mr Atherton, really," said Nurse Hacker, "You don't know what you're missing! You'll be thanking us all, this time next week! Besides, do you really want us to be the last hub in Region II to get their OHPC grant?"

"OHPC?" said Ziggy, in disbelief.

"Oh, for the Maker's sake!" Nurse Hacker exclaimed, to the delight of many around the hub who had begun to share her dismay with this unconnected heathen, "OHPC stands for One-Hundred-Percent-Connected! Wake up!"

There were cheers, in some quarters. And, whilst he couldn't hear them, Ziggy thought he could feel them. They were all watching. It had always been that way. He went limp. He wanted to laugh at the absurdity of it, but his captors were all too serious.

And suddenly, in one glorious, shining moment, he was overcome with his own thoughts - they were 'all too serious'. Perhaps that was it!

While he was planning his desperate course, he was being placed in the operating chair. Tetheril and Swanlake held him down and began fastening straps. He would have to be quick...

"OK, *nurse*," said Ziggy, "Are you prepared to die for your OHPC grant?"

Everyone in the room stopped and looked at him. In desperate hope, Ziggy surveyed them each in turn. Tetherill and Swanlake were busy looking at each other, then back to him, then back to each other. Nurse Hacker was looking at them both for an assurance which was not forthcoming.

He was right. He knew it, and it made him smile. At this, they looked even more nervous.

"What do you mean?" asked Nurse Hacker.

"The second your implements violate any skin or any orifice around my head," Ziggy said slowly, grinning darkly, enjoying the power, "That very second; the bomb goes off."

"What?" they all cried back, in a rare moment of involuntary unison.

"What's the matter?" he asked them, chuckling, "Don't you think I've got the know-how to install such a bomb? Do you think I'm scared of taking everyone and everything in a hundred-meter radius with me? You want your 'OHPC grant', fine. But if you're going to end my life as I know it, then I'll be the one who decides how I - how *we* - go."

"Where are you going to go?" Swanlake said, "Back into the Great Beyond? You're a nut case! There's nothing out there except a freezing death - and if not that then you'll be pulled to bits and eaten by the Skormolc!"

Ziggy whirled round to face him, growling, "I've been there before and I can do it again! I'll make it to another hub, or find out where the Fives go."

He used his one remaining free arm to grab a neat little metal incisor from the small table next to the chair he was sitting in. Holding it to his head, he said,

"Let me go, right now."

"You're mad!" cried Nurse Hacker, the tears welling up in her eyes.

"Am I?" he said, "Do you want to bet?" He pressed the incisor gently onto his cheek, making a little white nook in the pink flesh.

No-one moved but Ziggy could see their darting eyes, and he knew what they were doing.

"Yeah, that's right," he said, grinning maniacally, "Raise the alarms. Bring more people into the blast radius. Your epitaphs'll surely thank you for that!"

All movement in Ziggy's vision-field ceased, but he knew that meant nothing as far as the hub's internal alarm systems were concerned.

He looked at Tetherill. "Undo the straps," he growled.

Tetherill searched the ethernet around him urgently for a command or an inspiration. When the order came through, he began to be truly afraid. He lowered his zapper, as did Swanlake, and he undid Ziggy's restraints.

Ziggy kept the metal incisor close to his cheek as he rose, uncertainly, and backed out of the room, keeping his eyes on all three people.

All around the hub, more and more people were joining the enthralled audience, pondering his every move in silent awe. A daughter cried out to her mother, "Mummy, I thought no-one made bombs anymore!" Her mother replied, "Shh. No-one's got a bomb, trust me," holding the little girl close and looking around her in fear as she spoke.

Ziggy ran. He blasted through the complex like a thunderbolt, keeping the incisor up as close to his cheek as he dared. The passion lighting his eyes was awesome. Everyone in his path quailed and leapt aside, for all were now aware of the danger.

This time when Ziggy raced down funnel 0.0 towards the Great Beyond, he found there was no opposition whatsoever. He ran along whooping, delighting in the echoes he made.

Then, as the darkness of the Great Beyond came into view, he stopped abruptly. The way was barred by twelve police officers, all decked out in navy, crowd-control gear. Dull, bronze-coloured body-plating glimmered slightly. Twelve drawn zappers were being held down, patiently. Twelve visors in three different colours - dark ruby, grim sapphire and dirty emerald - all glared at him, motionless.

Ziggy drew out the scalpel and held it to his cheek. The zappers were all raised in reply.

For a few, long seconds, Ziggy faced them thus, quietly sweating.

Squad commander Lieutenant Wilberforce was unsure. He was searching involuntarily for Atherton's signature in the immediate ethernet, despite the fact he knew him to be unconnected. He couldn't even read that his mental efforts were being blocked, as he might with any other criminal; there were no indicators as to the intent of the man. Meanwhile, Corporal Thickett was badgering him to be allowed the shot. Thickett was a young officer, and far too keen. She kept reiterating that their prey was bluffing; that there was no way he had wired himself to blow up and even if he had, Thickett could zap him before he'd made the cut.

Yet Wilberforce couldn't be sure. There was an awful panic in Atherton's eyes, but also a serious determination.

Ziggy was sure his heartbeat must be causing an echo. He ground his teeth, then began walking towards them, making his intent plain. This was insane. They were going to kill him, but it no longer mattered. Those deadly, yet immobile weapons were getting closer and closer and he was surely only seconds away from -

- but as he drew near, all the officers lowered their weapons.

A fever rose up in Ziggy's breast. He increased his pace, eyes blazing, the scalpel held close to his cheek.

The line of officers parted silently, allowing Ziggy his path back into the Great Beyond. He edged his way past them carefully, keeping the scalpel against his skin and the passion hot upon his brow. His eyes twitched furtively from one faceless officer to the next, showing violent, venomous intent.

Ziggy didn't know how close he had come. The row which was going on between some of the officers and their Lieutenant over their connections, was bordering upon mutiny. Wilberforce managed to hold them back with evil visions of what was done to mutineers.

Ziggy knew they would be communicating silently, and he watched and prayed as he slid by. The silent visors watched, motionless as he receded into the black.

As he left the field of vision of everyone in Corporate Hub 337, a general cheer arose in his captive audience all around the city. It was soon checked by the flood of level Five disapproval across the hypernet, and many ill omens of what this unfortunate turn of events could precipitate.

Once he was back in that huge, dark tunnel, Ziggy began to jog along, faltering slightly as he went. If he could keep moving, he reasoned, then he could keep warm. The cold wasn't so bad that steady activity couldn't hold it back.

The strange, dank smell of the black emptiness ahead became less fearsome as he went along, breathing it in steadily, growing accustomed to it. The light behind him slowly shrank and shrank and eventually became a point. After a time unmeasured, it had faded altogether.

And so on, and so on, until time unmeasured doubled and redoubled and the blackness began to almost feel like home.

Ziggy didn't remember stopping, much less actually going to sleep, but in his dreams this time, his father's death came back to haunt him. His uncle and auntie had held him close as they told him he would never again see his father. Ziggy screamed. He fought, he bit, he kicked and he writhed, all to no avail. He would have failed to escape, were it not for the flying head butt which had landed so efficiently upon his uncle's nose. Despite the force of Ziggy's efforts, the poor man hadn't been expecting that.

He hadn't run far, that first time. Just away, to the nearest quiet corner he could hide in and give vent to the violent, helpless rage. A dead, stained, static, little niche, where he could hole himself within walls that couldn't be burst, no matter what he did to them. Back then, whilst these dreams were real, he had worn himself out with the force of his emotions. Now they were simply the desolate echoes of life's cruel lessons, still powerful and crushing.

Logic has never dictated the story lines of dreams. Somehow, from the horror of that little corner, he was now beginning to enjoy life once again, now he and Selene were together. It felt almost as good and as pure and as beautiful as his earliest childhood memories did - when he still had both his parents...

***

When Ziggy awoke, he felt an enormous pang when he realised that Selene wasn't there, and he struggled not to have to remember why. He took a moment to right himself, before reality sank back in. He felt the despair clinging, pleading with him, coaxing...

Yet it slowly set itself out in careful, pedantic totality, as he realised in dread that it was going to do, every day, for weeks to come:

His was the mystery which inspired her and made him so much more fascinating than any other man - he was the puzzle that lit her soul. Hers was the sweetness, the desire to please, and the obedience to the system that had betrayed the whole relationship. The law said 'Today', so 'Today' it had been.

It was faultless; it was unavoidable. Ziggy also would have called it 'grotesque', 'obscene' and a host of others, though there wasn't any point. He roared into the darkness, daring the lies to come in person and punish him, goading the darkness itself. He roughly pushed aside any thoughts of sentimentality.

There would be an end to this tunnel, and he would be the first to go where only the Fives had ever gone before. If not, he would die trying. He promised himself that and then he plunged onwards, heedless of danger, into the endless black.

Again, the monotony set in. Again there was the endless, chilling feeling that he was trying to escape from Hell. However, the slow, pounding rhythm of his jogging brought hope to Ziggy for many hours. Eventually though, the lack of food and drink started to tell. He was feeling increasingly weak and his fantasies about getting something nice and cool to drink were growing desperate.

He was ready to rest again for a while, when he thought he saw something ahead. He stopped and squinted, but couldn't be sure. Cautiously, he moved forward until he became sure what it was - a tiny point of light.

A shout of triumph escaped him, and immediately he regretted it. The echoes made him shiver and remember his lonely vulnerability. He raced on with renewed vigour towards the light.

Now every step seemed surer, though the light grew larger so very slowly. Still he pounded on, and on until eventually, he stumbled into the light.

It was coming from the left-hand wall of the tunnel, which had now become a large, blazing panel of weird lights in unusual shapes and shades. Ziggy barely noticed that the right hand side of the tunnel had fallen away into a vague, gloomy distance. The place in which he now stood was a great cavern, larger than any open space he had ever found in the hub.

He walked slowly up the powerfully bright wall, squinting as his eyes got used to the glare. As he moved the patterns of the indistinct, orange shapes and the billowing, grey shapes within the pattern stayed exactly the same, splitting the screen roughly in two, yet they grew outwards in all directions.

Staggered by this brilliant fractal program, he drew back. The image returned, more or less, to the one it was before. He moved right up to it again, and the effect was the same.

He did it again, marvelling at the smooth graphics and the unusual design aspect.

He tried moving from side to side, to find the image spreading always to the side from which he was retreating.

He looked as far left as he could, his face pressed against the glass. Now what was he seeing? He furled his brow in concentration, trying to make sense of the strange, silver curves at the edge of the display. They crept in from the top and bottom, and ran into a strange mass in the centre of the left-hand edge of the screen. There was something bothering him about this. He went to the right-hand edge of the screen, and noted the same, strange, silver pattern in reverse. There was a perfect symmetry to the edges of the screen.

He looked down to the bottom of the screen, where it met the grimy, metal floor. The orange colour of the lower display was ruptured here and there by troughs and peaks, making a perfectly randomised, chaotic pattern. He took it in slowly, enjoying it, then he noticed the small cloud of many hundreds or even thousands of black specks moving around each other fiercely, in front of and independent from the rest of the display.

Ziggy squinted at the specks of this cloud, a sense of dread growing steadily within. The cloud grew larger and fiercer, as did the flying specks. The panic struck him as he realised that these things were rising up, *towards him*. He knew it was only a wall display, but it was far creepier than any he had seen before. It made the background almost look like it was a real thing...

All at once, the cloud of flying things was right up around the glass of the display, banging against it, angrily. He gasped out loud at them, and backed away from the glass. The flying specks had grown quite big. Each one had a shiny, black, segmented body as big as Ziggy's forearm and was borne up by translucent wings almost twice as long, flapping furiously - faster than Ziggy's eyes could follow.

All at once, Ziggy realised - these were the *Skormolc*!

He screamed. The next thing he realised was that the display he had been looking at was no such thing. In fact, he had been looking out of a *window* - like the one above everyone living in the hub, the one which let in the light of the Maker when He deigned to shine down from above. And that meant that the orange of the lower display - lower *window*, he reminded himself - was the ground; the surface of planet Earth. And that meant that the place Ziggy was in now was far, far above the surface.

He screamed again and went on screaming, though the Skormolc seemed to be able to hear him and grew angrier in their attempts to bash through the glass. The clasping, spiked lips at the front end of each flying monstrosity scraped and buzzed against the glass and was flanked on either side of the head by two, bulging clusters of tiny, oily, shiny spheres which Ziggy somehow knew to be eyes. The creatures barged each other aside in their eagerness to get at him.

They couldn't get through the glass. It held them tight, but the sight and sound of them sent fierce, ugly feelings up Ziggy's spine. They revolted him and yet made him angry.

Part of him wanted to smash these disgusting creatures and grind them into pulp. Even though he wanted to look away, he couldn't. Neither could he help wondering at the vast, dark-orange landscape behind them, and at the sheer enormity of it.

"Ziggy?"

He spun around to see Governor Cary Loftin of Corporate Hub Number 337 standing stern in his enormous, purple, resplendent, level-five robes. Behind him was a twelve-squad of familiar, tarnished-jewel visors, all gathered around a large hovercar. Twelve zappers were trained on him.

Ziggy was dumbstruck. He had only seen Govenor Loftin in the flesh twice before, both times at rallies. They had never spoken.

"Ziggy," the Governor said again, "We should talk."

"OK," Ziggy said, panting slightly. The was no further need for the kind of reverence which the Governor could expect within the hub. Ziggy was past caring about the twelve zappers trained upon him.

"What the hell are those things?" he demanded, pointing at the beasts which were still clustered in an angry, buzzing mob behind the glass, "Are they the Skormolc?"

The Governor smiled. "They are," he replied, "But they aren't really anything to worry about. The glass is built to withstand many times more force than the Skormolc can ever offer."

Ziggy frowned. "So they aren't really a threat?" he said, "Not like in the stories?"

Governor Loftin shook his head, gently.

Ziggy felt the hyperactivity of mortal peril beginning to fade.

"And what in the name of the Maker is out there behind them?" he asked, "How high up are we?"

The Governor pointed down the tunnel from which Ziggy had emerged. "That way, as you know, is Corporate Hub Number 337," he said, then pointed ahead, "That way; Hub 336. Were you to cross over there -" he pointed to the gloomy, murky, low-roofed, distance which opened out to one side, "Then you can travel to Hubs 338, 339 and 340. If you can bring yourself to look closely out of the far side of either end of the window here, you can actually see Hubs 337 and 336. Each one - in fact our entire network of hubs is a standard of one kilometre above the surface of the planet."

Ziggy gasped. The strange, silver patterns he had seen were actually...

He ran back to the window, ignoring the rowdy Skormolc and gazed to the far left, at the hub he had grown up in. The silver pattern at the edge of the window was the tunnel he had travelled, running all the way into the distance, back to Corporate Hub 337. It was a long way away, a big, metal lump, sitting upon eight, giant legs.

"How far away is it?" he asked, quietly.

"Twenty kilometres," said the Governor, "You've shown extreme stamina and determination in coming so far. There are no longer any human beings of any of the lower classes who can manage such feats. You are to be congratulated."

Ziggy grinned, defiantly. "You're not transmitting a thing to your precious electorate, *now*, are you? Any of you?!" he said, looking with glee at the motionless visors.

Governor Loftin made no reply, yet he looked faintly amused.

"What is it out there?" Ziggy wanted to know, "What's all that orange? Why are we living so high up above it? The legend says we evolved underground, of how we worked our way up to the surface, and earned the glory of the rays of the Maker and His brilliance. That's a lie, isn't it? That's why we only have one big window *above*. What should I believe?"

"Out there is the true legacy of our evolution," said the Governor, and he noted Ziggy's confusion. "Don't worry," he said, "Let me take you somewhere safe, away from these unpleasant surroundings. There are many questions, I know, and I'll do my best to answer them."

"No," said Ziggy, "You're just trying to bring me in to connect me, aren't you?"

He fumbled for the scalpel, then held it up to his chin once more.

Governor Loftin sensed the alertness and the requests of his squad, and firmly denied them. All Ziggy could see of this exchange was some of the officers behind the Governor shifting uneasily and fidgeting with their weapons. He backed up towards the window, forgetting all about the cloud of angry Skormolc outside.

"Ziggy," said the Governor, "Forget my squad, they mean you no harm. Nor do I. On the contrary, But first I need to talk to you in private. Won't you come with me?"

Ziggy didn't move.

The Governor sighed. "Go ahead Ziggy," he said, "Cut your cheek. Cut it wide open and bleed on your overalls."

"You know what'll happen!" Ziggy shouted, desperately.

"Yes. You'll bleed, you'll look silly and then I'll take you with me anyway. Why not try retaining a little dignity?"

Ziggy felt the panic again, saw a vision of himself lying on the operating table as they opened up his brain, his ears, his *eyes*... Yet he had no answers left. He dropped the scalpel, and it was swiftly retrieved by a nimble-footed officer.

All at once, the squad began moving slowly and sullenly back into the hovercar. They waited longer than necessary, and at a further, silent command from Governor Loftin, the car moved away.

"Trust me, Ziggy," said the Governor, softly, "I am not about to connect you. I'm taking you to the home of the Fives."

"The *what*?" Ziggy said, gaping, "Fives live in the hub, like everyone else!"

"No," chuckled the Governor, "Fives do shifts in the hubs, like everyone else does shifts in their offices, shops, maintenance depos, labs..."

Ziggy shook his head. "But, but... Why would you tell me this, if it's really true?"

Governor Loftin gave a dazzling display of shiny, white teeth, and said,

"I intend to make you a Five. You have all the right qualities."

The Governor turned and headed out into the gloom of the cavernous space, away from the window and the frantic buzzing of the Skormolc.

Again, Ziggy was completely still.

"Come on," the Governor called out, "In the home of the Fives you won't be troubled by the lack of a connector, I promise you!"

Ziggy followed, slowly.

They walked right up to the huge, central pillar of the shadowy cavern, and here the Governor touched a hidden point on a curve of the pillar. A panel opened, revealing a small keyboard. Ziggy watched, quietly.

Governor Loftin quickly typed in a sequence which Ziggy couldn't make out. A large doorway opened in the pillar and a familiar, bright-green light shone out of it.

"What is it?" asked Ziggy, fearfully, despite the appearance of the doorway being that of an everyday zip-stream terminal.

"What does it look like?" laughed the Governor, "Do you want to see the home of the Fives or not? I can promise you the best meal you've ever had, and answers to all the questions - or you could stay here and try to tame the Skormolc?"

Ziggy followed.

The zip-stream was the same as ever; the overwhelming rush of energy, the buzz moving like a wave through his entire body, rattling his every atom and tickling him to the point of distraction - at which it faded and the new surroundings took shape through the brilliant, green haze.

Then Ziggy was standing beside Governor Loftin in a bright, warm place. Water ran freely over rugged stone to his left, and motionless, rolling tides of green stretched away to his right. The sky above was still a deep, dark grey, and it filtered through the enormous glass-plated roof whose end was out of sight in the distance. Despite the grey coming down from above, sunny light was bouncing everywhere from subtle reflectors and up-lighters.

The Governor led Ziggy round the back of the terminal they had passed through, onto the spacious veranda of a big, pleasant-looking building with two storeys and a profusion of elegant, curved windows.

A server droid was standing by a white table, pouring two glasses of drink. They sat down to the meal which was waiting for them, steaming.

Ziggy didn't bother waiting to be invited. He sat down, took up his knife and fork and tucked in, greedily. The Governor laughed out loud.

"My, what a good appetite!" he said, "That twenty kilometre hike left you a bit worn out, didn't it?"

Ziggy nodded, trying to close his lips around the sumptuous food. He had no idea what it was, but it was as good as he had been promised. Succulent, juicy flavours were married with pleasant, tender textures in his mouth.

Governor Loftin raised his glass in a toast -

"To the human spirit!" he said, "To you, Ziggy, for demonstrating it with such verve!"

He drank, and Ziggy, after forcing food down his gullet, followed suit. He was immediately struck by the pale, cold yellow-coloured liquid. It had a rich taste; sweet and fruity.

"What's this?" he asked, "I've never had anything quite like it."

The Governor leaned back in his chair, unbuttoning the top of his stately robes, slightly, to reveal a gigantic fold of flab, hanging under his chin. While Ziggy goggled at this strange and unpleasant sight, Governor Loftin, oblivious, said,

"This is called 'champagne'. Good, isn't it? That's another little perk which we Fives are privy to - alcohol."

"*Alcohol*? What's that?" said Ziggy, trying to stop staring at the Governor's bulbous, flesh-necklace.

Governor Loftin laughed. "Keep drinking," he said, "You'll find out!"

Ziggy swallowed some more, ate another couple of hurried mouthfuls of the delicious meal and then finished his glass. The droid reappeared straightaway and refilled it.

"So," he said, "Why're we living so far above the surface? What is going on? Where are we now?"

Governor Loftin didn't stir an inch but the holographic display system became active. The table became a torn, rugged, orange landscape. Large, silver structures grew up out of the ground and became a great, interconnected mass, held up above the surface by many legs.

"Here is Corporate Hub 337," he said, highlighting a section of the model in bright gold for Ziggy's benefit.

Now Ziggy understood. In the main body of the display was a pentagonal network which connected the hub he had lived in with four other hubs of equal size and shape. The connection network was in the pattern of a fat star, with five, much smaller, inner buildings in a lesser pentagon where the tunnels linked up. Ziggy pointed at one of these.

"Is that where I'd got to?" he asked.

"No," said the Governor, his collage of chins wobbling slightly, "This one here, see? And here's where we are now," he said, highlighting the giant complex in the centre of the pentagon. It dwarfed all the hubs around it.

"Fives have a big place, don't they?"

"We do. You'll like it here."

"This can't be right, though," said Ziggy, "This makes it look like the entrance to the Great Beyond splits into four different tunnels!"

"That's right, it does. You just have to know where the doors are, and the right passwords, obviously."

"And where do these other tunnels go?" Ziggy asked, indicating the outside of the hubs, where other strands of silver led away, off the edge of the display.

"Those are the other exits which only Fives can access. They lead to other pentagon-networks of hubs."

"So how many hubs are there in the world?"

"Over eighteen hundred and still counting."

"The Maker sideways," Ziggy murmured, grinning. He felt a little light-headed. "But why are we all so high up?" he said.

Governor Loftin sighed. He had seen these wretched clips a thousand times already, but still, the youngster had *not*...

The miniature, orange landscape dissipated into nothing and the space above the table grew dark. A three dimensional image of Planet Earth coalesced and took shape. It was a metre in diameter and it hung, spinning very slowly above the table.

A disembodied voice spoke out from concealed microphones,

"More than two thousand years ago, human beings lived happily upon the surface of this planet."

Planet earth expanded vastly, and the viewer was taken to the surface, to witness scenes of city life and sky scrapers, of village life and pub gardens, of farm life and herds of dirty cattle, of plantations where fruits and vegetables grew directly out of the ground. The viewpoint zipped quickly through the atmosphere of the computer generated planet, from one scene to the next; demonstrating that every one of them had been filmed under an endless, unrestricted sky.

"Everyone was safe to walk under the suns rays without fear of harm," continued the voice, "The world was prosperous and everybody was happy. Then one day, the balance was upset."

The view shifted, to show vast, bottle-green clad armies and then these armies were manning endless ranks of armoured vehicles, both airborne and ground-based. Soon, explosions were tearing up and decimating the entire plethora of visions.

"Evildoers, lacking even the most basic principals of decency and fairness, hijacked humanity's blessed civilisation and turned it to purposes of evil -" the voice said, sorrowfully, "- And human societies across the globe began to turn upon one another in their desperation to keep control."

Ziggy watched the holographic file with a growing consternation. The scenes had begun depicting all manner of horrors; brutal torture, gang-rape, mass murders with terrifying, rapid-firing guns that blew holes right through people, vast explosions which tore limbs apart and shredded spines.

He gasped, and covered his eyes.

"Before long," the voice continued, "The evildoers came to use Nuclear Weapons to win their war, and the earth was lost."

"What?" said Ziggy, reeling from the awful imagery, "What are nuclear weapons?"

"Shhh," said the Governor, "They're bombs powerful enough to wipe out a hundred corporate hubs in one go - look!"

The images became those of gigantic, fiery mushroom clouds, blasting landscapes into ash and rubble. After a prolonged bombardment, the images faded into bleak, amber horizons.

"The Nuclear winter is a deadly disease which our ancestors bestowed upon planet earth," the voice continued sadly, "It wiped out all the larger plant and animal life which wasn't saved in the Arks, including the majority of the human population, and has now has been going strong for over two millennia."

Ziggy was horrified. "*What*?!" he cried, and was answered by the narrator -

"The devastation of this winter is set to keep human beings living inside radiation-proof glass and Starmite structures for a further eight more millennia."

Ziggy sat, stupified. "Nuclear winter?" he repeated, as the images vanished and the table resumed its normal appearance, "What's a Nuclear Winter?"

"It's what keeps us up here in the skies, Ziggy," the Governor replied, "Ground level radiation could be dealt with, but at a much higher cost. It became obvious to our ancestors, hiding in shelters underground, that if they were ever to live under the sun again, it would not be easy. Fortunately, they were saved by their excavations into the earth's crust. They dug further and deeper than anyone had before the wars, for the deep underground was now their only hope for the continuation of humanity."

Ziggy's head was in his hands. "How were they saved?" he asked, "What did they find?"

"They found virtually endless fields of Starmite - the material which allowed them to build up and out of the ground sooner and with more confidence than anyone had believed possible. Its what all hubs and interconnections are built from. It truly is a miracle, what some of we Fives refer to as 'our Redemption.'"

"This kind of a war, could it ever happen again?"

Governor Loftin shook his head. "Not any more. We've reordered the entire sphere of humanity to ensure that war is no longer possible. All hubs are of a similar size and reasonably governed by we Friendly Fives who are very well-trained at our jobs. Only the Fives can ever travel from one hub to another with impunity, barring odd exceptions who can always be won over to our cause."

Governor Loftin gave Ziggy a knowing smile and continued -

"All Fives are colleagues, hence there is only one ruling class in the world. This means that shortages are spread evenly amongst the majority of the population, as are some respectable surpluses. This majority will never leave their respective hubs, and now they are all connected, there will never again be any voices of dissent to rise above the hum of the crowd."

The Governor grinned. "They keep us very well," he said.

Ziggy swigged hard, then took in his surroundings once again. The exotic growths which covered the landscape, the subtle, warm lighting and the gigantic domicile of Governor Loftin.

"They do," he said, "*We* do."

"Come now Ziggy, you're one of us yourself, from this day forth! You can have a house just like this one! Better, in fact, you can have one of the brand new ones being built in the Benzie district."

"A house like *this*?" Ziggy gaped up at the structure. "I've lived in a Three Cube for ten years, like every other singleton. How many would I be sharing with?"

Governor Loftin was laughing at him again. He thinks I mean it, thought Ziggy, maintaining a look of mild indifference.

"As many or as few as you like," said the Governor, "It would be all yours, to do with as you will. There will be no more living like a common singleton in a three-metre-cube, for you. Now, you'll be a very eligible bachelor!"

"Could I bring Selene?"

Ziggy heard the words come out before he could stop them, and he cursed himself, silently.

"I'm very much afraid that you may not. You won't be seeing anyone from Hub 337 again. There'll be many other hubs for you to roam in, but the legends of Hub 337 will have to be repaired with some quite horrific stories of what became of you. We can't have others of a lower level deciding to follow you, connections or no."

"Why not?"

"Ziggy, Ziggy," the Governor tutted, unbuttoning his robes of state still further to reveal voluminous expanses of pasty, rolling flesh.

Ziggy looked away repulsed, and concentrated on paying attention. He was feeling strangely light-headed. Were all Fives like that, under their giant robes?

'The resplendent robes of the Fives' ran the religious texts of the Maker, 'Are symbolically large in order to represent the awesome responsibilities of care and fair governance which are placed upon the shoulders of every Five in the council's employ.'

Ziggy had never really thought to question the texts before.

Another line came into his head;

'While the rays of the Maker may sometimes bless us with the ethereal light of His divinity, they are poisonous to naked flesh, and therefore we must be contained under our giant screens until such a time as He makes us strong enough to stand proud under His brilliance, without protection.'

For so was it written.

Was it so? Ziggy wondered, or was it simply the 'Nuclear winter' that Loftin had mentioned? According to him, humans had once before stood under the Maker's 'brilliance without, protection.'

"There are other women in the world," the Governor was saying, "You'll soon be forgetting all about Selene. Besides, if you were to see the interview she gave about you earlier, I'd be surprised if you still wanted her."

Ziggy closed his eyes. He could see it already.

"I don't need to see that, thanks," he said, "What the hell are the Skormolc?" he asked, feeling the need of a new subject, "And why hasn't the nuclear winter killed them, if it's so lethal?"

"The Skormolc would not exist without the nuclear winter," said the Governor with a sigh. "They've grown by around a thousand percent in every direction in the last two thousand years - a direct result of nuclear radiation mutating a once harmless insect species beyond recognition. They wiped out all the other mutated, insectoid competitors long ago. They live only by feeding on the vast numbers of much smaller insects which still plague what vegetation there is left on the surface. The only other species to survive were the arachnids."

Seeing Ziggy's blank look, he explained, "The arachnids are now even bigger than the Skormolc, and even more fearsome and deadly. They feed upon everything else, including the Skormolc although - thank the Maker - they don't swarm and their population is not enormous. We still have many wars to fight, if and when we ever evolve beyond the confines of our radiation-proof surroundings. Retaking the bare surface of Planet Earth will be a great test, though you and I won't live to see it."

Ziggy had finished his meal, and he leaned back in his chair, enjoying his third glass of 'champagne'. The feelings in his head were growing stronger. He felt at once dizzy and very strong and powerful. He wasn't as interested in what the Governor was telling him as he was with his own exploits. He had escaped the hub, to become a *Five*? He was the Maker's chosen boy!

"Now," said the Governor, "Why don't you and I enjoy some of the other delights which we Fives are privy to?"

As he finished speaking, they walked around the corner. Two, smiling, barely-clothed women, a blonde and a redhead of extremely generous proportions. Their full folds of flesh bounced slightly as they walked towards the veranda.

"By the Maker!" cried Ziggy, "You're all gigantic!"

As soon as the words left his mouth, he cursed himself

inwardly, once again. Why was his tongue running away with his brain? The two women had stopped and looked at each other in shock; Ziggy knew this was a much bigger blunder than the last.

"Are you sure he's right in the head, Cary?" one of them asked Governor Loftin, frowning angrily at Ziggy.

"Yeah," said the other, "He's still not connected, is he?"

"I'm sorry, my dears," the Governor replied, looking rather embarrassed, "Perhaps we should do this some other time. Our Mr Atherton here still has rather a lot to learn."

The women wandered away, grumbling to each other.

Governor Loftin's head was in his hands. Ziggy didn't feel particularly uncomfortable about what had just happened, though he thought he should try to divert attention away from what he had said.

"What did she mean, 'still not connected'?" he asked.

The Governor stood up. "Walk with me, Ziggy," he said, "There are some more things I need to show you."

"Do you mind if I bring this?" Ziggy asked, pointing at the bottle.

The Governor chuckled. "Is it kicking in yet?

"What?"

"The alcohol. It gives you a bit of a rush, doesn't it?"

Ziggy stared at the bottle, fascinated. "Is that what it is?" he said.

They left the veranda and passed once again through the zip-stream terminal, to emerge in a very clean, fresh, spacious and subtly decorated room. The walls were adorned with scores of portraits of very large, proud-looking men and women.

The Governor waited as Ziggy walked slowly along one wall, taking in the magnificent view.

Ziggy's mouth fell open as he looked from one to the next and the next. All the pictures were very different. One man had the uniform of a police officer, another wore the sacred robes of a preacher. There was a frightening-looking woman wearing a rainbow of floral colours and one wearing the kind of suit Ziggy might have expected to see in the office. The one thing which all these people had in common, was their proportions.

Ziggy raised the bottle and gulped back most of what was left.

"Our size is our divine right," the Governor explained, "We are the rulers; we brook no shortages, although anyone of ranks one to four may, on occasion. We eat what we like when we like, in the age-old tradition of our forefathers. Our flesh naturally swells with the sustenance."

Ziggy finished the bottle and very nearly fell over.

"Wow," he said, "No shortages? *At all*?! Get me a cheeseburger!"

The droid appeared with a freshly-made cheeseburger, some thirteen seconds later. Ziggy laughed out loud, and then munched on it, eagerly.

"So what else do you want to show me?" he asked.

The Governor led him through the zip-stream terminal once more.

Ziggy gasped. They were standing on the balcony of a large tower, over looking a vast, industrial complex. The roof, way above them, had a few skylights and a huge array of cables and pipe works.

"Where are we?" he said.

"This is the centre of communications for corporate hubs 336 to 340," said the Governor, "Follow me,"

They went into the tower. Here, in a dark, circular room were five big displays. Each one stood proud of the floor by at least eight feet, and each one was an intricate, four-dimensional pattern of thousands upon thousands of coloured arcs and points of light, all swirling, flowing and dancing with each other.

Ziggy stood, entranced.

"Beautiful, aren't they?" the Governor said, quietly, "From here Ziggy, we co-ordinate and control every channel in every brain in five different hubs.

Ziggy said nothing.

"Doesn't it excite you? Here is where we build dreams for

people, where we create and direct a million virtual lives. This is the true centre of our power."

"Slaves," Ziggy murmured, remembering a forgotten word from an old story from the tomes of the Maker, "It's like everyone else in the world is a slave to the Fives."

"Oh, Ziggy!" the Governor chuckled, "When is a slave not a slave?"

Ziggy shrugged. "When?"

"When he doesn't believe he is. Do you know the real reasons why entering the Great Beyond is such a heinous crime?"

Ziggy shook his head.

"It's a measuring device."

Ziggy frowned. "What?"

"Every hub in existence has a similar religion, similar laws and a Great Beyond to measure them all by. The trick is lowering the numbers of people who flee any one given hub, to zero. You yourself know only too well the stigma attached to those who enter the Great Beyond, you understand the alienation. Anyone leaving the hub is taking on the Maker himself, as it is written, and so any such person is to be shunned. Can you imagine what a person would face if he left one hub and *arrived in another*? He'd be an outcast, as many have been in the past. The system works for us on many levels. The best way of keeping people in their own hubs, is to make them make each other stay. It works in almost every case. These days, now that everyone is connected, leaving a hub would be even harder for anyone of rank one, two, three or four because all connections would end the very second he crossed the threshold. You didn't have that burden, and aside from you - the rate of deserters in hub 337 has been at zero for decades."

Ziggy felt tension in the air, but he wasn't sure why.

"You know one other privilege we have?" the Governor asked him, quietly.

"Go on."

"We can turn our connections off, whenever we like."

"I see," said Ziggy, watching the mesmerising displays, "Does that make them more bearable?"

"You'll see."

That was it, thought Ziggy, that was what the Governor was hiding. He was still to be connected.

"These displays are almost magical, aren't they?" the Governor said, "Look at them - the nerve centres of five entire hubs of our people. Don't you even want to try the experience? You're a Five now, you'll be able to turn your connections off, just like me."

Ziggy was struck by a sudden realisation. 'Lurking in the bowels of the Great Beyond are the evil Skormolc,' ran the Maker's texts, 'Beware of them, for they shall eat men alive.' And here he was, talking to one of them. The Fives were the real Skormolc, not those weird, flying things which were forever locked out of the human environment! And here he was, about to be made one of them.

He was getting deja vu. He screamed. He smashed the empty bottle over Governor Loftin's head.

As the Governor was collapsing, Ziggy, howling in rage and drunken frustration at fate itself, tore into the display of hub 337, hacking at every optic and terminal with the broken bottle, smashing everything he could.

The police officers came storming out of the zip-stream terminals as Ziggy's efforts destroyed the connections of his former hub. He moved onto the next display just as the officers flew into the room from all sides.

"Freeze!" they yelled at him, at which Ziggy lobbed the remains of the bottle at the nearest one and continued the demolition with his bare hands.

Governor Loftin, stunned and bleeding on the floor, tried to cry out the words, "Don't fire!" but he couldn't speak.

The officers, their connections coming down one by one, lost their thread of command. The military instinct took over, the threat had to be stopped.

Ziggy was ripped apart and turned inside out by the wild blasts of the zapper guns. Unfortunately for all the Fives in the immediate vicinity, these untamed volleys also shorted out what remained of the other four displays.

Suddenly, in five separate hubs, all connections were down

and they were going to stay that way for days.

Governor Loftin groaned in horror, clutching his face as pieces of Ziggy Atherton dripped off the walls. "By the Maker, *oh by the Maker*!" he cried, softly, "I should have known, I should have known! Like father, like son."

The smell of champagne was in the air.

***

It was a mid-afternoon on Friday when the entire hub's connection grid went off line completely for the first time in almost two decades.

Everyone in funnel 3.23 had sat down on the floor, unsure how to move or react. Until that moment, everyone in the entire hub had known exactly where all their friends and family were.

After a few seconds, the dull voice sounded out in the old speakers in all the funnels, shops, apartment blocks, offices, factories, churches, hospitals and fire and police stations within Corporate Hub No. 337;

"Ladies and gentlemen, please do not panic, we are experiencing minor technical difficulties with the connection grid but we hope to have it back for you, as soon as possible. In the meantime, all work and deadlines are suspended. Please relax and enjoy some classical music."

Peter and Jane, a pair of courting sixteen year-olds, were sitting on the floor together in funnel 3.23. They looked at each other in surprise as a faded, crackling, forgotten piece of music from centuries ago began to play.

"What the hell is this?" said Peter, looking around him with an suitable degree of disgust apparent on his face.

"This is deep, this is," Jane replied, gazing around her at all the people sitting, listening to the fierce, yet beautiful song.

"Hmmm." said Peter, his eyes skirting her breasts. Careful! he reminded himself. Then suddenly he realised that because *her* eyes were averted and their connection was down, she had no way of checking *his*...

Jane was staring around in fascination at the once in a lifetime sight of a crowded funnel of people, all sitting on the floor looking at each other. She could hear snatches of an excited conversation -

"I bet it was that Ziggy Atherton!", followed by, "You what? Why him?", followed by, "Well they couldn't stop him before, could they?"

- and others. These were mostly people lamenting with total strangers over the loss of the conversations they had been having, the soap operas, sitcoms, films and sports they had been watching, now all lost to the blackout.

Strangers were gathering in groups with a common, physical interest. Liveliness was spreading rapidly through the crowd.

Peter was staring in fascination at Jane's tight top, looking for much longer and paying far more attention to the curves of her sweet young body than he had ever been able to before. His eyes ran away with him, trying to map her every curve into his memory.

All at once, Jane turned back to find him thoroughly absorbed.

"Peter," she said.

Nothing.

"Peter!" she demanded as she noted the line of his gaze.

"What?" he remembered himself, and looked her in the eye.

"What were you staring at?"

"Nothing."

"*Nothing*!?"

"I wasn't looking at anything, in particular."

"Yes you were! You were staring right at my tits!"

"I wasn't."

"You bloody were!"

"Can you find a file on it?"

But of course she couldn't; the server had stopped saving short-term memories when it went down - and their link was gone.

"You bastard!"

"What? I wasn't doing anything!"

"You were ogling my breasts, Peter, that's *not* not doing anything!"

He felt a whole new level open itself before him, and it was sublime. He looked at her with a friendly pity.

"If you can't show me the file," he said, gently, "It never happened, did it?"

She stared at him in surprise and indignation.

"It not fair!" she pouted, becoming aware of the fact that they were both totally cut off from their parents for the first time ever. In order to ensure full parental responsibility, no-one was usually able to cut themselves off completely from their parent(s) and/or guardian(s) until they were eighteen.

Something was making her breathe faster.

"Why not?" Peter asked, grinning, "Look at it this way; even if I was staring at your tits, which I wasn't, it only shows you that I like them! What's so wrong with that?"

Jane's mood had changed. She cast an exploratory eye over her boyfriend, then drew her head closer to his.

"What's wrong is that you can see more of me than I can of you," she said quietly, looking deep into his eyes. She noted the transition with satisfaction, and to stay ahead she asked,

"Are yours home yet?"

Peter's eyes were wide, his heartbeat was thumping harder and harder against his ribcage, the warmth was spreading uncontrollably through his midsection, and yet he tried to stay cool.

He replied - his voice bouncing and almost seizing up - "They'll be sitting at work, for now,"

Jane slid her hand into his. "Come on," she whispered, every word tingling with the hint of adventure in her mind, "My mum's probably back - let's go to yours."

"You know the server could be back up at any minute?" Peter whispered quickly.

Jane tutted as quietly as she could, her eyes rolling with impatience, "Don't you want to risk it?!"

Peter's head was spinning as they nipped into the nearest zip-stream terminal. Most of the other people in funnel 3.23 were now standing up, having animated discussions. Laughter broke out in uneven pockets of random members of all the common ranks, one to four.

No Fives were present, though the smart cameras kept their vigil.

© H. R. Brown, 08/12/2002

SCRIBBLED NOTES FOUND AT THE SCI-FI CONVENTION

[TITLE:] Evolution? Justice is Blind? HOPE?! Yea, Though I Walk..? The Poisonous Pissings of a Diseased Mind?! We Are God's Protective Nanobots!!! - ? (TBC)

"Ladies and gentlemen of the jury, you've heard the argument that I am guilty of inciting violence against the United States of America. I would like to present to you now, my defence. What I'd like to do is to read to you, in full, the contents of my manifesto, a political manifesto, that is, with which I had hoped to mount an insurgent challenge for the leadership of the Monster-Raving Loony Party. This is a fringe political party in Britain (or what *was* Britain), which I'm a member of."

"The Monster-Raving Loony Party has never had any real power, nor has it ever posed the threat of gaining any. I had hoped these ideas were just about bat-shit crazy enough to help me become leader of a party most people regard as a joke, but one in which I find potential in these bewildering times. This document has been published online, which is of course, why I'm here. OK, here goes:"

The defendant cleared his throat.

"The Future of Humanity: My Manifesto for the Leadership

of the Monster-Raving Loony Party.

Hey christians, guess you'd have to agree that God is the Universe, right? God is everything, so you'd have to accept that. Hey scientists, wouldn't you agree that if there is such a thing as 'God', then he, she, it or they must be the Universe itself? I think there's agreement we can find here.

Now, the Universe has been diagnosed by scientists as 'mortal', i.e. it will one day suffer a heat-death. If this is true, don't we have work to do? Scientists are constantly trying to expand our knowledge of the universe, and I salute you all – especially for bringing this issue to our attention. I say to to my christian friends; if you could help prevent the death of God, what wouldn't you do to help?

Granted, the Universe will destroy planet Earth long before its own demise, when, in four billion years or so, the sun begins to expand. Overcoming this problem by emigrating the planet, sometime within the next four billion years, is just one of the first steps in a grander scheme which humanity must commit to, in order to ensure our own survival, first of all.

That scheme is to continually build our knowledge and understanding of the universe to the point where we are able to find a way to allow both the universe and the human race, to survive, *literally*, forever. This would presumably involve us evolving and learning until the point where we might manipulate the galaxies themselves, and their black holes. We would need to evolve into a type IV or even a type V civilisation on the Kardashev Scale to achieve this, however we are not even anywhere near a type I civilisation on this scale, as yet.

This is a massively long-term plan, I grant you, but a worthy one, surely? To save God's life, and to save our own race? Surely both scientists and christians can agree that this should be the course for the future of our race? For who else in this entire universe do we yet know – except ourselves – who are even aware of the eventual death of God? Who else is there to make the diagnosis, or to even try to help?

'What a piece of work is man, How noble in reason, how infinite in faculty, In form and moving how express and admirable, In action how like an Angel, In apprehension how like a god.. '
- Hamlett, Act II, scene 2

I ask you, scientists and christians both; what are we here for – if not this eventual purpose? What did He in His infinite wisdom put us here for; to discover this fate and to do *nothing* to prevent it?!

My friends, I don't just call for a truce between scientists and christians, I demand an alliance between you guys! Because now, I say to you scientists; have you not found machine code underlying the mathematics which describes our universe? And does this not make you wonder who wrote the code, or at least *how* it was written?!

What a great thing would it not be for the future of our planet if you guys could agree and join forces for once?! I say to you: we are here, as a species, to keep advancing our knowledge base for this purpose – we are – or we will be, one day; God's protective nanobots!

We will exist in perfect symbiosis with Him; or She/He/It/They/the Universe, whatever; this will live forever and sustain the human race forever. I am not talking about immortality for any individual human, just the perpetual existence of both God, or the Universe, per your perspective, and the human race.

First up, on the agenda of advancing our understanding of the Universe, of God himself, my dear christians, my dear scientists; you need to gang up together on the governments of the world and pressure them to ensure the release of *all* of Nikola Tesla's files, in full. We know his knowledge is not allowed because it might mean the end of the petro corporations, via clean energy for all – but we have no more time to waste; climate change is upon us.

This is not – and should never be – about money. It's about knowledge which should belong to all of us. It's about the future of our world and of the human race and of the Universe itself.

Release the files!!! Let's get this party started, let's GO!!!

Also on the subject of climate change; I intend to invest in wave power to bring secure jobs and clean, green prosperity to the UK. We are an island nation, surrounded by an ever-moving ocean – why not make proper use of this perpetual motion machine??

Next on the agenda for the future, my dear scientists and christians, is to maintain the knowledge base we have here on earth, right now, by convincing the governments of all the globe to work together on preventing the next asteroid strike which could destroy our whole civilisation, and send us back to the stone age. This project alone would require the coordination and cooperation of all world armies and world leaders. We need full cooperation to fully monitor the heavens and coordinate a viable response to any potential asteroid strikes. I say I can make this happen, or at the very least pull a Thunberg and get all the globe talking about it!

Also, as a back-up plan, we need to build a series of arks around the globe, each of which will contain the full store of human knowledge and technology. These should be ready to go, and ready to save as many as possible, at all times, in case earth's defences should ever fail and the dread times come again.

This issue is actually more important than anything, other than climate change.

The Pyramids of Giza. Göbekli Tepe in Turkey. The giant stones at Baalbek in Lebanon. Countless other structures and ruins still found all over the globe on land and under the sea; these show us that great knowledge has been lost to our race, from a time before history as we know it even began. We are a species with amnesia, as Graham Hancock says. We have already, *literally*, been bombed back to the stone age, more than once, by many cataclysms in our past.

Don't we owe it to ourselves and to future generations to *not allow* further centuries of dark ages, intolerance, barbarism and religious genocide to descend upon us again, in the wake of any great calamity, as they surely have in our past?

We are smart enough to make this possible. And we're smart enough to evolve, potentially, into infinity. This is my manifesto, thank you for listening."

The Judge looked at the defendant over his glasses. "Do you have anything to add?"

The defendant gulped. "My lord -" he began but the Judge cut him off with -

"Son, I ain't no Lord!"

General laughter followed this around the courtroom, before, he added,

"*Sir*, will do just fine."

The defendant's stomach tried to assume the foetal position, and he shivered. A decreasingly small part of him was still in denial, believing this whole terrifying thing simply a nightmare.

"Sir," he stammered, "I never thought this manifesto would be read by even hundreds of people, never mind millions! I never thought anyone might take it seriously, outside of a political party which is literally a joke to the vast majority of people in my country. I certainly never thought I'd be extradited here, to answer for crimes which were clearly perpetrated by others, whom I've never met, and who are already answering for those crimes. I don't believe I should be criminalised for the crimes of people I've never met, who claim to act in my name or on my behalf. I have nothing to do with the attempted break-in at the FBI building. I have never been to the USA before, and with the greatest respect to you sir, and your great country, I don't believe I should be here now."

The Judge sighed. "That it?" he asked.

"Sir, I have never incited any kind of violence or law-breaking, and I never wished to. I'd like to point out that my manifesto requested aid in the cause of getting Tesla's files released, from scientists and christians, preferably working in unison. This is specifically because I wanted only to appeal to those people whom I would trust to apply pressure to governments in a non-violent, diplomatic, civilised, and perfectly legal manner. I abhor violence and theft, and I condemn that break-in and the actions of those involved, unreservedly."

"Uh-huh," said the Judge, "So.. That it?"

"Sir, I, I guess so, sir."

"Huh," rumbled forth from the Judge, "Ain't no sergeant-major neither. Are you saying you rest, son?"

"Ah, yes sir, I rest my case. And beg humbly to be released, if only so as to not be any further burden on the tax dollars of good Americans, in the act of incarcerating me unnecessarily."

The Judge had to take pity on the boy. "Son, you absolutely sure you want this – you don't want no lawyer?"

"I can't afford a lawyer, sir. Or at least, not one who'll argue my innocence."

"Damn boy! This shit went viral, landed your sorry ass in my court and you didn't even make out on it?"

The defendant shrugged, miserably. He lowered his head.

The Judge gave the jury a reasonably-impartial summing-up and then let them retire to consider their verdict. The defendant retired to his cell to sweat and stare at the cold, grim walls.

***

- LOOK UP - crimes of inciting violence/theft against USA, potential sentences, etc.
- Check dad OK with takeaway when D & L come over (timing, etc.).
- Washing.
- Money for tonight, shower, TICKETS!!

© H R Brown, 24/12/2019

Sunny Uplands

Lying in bed together, a dozey ten minutes or so after a good, zesty session, Helen stared at Tim.

"45 pence?" she said, "45 *pence*?!"

He nodded.

The look on her face became one of wonder. "That means you've broken the basic all-time rule of getting high," she said, "You can get more high for your money by eating this hash-cake than you can by smoking the same amount of hash! That goes against the rules, it was always smoking that delivered best value for money, always."

He held up his hands. "That's what I've been trying to tell you!"

Her eyes narrowed. "I call bullshit!", she declared.

"In what way bullshit?"

"There's no way what you gave me tonight cost you 45 pence to make. This is fucking crazy, dude! I mean it was like coming up on an E, except it's a massive hit of pot, and I might just be starting to come down now, but I've been high for... oh shit, what time is it now?"

He rolled his eyes, glanced at his watch; "It's half an hour since we last worked it out, so it's now four hours since you first said you must be at the peak, and that was an hour or so after you ate it."

"No way," she said, suddenly remembering to eye him with suspicion, "You're trying to make me think you're a genius and get me to suck your cock. That's what this is. Admit it."

He took her hand and kissed it. "I can assure you my dear, that was furthest from my mind. I just wanted to spread the good old-fashioned Bob Marley-style love to one and all! And I don't have that many mates who might partake these days, because you're right; everyone who's a pothead's a smoker, and everyone's trying to quit that shit nowadays."

She smiled. "I was gonna fuck you anyway, you know."

He smiled back. "Well clearly, and a delight you are to fuck babe, as ever! I'm not shittin' you about these biscuits though; I can do the sums again if you like."

She frowned, "OK, I did at least begin a Maths degree, once upon a time, let's give it another go."

"75 quid for a good half-ounce of hashish," he said, "It's gotta be hash to make these biscuits; I've tried it with bush and with skunk but it's only hash – good quality hash – that really knocks it out of the park. Then add a bit extra for flour, eggs, caster sugar and so on; the other vital ingredients, plus the cost of the heating. Call it 80 quid, average. Still with me?"

"I'm not that fucked."

"OK, so the way I do it, with a half of hash I make at least ninety of these biscuits and each one will get you fucked outta your mind for hours, as you've been so eloquently describing for hours now! 80 quid for 90 biscuits makes it 88.9 pence each, I just round it up to 90 pence."

"You said 45 pence," she chided.

"Yes babe, but remember you're a pussy; you only had a half!"

"I'll have you know my father was a weed dealer! I'm steeped in weed!"

"I know, agreed, but you haven't actually had any in years, have you? Which makes you now a lightweight. Anyway, yeah, a half of one of Uncle Timmy's Amazing Hash Cakes is 45 pence to make, that is the sum total cost of its production. Providing the hash is good, of course. If it's average, the biscuits aren't quite this good – you're lucky you got me on a proper Moroccan Squidgy Black vintage; they're not always *this* amazing! You just can't always get it this good. Either way, hash is still better, pound for pound, than using bush or skunk."

She smiled, spanked him several times on the behind and then looked confused. "OK, but what point was I trying to make?"

"Err.. Was it that it's basically a fucking odyssey whenever you get high again for the first time in ages?!"

"No, well yeah, but no there was something else.. What was it?"

"No idea," he said, "Remember, I had a whole one!"

"Yeah but you're used to it, you said you've been eating it like this for years."

"That is true. Hang on, wait a minute, weren't you so turned on by my genius at hash-cookery, you were gonna give me a blow job?!"

"Oh yeah, that's right," she said, "Just let me sharpen my teeth."

He laughed. "Never mind."

"No," she said, "No, I remember now; you've broken the law. You've broken the law! If you aren't bull-shitting me, *if,* you aren't bull-shitting, you've found a way to get higher on weed cakes than by smoking weed, pound for pound. You could sell whole ones for four or five quid each, easily."

"I know," he said, "These biccies beat anything Amsterdam has to offer – and I know 'cos I checked. And if it was a business, working in bulk would be potentially even cheaper – at dealer's rates you'd get a half an ounce for forty quid or less."

"And in clubs..." said Helen, oblivious, "Maybe double that! And they're so much healthier than smoking! And you don't smell of it, you can get wasted on these and never have to worry about it."

"I think there'll still be a carcinogenic effect," he said, "Do enough of them, for long enough, and you'll probably be risking some kind of bowel cancer or something. Also if you take one when you're already pissed, you can throw the mother of all whiteys, trust me!"

"So how do you make them?" she wanted to know.

He grinned, "It's all in the heating process!"

"Alright, but how?!"

"I'll tell you. One day. Probably!"

"Are you actually thinking of selling them?"

"I'm not going to prison, no," he said, "Which is what would happen within the first week of me making any serious attempt to become the Walter White[1] of hash cakes. But..."

"But?"

"But now they've legalised it in quite a few places on the planet, I'm actually thinking about emigrating."

She frowned at him. "Really?"

"Well, no, I mean I don't want to, but, I think too many people know about these biscuits now. Like those two this afternoon."

"Which two?"

He looked at her and chuckled. "That's where this all began, remember?! That lad with the massively missing tooth? And the girl with the half-shaved head?"

"Oh, they said your biscuits were amazing and cool and

trippy!"she said, now remembering the events of seven hours ago like they were seven years since.

"Yeah," he said, "This is what I mean, and since you wouldn't let it go and I told you what the biscuits are, and now you know from first-hand experience too, I know it's my own fault and I've let too many people in on this, but it's getting dodgy."

At the look on her face he said, "Oh I'm not worried about you knowing babe, you know I trust you, but too many other people know because I've thrown them around at parties and in clubs. I didn't even recognise that lad with the massively missing tooth but I've clearly let him have one as well, at some point. And it's not the first time that's happened either, where I don't even remember someone but they remember me – and my biscuits!"

"You've never charged for them?"

"Why bother? If, *if,* I take five of these little beauties out with me on a good night out, then for less than a fiver I can take me and four others to Mars on the same evening. Compare that to an average round of drinks. And when you all take them at the right time, just a few pints in, then you all come up like you're on E; they're great for dancing on too! Sometimes I get to be where the party's at."

"So where would you go if you left?"

"I don't know, I've just started to think I might be better leaving, going to a place where it's legal and setting up a biscuit shop, or web delivery service or something like that. Otherwise sooner or later, someone I don't want to know is coming to make me show them my method, whether I like it or not."

It was her turn to giggle at him. "Paranoid much?!"

"It's not paranoia if you know for a fact you can't even remember everyone you've let in on the secret; weed's still illegal you know."

She began chanting, "Para, noia, para, noia, para-"

"Oh maybe you're right," he said, "Maybe it's that part of me thinks making a business out of this'd be a much more honest way of making a living than the shit I actually do. It's just I'd have to emigrate to do it because there's no way the fuckers'll legalise it in this country. I mean, I could lead a healthy revolution in marijuana; bakery not smoking, could provide jobs to loads of people – for the good of Britain, you understand!"

Helen smiled. "You could get involved with that campaign, Free The Weed! Because you're right you know, you can offer a really healthy alternative to smoking it, could even become a centre-piece for them."

He thought about it, and the doubts quickly multiplied. "Sounds like a lot of effort, and unwanted attention," he eyed her suspiciously, "And the last thing you want right in the middle of any fucking campaign is anyone on this shit!"

She giggled and he grabbed her and they became lustily entwined again.

***

Although they had had a lovely evening, Helen didn't want

to stay the night. She left his house with a cheery,

"I'll see you later in the week!"

"Hey," Tim called after her, from his doorstep, "Does this mean we're going out again?!"

"Let's just be fuck-buddies for now," she yelled at him, laughing – and laughing all the more for seeing the horrified look on the face of one of Tim's neighbours, staring at her from his window - "And if anyone asks, just say 'it's complicated'!"

After she had gone, Tim thought again about Helen's idea of contacting the Free The Weed campaign. The more he went over it in his mind, and with the endorsement of a former weed-dealer's daughter, no less, recurring through his thoughts, not to mention the better part of a bottle of red wine and another half a biscuit, Tim decided to let his wild hopes attempt to engineer the future in his favour, and he googled the details.

When he found the address on their website, Tim sent the following email to the offices of Free The Weed:

From: Tim (the guvnor) Holmstock <timtheguvholmstock@deadzedmail.com>
Sent: 27 July 2021 20:47
To: enquiries@FTW.qui.ck
Subject: Cheap & Powerful Hash Biscuits...

Dear Sirs

I note the mission statements on your website and in particular your primary aim, "to end the prohibition of cannabis". I agree wholeheartedly with your mission and would seek to assist you in it, if possible.

However, I do not have money to spare for your charity I'm afraid. What I would like to offer to the cause is the recipe and the method for making the most powerful – and inexpensive – hash biscuits on planet earth.

Whilst I support your cause, I no longer smoke weed and hope to never do so again – because my product has removed the need for smoking or even vaping cannabis. I can get ridiculously high, for at least five or six hours, on just one of these biscuits (total production cost = 90p each) and then go cross-country running because I can be fit and healthy *and* a pothead. In these fiercely anti-smoking times, I hope you can see the value in my offer and hope to hear from you soon.

Regards,

Tim Holmstock

PS: Also; do you think "WTF?FTW" might work as a slogan? It's all yours!

B-)

After he had sent this, Tim sat down to watch an old movie he'd not seen before, called Multiplicity. Starring Michael Keaton, it's a film about a man so constantly pressed for time by job and family that he agrees to have a clone of himself made to help ease the burden. Tim watched it for a while but he lost interest, then he whiled the remainder of his evening away channel-hopping and phone-surfing.

***

It was in his dreams that night the cloning theme of the film took control. Tim could never remember afterwards what reason he had had, in this dream, for wanting to create a clone of himself, it just seemed like a good idea at the time.

Tim gave hair and blood samples (as per the plot of Multiplicity), and watched as Tim Number 2 was brewed up, solidified and created.

Tim 1 then had to convince Tim 2 that he was in fact the clone, not the original. This wasn't easy because Tim 2 was a perfect clone, both in body and mind. However, as per the film, Tim 2 was revealed to have the number '2' tattooed behind his ear, thereby confirming him as the clone, not the original.

At this point both Tims faced each other; Tim 1 looked on his clone with compassion, whereas Tim 2 stared past the original, as the understanding of his situation sank in. His psyche raced to new horizons which took flight before his wild and fleeting gaze.

Tim 2 focussed in again on Tim 1. He took a deep breath, then smiled.

"You had me made to make your life easier," said Tim 2, "And in some ways just for the thrill of it. But you didn't think through what this actually means for me. I have your skills and your potential, yet by your own admission, *you* are the original Tim. Your job and your house and your mortgage are just that; *yours*. Not mine. I am not bound by them as you are, and my life is my own."

Tim 1 felt the walls of the dream closing round him as his clone and sudden nemesis continued,

"You, Tim my friend, would never dare leave your house on a warm summer night like this and go and sleep on the grass in a field, or in a bed of leaves in a forest, under the stars, like the blokes in *Tortilla Flat*[2]. You wouldn't wake up in the dew and the glow of the dawn, see the sun rise and then get up and just keep walking, to find what I may find, see what I may see and go wherever I may go. I have no boundaries. I am free. I can just go wherever the wind pushes me. And tonight, I sleep beneath the stars."

Tim 2's eyes were so bright and intent, Tim 1 realised with a shock - they were crying! Were those tears of *joy*?!

Tim 1 felt the same wide-eyed rush of understanding Tim 2 had had before him, coupled with a surge of green-eye for this crazy version of himself who was utterly free and whom he had released into the world.

There was a wild, reeling sense of vertigo within the conflicting ideas; sudden and total freedom on Tim 2's part, and Tim 1's immediate jealousy of this freedom in his double. This madness broke through the bubble of the dream, and he was both Tims once more.

Breathing hard, more disturbed by the dream than any he'd had in a long time, Tim went over and over it in his mind. His alarm then went off, maliciously, only a minute after the dream ended. Tim cursed and kicked his body out of bed and carried on cursing, viciously, at no-one but himself.

Though the words of his doppelgänger faded and became jumbled over the course of his day, Tim could not forget their basic meaning, nor his response to it. Both the Tims in his dream, he knew, were constructs of his own subconscious mind.

***

Leaving the office late that Monday afternoon, Tim remained unsettled and beset with anxiety. He had forgotten the joyously crazy, wannabe tramp of a clone from his dream; now he was far more concerned about the very real email he had sent the previous evening. Stupid! Why had he done that?

Although he knew full well why he had done it; half drunk and twisted on hash cookies, loved-up by the recent intervention of his ex Helen, who wouldn't want those warm and wonderful feelings to be spread to all other members of the human race?

Fucking idiot, he told himself. And again.

It was exactly the same way in which he'd left himself unguarded before in pubs and clubs; getting drunk as well as high - and throwing his excess supply around. He had said as much to Helen the previous evening, then done the exact same thing again – only this time he'd left a digital trail, no, a *confession*, and sent it out unencrypted over the fucking internet. He could only hope it was lost in the general oceans of info and would only be read by the folk at FTW to whom it had been sent. Then he hoped the folk at FTW would be understanding of an idiot who had too much to drink one evening and shot off his stupid mouth.

As he rounded the corner, not far from his bus stop, Tim froze.

The street between him and his stop was a party, a rally for the Free The Weed campaign. Red-yellow-green marijuana banners flew everywhere. Reggae music played. It was a carnival. Happy hippies were everywhere, many of them dancing. Everyone with dreadlocks in the county must be here, Tim thought. Around the edges of the event, thirty or more police stood impassively, keeping watch.

The sudden burst of massive paranoia almost choked him. Were they waiting for him? Surely not.

Some of the faces in the crowd he knew and recognised as fellow stoners, which meant – he already knew – there would be more in this crowd who recognised him, than he himself could recognise. More paranoia.

Under other circumstances he would have loved this gathering and would have wanted to get involved and have fun, but after his email last night, this was too much. This was made worse because he was just out of the office and wearing his shirt, black trousers, black shoes and he had his rucksack on his back. Decidedly not party gear.

"Hey Tim!" a voice said behind him, "Nice to see you here!"

It was the young man with the massively missing tooth who knew Tim, and his biscuits.

Tim smiled at him, panicking, "Hi!", he said, too high-pitched, then coughed.

The young fellow grinned, held out his hand, "Leo," he said, "In case you forgot!"

The relief in Tim must have been obvious as he took Leo's hand, for Leo chuckled and said,

"I knew you couldn't remember me yesterday! Don't worry about it, you were completely mashed at that party. So was I when I had your cake!"

"Pleasure's all mine mate," said Tim, "But I have to ask - what's all this?", he gestured around at the rally, "And when are those cops gonna move in?!"

"It's four-twenty mate! said Leo, "Don't you know what fucking day it is?!"

Again Tim was relieved, and also massively annoyed at himself for thinking this whole carnival could possibly be about – or anything to do with – him. He chastised himself further for forgetting about the internationally renowned weed festival 420, held all over the planet, once a year. He'd been meaning to get to this for a few years now, and kept bloody forgetting -

"Damn, you high right now?" Leo wanted to know, "Listen, don't worry about the cops kicking off man, there's way too many of us for that! No-one's breaking any laws anyway. Well, except for the obvious!"

Obvious it was. It hung in the air, a delicious, sweet reminder of Tim's smoking days. Golden, early evening sunlight bathed all. One reggae number finished and the crowd roared, then roared again as the band struck up an excellent cover of Bob Marley's *One Love*. Green, yellow and red colours flew everywhere.

"Oh, wait," said Leo, taking out his mobile. A moment later

he smiled and said, "That's pretty good!"

Tim was about to wish him well and slip away, when Leo took out a fat green marker pen and used it to scrawl in big, thick, green ink on the nearest lamp post:

WTF?FTW

Then time slowed down and the colour drained from Tim's face. Leo looked at him. "I've got an extra marker pen dude, you wanna help spread the word?"

In shock, with cold sweats suddenly bathing the small of his back and beginning to radiate outwards, Tim tried to speak, coughed, had a minor coughing fit, then said "Where did that come from?" he coughed again, "It's pretty good."

"Text update from management," Leo told him, "They don't encourage graffiti, just the slogans!"

"Management? You work for Free The Weed?"

"Just on the door-knocking side, armed with leaflets."

Tim was caught between panic and the need for flight – and the awareness of the need for information on potential threats to his existence.

"Nice," he said, "You got any leaflets then? Can I have one?"

"What, like you aren't already a convert to the cause?!" said Leo.

Again the paranoia. Who exactly was Leo? And what did

he really know?

"No, I just might want to get in touch with the movement."

"I've run out, sorry. Try over there, there's a dude with hundreds of them."

Fortunately, Leo pointed in roughly the direction Tim wanted to go to escape.

"Cheers dude," said Tim, "I'm gonna check it out and get me one, maybe you'll have me for a colleague sometime soon!"

They bumped fists and Tim nearly bolted away in the direction of freedom. Within five seconds he was painfully aware how his furtive movements stood out in the happy crowd, because he was also very aware that several police officers had noticed him and were now focussing on him, highly alert.

As he left the throng and headed up Gothlorien Street, Tim knew that two of the coppers were leaving the edges of the street party and bearing towards him.

Shit. Fuck.

Tim decided to walk faster, but knew he'd only be able to speed up steadily, in the hope the cops didn't realise he was trying to get away from them. The cold sweats definitely had him now. Half his body felt numb but the numb areas were shifting, around and about him.

As he walked down the street he increased his gait gradually. He was fighting the urge to look over his shoulder and not to lose his shit completely when he noticed another hippy type, with long hair flowing behind him as headed directly towards Tim. As he approached, the fellow beamed hugely at Tim. Tim was nonplussed and became more so, as the man also winked at him as he passed and headed towards the throng, the crowd and the two policemen.

Tim couldn't help but look over his shoulder now, wondering if he knew the bloke; was he one of these Brambleby hippies he'd given a biscuit to, once upon a drinking session?

Whoever the hippy was, he was he marched straight up to the policemen and stood in front of them, barring their path. Both coppers stopped and looked at the man.

Tim couldn't catch what the man said, but both the police rolled their eyes and one said something to the hippy which came with a sneer.

The long-haired dude then hopped out of the coppers' way and nipped off into the rally.

Tim grinned, wondering what the bloke might have said. He walked away steadily, as now the coppers were looking back towards the busy square, and the fellow who'd clearly irritated them.

Tim carried on walking briskly, imagining the hippy fellow having no trouble in escaping through the crowds.

***

Once back inside his house, the front door locked behind him, Tim felt a little safer, but only a little. His email had been read and at least some of its contents disseminated amongst the staff of FTW, that much was certain from the slogan "Leo" had scrawled on the lamp post. And why was the rally held there? Had they actually set up the rally there because they knew he would walk that way home? Surely he had not given that many biscuits away, and he'd sent only one email.

He knew he now had to decide if his house was safe for him to stay in or not.

This question was more pressing and pertinent than he realised, he realised, as he entered his kitchen and saw the same hippy who had just effectively saved him from the interest of the police, sitting at his table and drinking what looked like a beer from his fridge.

"Helped myself to a beer," the fellow said, "Hope you don't mind."

Tim's mind, bent out of all shape with his current realities gave up trying to control anything.

"Why would I mind?" he heard himself say, "Some random dude illegally breaks into my house and starts drinking my beer, why would I mind, I've got at least another seven, think I'll get me one too."

"Way ahead of you," said the hippy dude, holding one out to him.

Tim took it, popped it, sank a good third straight away.

"So who the fuck are you?"

"I'm the dude who stopped the cops checking you out," said the long-haired interloper, "My name's Ash. And I'm here to help."

"Why?"

"I work for Free The Weed, they told me to look out for you. They liked your email. But they worried it was sent insecurely, and put me onto you to make sure you're OK."

Tim said nothing, just drank some more.

"It wasn't just the email though," Ash continued, "Free The Weed have contacts in Brambleby, obviously, and some of them recognised the biscuits you talked about in that email. They know the stories are true."

Tim was equally humbled and frightened by this.

"So, am I in danger?" he asked.

"Well, you aren't in no danger at all. Free The Weed have assigned me to you because they already know your email was read by people you never intended it to reach. There are criminal gangs known to monitor the communications of Free The Weed, for any worthwhile info. I have to tell you; our security systems say that information regarding you has been passed to the head of the Outta Towners."

At that name, Tim felt genuine fear. He'd heard horror stories before about the Outta Towners; a hardcore gang of criminal nut-cases whose paths you didn't cross - without ending up maimed, raped, crippled, killed - or some combination of the above.

Tim's head was in his hands, "What can you do to help?" he moaned.

"Well, Free The Weed like your idea but they aren't ready to use it; weed is still illegal, after all. For now, keeping you safe is the mission."

Tim looked at Ash. He was average height, lean, dressed in colourfully shabby clothes, unkempt and he had long hair. "How are you gonna keep me safe?" he wanted to know.

"I was a soldier once," the hippy replied, "I'm handy enough but there's only one of me. The longer we stay here, the more likely it is someone is going to come looking for you or your recipe. We need to leave."

"And go where?"

"In the immediate term we need to find somewhere safe to have a full and frank discussion on the best course of action. So pack a rucksack with clothes for a few days – and bring all the hash biscuits you have too. And don't leave any copy of the recipe in this house."

"Yes sir," Tim muttered.

"Problem?"

"No Ash, everything you say sounds right, it's just a lot to take in all at once."

"If I'm curt with you it's because time is a factor. I think fast, I talk fast and I need you to act fast if you wanna get out of this. So pretty please, with sugar on top, pack a fucking bag."

Tim stared at Ash in resentment, "You did not just rip off

Pulp Fiction[3] to smack me down with!?"

Ash grinned.

"Twat!" Tim shouted.

"Just get a fucking move on," said Ash.

"Just tell me one thing first," Tim said, "What the hell did you say to that copper?!"

Ash slowly rolled his head round to give Tim a hard, dead-eyed look. "Pack a bag," he said, "We don't have time for this."

Tim grumbled but he got on with it.

Ten minutes later he was good to go, although he was not at all happy with the fact he was now carrying more than fifty, high-powered, hash biscuits in his rucksack. They were sealed in a tin, wrapped in a plastic bag and stuffed down deep, beneath some spare clothes, but still he knew he would worry about them constantly.

As they left his house, Ash told Tim to turn his phone off, for now.

Tim complained but Ash was not to be dissuaded.

"You've seen enough movies to know you can be tracked via your phone. Turn it off, *now*."

In the movies they would usually toss the phone out of the window of a moving car, Tim thought; at least Ash hadn't gone that far. He turned it off and pocketed it.

"Now then," said Ash, "Name the nearest pub you never go in."

"White Lion," said Tim, "It's a proper old man's pub, the beer's shit and overpriced, there's no -"

"White Lion it is," Ash announced, cutting him off, "And it's your round old man."

***

In the White Lion, Tim could swear he was eyed with suspicion as he bought a couple of pints. He ignored this and sat down with Ash.

"Maybe you'd better put something on the jukebox," said Ash, quietly "So people can't overhear."

"I got the beer," Tim said, "You can sort the jukebox. Impress me!"

Ash slid out of his seat, sidled across the pub and put a few tracks on the jukebox.

As Ash took his eat again Tim realised the song which was beginning to play throughout the pub was *Just Dropped In*, by Kenny Rogers and The First Edition.

Again, Tim felt his ears begin to burn. "Was that really the best song to put on, *now*?!" he hissed at Ash.

Ash grinned. "No-one else in here's thinking what you're thinking. They've no reason to. Paranoia's getting to you mate."

Tim took a deep breath. "OK," he said, "Now what?"

Ash looked at him. "This recipe of yours; what's it worth, really?"

Tim explained by going over the economics of his product, as discussed previously with Helen.

"So, in the right market conditions you can make a three to four hundred percent profit on each unit sold. Not bad. Can your recipe be replicated?"

"I should think so, but I don't know if anyone else knows the tricks I found out by cooking these biccies over and over again for years."

"So if you did ever successfully market them, someone would sooner or later figure out the same methodology, given your ingredients? I mean, there are only so many ways the ingredients can be put together and cooked; a professional operation could probably work it our pretty quickly, yes?"

Tim knew this was entirely possible. He had stumbled across his method via years of practice and learnings made from mistakes; a commercial venture aiming at the same standards would undoubtedly soon achieve them. He gave a reluctant nod.

"So don't be greedy. Publish your recipe anonymously on the internet and everyone can enjoy it, right now. Once it's public knowledge then you're safe; no-one's coming to your house all tooled-up for what they can download for free off the net."

Tim took a good swig of his beer. Ash was right. He knew it. He knew it was the right thing to do; to give this fantastic recipe, for free, to the whole of the human race. Yet he paused, supping his pint, thinking. It was still a risk to post such a thing on the internet, even anonymously. And, at the back of his mind was also the ongoing sliver of self interest which really stole the show; the unmentioned knowledge that he could yet make the biscuits an integral part of the financial planning for his retirement years. God only knew what his pension would be worth, but he knew it wasn't going to be much. Almost certainly not even enough.

"Still a risk," he said, "Posting it on the net."

"Dictate it to me," Ash said, "I can then post it unencrypted and unashamed from another country whilst you are verifiably here; you'll be safe and no-one's catching me at it."

Tim's paranoia expanded at this point to include Ash; who really was he? Ash could see this in Tim, but he said nothing.

"Are there any other options?" Tim asked, tight-lipped.

"Move abroad to where it's legal."

"I'm English!" Tim moaned, "I don't speak other languages well, and all right, there parts of America where it's legal but I'd get shot dead in six months if I went there, I just know it!"

Ash raised his eyebrows.

"All my friends and family are here; there must be another option?"

Ash sighed. "Was afraid you might ask me that."

Tim said nothing, waited to hear what else might be done.

"We can't just delete what is already known about you by the Outta Towners. And we can't stop them. If they are coming for you, they always will be. If you don't want to give them the recipe, nor the rest of the planet, then you have to change the rest of the planet."

Tim frowned.

"However in your case," Ash continued, "Just changing England would do."

Tim's expression didn't change. "The whole planet," he said, "Or just the whole of England, it's still a bit of an ask."

"If we could kick-start the government into legalising weed," said Ash, "Then you could copyright your recipe without repercussions."

"Legalise weed?!" Tim laughed, "That's Free The Weed's job, and I don't see them sorting it out any time soon."

"No, they won't. I mean I like my employer, don't get me wrong, and I like the line of work, I've grown into quite a hippy in my old age – but they're not serious about actual legalisation. What's the reason for their continued existence once weed is legalised? They're all on the dole the minute it happens, so there's never gonna be any rush on their part."

Tim nodded. "Makes sense. Cynical, fucked-up, but makes total sense. So how do you propose to legalise weed in this country, preferably before Christmas?!"

Ash took in a good amount of his beer. "I've often thought about what would be the most effective way of achieving legalisation," he mused, "And I usually come up short. However..."

Tim tutted. "However?"

"However, I've never before had the potential I have right now. Assuming you and I can fully, and honestly, work together, then I think the sky's the limit. Can we work together?"

"What is your plan?" Tim said, "Explain it to me, and I'll tell you if we can work together."

"Well, let's start as we mean to go on," Ash said, "You've got a couple of hash cakes in your pocket right now, yes?"

Tim stared at Ash, his paranoia screaming in his bones and his blood; "*How do you know that?*" he hissed.

"I saw you slip them in there when you thought I wasn't looking," Ash said, "By the mirror in your hall."

Tim was caught out. He went over the incident in his mind; he had taken the biscuit tin out of his kitchen cupboard and packed them whilst Ash waited in the hall. As he was doing this he had quickly concealed two of them in a little bag in his jacket pocket; he had to accept Ash could have seen him doing so.

"I can tell I'm making you more paranoid," said Ash, "And that's understandable, given the circumstances. So why don't I put your mind at rest? Once I've eaten one of your biscuits you can be sure I'm not working for the police, yes?"

Tim nodded. He had indeed secured two of the biscuits in his jacket pocket in order that he and Ash could both have one and come-up together, at some point – without having to delve deep into his rucksack. He hadn't been expecting Ash to be such a ninja that he already knew this. What the hell, he thought; now was as good a time as any.

He went in his pocket and brought out the plastic bag, inside which were the two hash-biscuits. He and Ash took one each, and washed them down with beer.

Ash grinned widely. "Ooh," he said, "They taste good. Think I'm gonna enjoy this!"

Tim relaxed a little, now he knew Ash couldn't be a policeman, although he still didn't fully trust him. "You are definitely gonna enjoy it," he said, "But now we're on a timescale. We want to be somewhere safe for the night, within the hour, 'cos when we come up on these..."

"I can tell they're hash cakes, they're really strong," said Ash, ignoring Tim entirely, "But they're sweet, well-made and the ginger hides the taste of hash pretty well. If you covered them in chocolate too, they could be the perfect weapon..."

"Ash, focus; what's the plan? How are you gonna weaponise my biccies with chocolate!? And where are we going; we're both going to be really fucking high in an hour!"

Ash's eyes lit up. "We get the next train to London," he said, "Tonight, right now! It's the only way!"

"What? I have to work tomorrow!"

"Wrong," said Ash, "You have to stay alive. And you can call in sick for now. We have to go to London."

Tim sighed. The prospect of a several-hour train journey, in the heightened state they were both now soon to achieve, could prove problematic in many unforeseen ways. "So," he said, "You gonna tell me the plan on the way?"

***

Tim would soon wish he had simply acted on his own words and moved abroad.

The train ride with Ash was a blinkered hell of over-bearing bright lights, paranoia and crazy notions. Remembering it later, Tim was fairly sure much of the horror of it must have been part of his internal monologue, but at the time he became utterly convinced they would not survive the journey and everyone on the train was a spy who already knew what they were up to – and what he had in his rucksack.

Outside the artificial lighting of the train carriage, a shadowed and threatening dusk became lost in streaks of night and rain. The branches of trees raged past, slinging forth wraiths, gargoyles and other demonic forms to howl around the train as the drums of hell shook the cowering, rain-battered world through which they fled.

All of which, with hindsight, was probably just the train

passing though a thunderstorm.

The conversation with Ash on their plan of action was the only thing he remembered with any clarity.

Ash's idea to get weed legalised was dangerous and bizarre, but it had the definite advantage of being a surprise attack, albeit illegal and immoral.

"Who are the main obstacles to the legalisation of weed?" Ash asked him.

Tim wanted to say; the multiple assassins sitting all around them - disguised as passengers - were the most immediate obstacle, but he settled on; "Politicians, left and right."

"Wrong," said Ash, "The main obstacles are the Daily Stun and the Daily Stale. They're the papers the government doesn't want to get on the wrong side of. They're the most moralising of the tabloids when it comes to weed and drugs in general, and yet, despicably for twenty-first century Britain, they're also the most well-read papers in the country. What we have to do is show up the Stun and the Stale as total hypocrites on the subject of weed – and to do that we need to get the staff, and preferably the proprietors, high on your biscuits. Then we drop them in it, one way or another. Once the public know these guys have been getting high, Free The Weed will jump to campaign against the hypocrites of the tabloids spoiling everyone else's fun. Various liberal politicians will find their backbones and join in on the side of legalisation; we can create a snowball effect with the right catalyst. And right-wing, moralising, self-important media moguls who get caught doing that which they always preach against, could be just exactly the right catalyst."

"They'll know they've been spiked," Tim retorted, "And they'll catch us."

Ash grinned. "We have surprise on our side, remember? Who would expect to go off their tits, an hour after eating one innocent little ginger biscuit? We can be long gone before anyone knows they've been spiked."

Tim, at this point, had his head in his hands again. He was partly convinced the conductor was a zombie in disguise, and was standing behind him, ready to bite his neck. He was also frightened by Ash's idea. It sounded like plain horror to him.

"I can't spike people with my biscuits," he whispered fiercely at Ash, "I won't."

"You can and you must," said Ash, "Forget about you and your position; this is also for the greater good! We're talking about a set of scumbags who have no problem in seeing people jailed and having their lives ruined, just for having weed. Just for *weed*, man! It's senseless, it's barbaric and it must end. Right now, you and I have the wherewithal to make it happen, and if all it takes is to spike a bunch of twats with these brilliant little pot-bombs of yours and watch them lose their shit for a few hours – I say so fucking be it! Come on!"

Tim sighed and he nodded. He didn't want to; he did agree but he didn't want to be the one responsible for enacting the plan, and certainly didn't want to take the risks involved. Right now he only wanted Ash's relentless argument to stop. At this point they were already halfway to London, and Tim was sure he'd find a way to wriggle out of this before putting himself into actual danger.

"OK," he said, "Say we really can do this; how?"

"Give me five minutes on your phone and I'll tell you."

"Whoa," said Tim, "I thought we're off grid?"

Ash tutted, "I can encrypt your phone in ten seconds flat," he said, "And it's not too big a risk, I just need to check something."

Tim found himself handing over the phone. He balked slightly as he realised Ash didn't need to ask for his unlock pattern – he already knew it. He worried about this, but he also felt somewhat reassured by Ash's obvious field skills and keen assimilation of important information. The man was definitely a ninja.

The walls of the train were moving gently in and out, as if the train itself was breathing. Tim shook his head and rubbed his eyes.

Within a minute Ash laughed out loud, "We could not have picked a better time to head to London," he said in triumph, "Perfect opportunity!"

"What kind of opportunity? What do we have to do?"

"Well, Rudyard McKintock is arguably a better choice, but he's not often actually *in* the UK. Sir Dickie Padre however, top dog at the Daily Stale, is attending a press bash tomorrow evening!"

Tim's stomach lurched and growled at him. This was all sounding too real, too intense and too fucking soon.

"And how are we going to gatecrash this bash?" Tim found himself saying.

"More important right now is where to stay tonight," Ash said, "But I have a few ideas..."

***

On the way to their digs, hastily arranged by Ash on Tim's phone – which had now been turned off - they took a detour to go shopping. Ash purchased two large bars of finest milk chocolate and one of excellent dark chocolate (to 'zshuzsh-up the mix a bit'), a flattish stone bowl, a bunch of cock-tail sticks, grease-proof paper and a spoon.

"We're staying in a crap hotel," Ash explained, "And to chocolate-coat the biscuits we just need these – and an iron, which even a crap hotel should be able to provide."

They travelled by tube to the accommodation Ash had arranged; this was a drab, tiny little room and clearly one of them would have to sleep on the chair in the corner, as there was only a single bed. Tim was glad when Ash called the chair, saying he was used to it.

That night, in their hotel room, they heated the chocolate by placing it in the bowl and a hot iron over the top. They stirred it occasionally until it was thoroughly melted, then used the cocktail sticks to dip each of the hash biscuits in the chocolate before letting them cool on the grease-proof paper.

Whilst this process was underway, Ash explained to Tim what the next day would entail. Early on they would 'case the joint', meaning they would check out the hotel where the

Press Association were holding their party, and discover what uniforms the staff wore. There would be a back way in, Ash was sure, via the kitchens. They just had to get the right uniforms to match, then turn up there in good time and wait for a member of the kitchen staff to go for a fag break, and then get past them into the building. Tim had queried this part until Ash pointed out they could just act like they were late, apologetic and keen to get started; it was doubtful anyone having a fag out of the door would question this, as long as they looked the part.

***

The next day, after a fitful sleep, Tim found himself believing they could pull it off. Perhaps due to Ash's supreme confidence in the scheme, perhaps because he was becoming convinced himself that what they were planning was such an unexpected attack, that there was every chance of their success. Also, looming over everything was the spectre of the Outta Towners and the multiple, brutal versions of future tortures which they might inflict upon him.

His position was made easier for him by Ash, who was an excellent commander for their situation. Tim would never have thought of himself as a recruit, but this he had effectively become. Their morning breakfast was coffee, croissant and apple, which Ash had popped out early to buy pairs of. They also both had another hash-biscuit with their breakfast, just for good measure, as Ash had it – and also to road test the new, chocolate-coated version.

"Awesome!" Tim said, munching on his, "Normally I'd have to worry about chocolate melting in my pockets, which is why I've never bothered with chocolate, or icing for the same reason, but now..."

"Now you need to call in sick," said Ash, "Then we just put these all back in your tin, sneak into the party, place them all on some nice silverware and pass them out to the party people; Sir Dickie Padre in particular."

Tim turned his phone back on and made the call to his boss, telling him he'd had some kind of food poisoning and couldn't move far from his toilet, for now. His boss was understanding and said to update him tomorrow.

Tim turned his phone off again, grinning. "So, first we case the joint, right?"

Ash grinned. "That will be the easy part!"

He was not wrong. In the alleys behind the Metropolitan they saw various staff taking fag or vape breaks. They took note of the uniforms and also spent a few minutes milling around the hotel lobby doing the same.

In the lobby, Tim was asked, by a sparkling young lady in a spotless uniform, if he needed any help. He replied that he was simply waiting for a friend, then a few minutes later when he was satisfied he'd seen enough, he pretended to receive a text which re-directed him out of the hotel.

Buying the uniforms to match was straight-forward, although not cheap. They finished their preparation for the evening by the early afternoon. They went to the nearest pub with a pool table and played for a while, to calm their nerves.

Dinner was a takeaway meal and another half a biscuit each. Ash had wanted a whole one, but Tim didn't want to be too high for their performance tonight.

When they arrived at the alleys behind the Metropolitan they were well scrubbed-up and neatly dressed in their waiters' uniforms. Tim had the package of chocolate-covered hash cookies sealed in the tin in his rucksack.

They waited three minutes before a podgy young apprentice chef appeared from a side door to light up a rollie.

"'Scuse me mate," said Ash, stepping past him, "Hangovers, don't ask!"

Tim followed with a nod, as the chef nodded to them and carried on smoking.

Inside the kitchens was what looked like pandemonium, although there must have been some organisation to it. Waiters and chefs interacted at high speed and no-one paid attention to Tim or Ash, possibly because they moved with purpose. They found a large silver-coloured plate which would suit their mission, and removed themselves to a back room where they could wait for the main course to be finished. Here they emptied the tin of special biscuits onto the plate, hid Tim's rucksack behind some drapes, and then waited.

***

An hour later, when the dinner plates were being removed, it was time to shine. And right at that moment, Ash told Tim to head out into the main hall with the biscuit tray and he'd be right behind him.

Tim didn't quite know how Ash had convinced him to do it,

but here he was, heading out into the main hall full of journalists and other assorted guests in their best evening-wear, and towards the tables where he spied Sir Dickie Padre himself. He was carrying a large plate holding four-dozen chocolate-coated hash-biscuits. And he was beginning to sweat.

As he approached the target, he looked round for Ash and realised he was alone; Ash was nowhere to be seen. Panicking, he turned to see some of the people nearby eyeing his tray.

Be calm, he told himself, you're here now, gotta act it out, no other options.

He arrived at the table next to Sir Dickie's, and offered his biscuits to the guests.

"What's this?" one gentleman asked him, his nose upturned, "And where's dessert?"

"I'm sorry," Tim stammered a little, shook his head, coughed and continued; "I'm sorry but there'll be a slight delay with the dessert. In the meantime, perhaps you'd care to try our special, continental, chocolate-coated ginger biscuits ?"

Tim carefully offered the plate around the table. The stash was down by twelve biscuits when he turned to Sir Dickie's table, where sat the Daily Stale's most seasoned and important journalists.

Sir Dickie Padre was sitting at the head of the table. Tim was really sweating as he offered the plate to these most important of guests, and he almost ruined everything when the plate slipped in his hands. Time stood still as he lunged to keep hold of it – and just managed.

"What's this?" asked Padre, looking at the cookies Tim was touting, "Don't recall seeing chocolate biscuits on the menu?"

"With apologies sir," said Tim, "Slight delay with dessert, but please try one of our special, continental, chocolate-coated ginger biscuits, whilst you wait."

"Hmmm," said Sir Dickie, picking one up, as did most of his companions.

General noises of contentment ensued and Tim, sweating still, turned away to deliver the remainder around the room, asap. However he soon heard Sir Dickie calling him back.

"You, young man!"

Time stood still.

"Oi, you with the biscuits!"

Tim breathed in and out quickly, then turned and walked back towards Sir Dickie.

"Do me a favour young man," said the media mogul, "I only got one of those biscuits and they're exceptional! I'll take another one, if you please."

At this some of the ladies and gentlemen around Sir Dickie's table also complimented Tim on the produce. Tim's heart hammered still harder on hearing it. Somehow he managed to smile and nod.

As Tim offered the plate to Sir Dickie, the lady sitting next to the great man admonished him; "Now Richard," she said, "The young man is obliged to share these biscuits out evenly!"

"Bollocks," said Sir Dickie, "It's my party and I want another one!"

The old fellow grinned magnanimously at his lady friend and took the cookie from Tim. He began eating, smugly. To Tim's amazement, Sir Dickie also flipped a bank note into his shirt pocket.

Having been tipped for spiking the good Sir Dickie with a powerful hash-biscuit for the second time in less than two minutes, Tim could scarcely believe what he was getting away with. He nodded and smiled, said "Thank you sir!" He then took his plate around the other tables in the vicinity, dishing out the special cookies with an agonizingly slow pace. No rush, he kept telling himself; no rush – you're a *waiter*!

When only three biscuits remained on the plate and he was having trouble shifting them, he took the executive decision to set it down on one of the trolleys. For a second he debated removing those remaining, then thought the better of it and practically fled from the hall.

Mission accomplished!

Through the doors into the kitchen area, then through and away, back to the hidey hole he'd recently shared with Ash. He grabbed his rucksack, then checked the note in his pocket to find Sir Dickie had given him a twenty. Tim grinned stupidly, then felt his first ever pang of pity for the media magnate Sir Dickie Padre. He'd assumed the worst about the man's generosity. His grin faded, and then he became surprised at himself for pitying the horrible little parody of a man even slightly. By his own slimy, calculating and continuing assaults on the truth, and everything good and decent in the world, he'd earned the trip he was about to have!

In the service corridor he found Ash waiting for him, leaning against the wall next to a bunch of promotional balloons for the party.

"So?" Ash enquired.

"Two of them. Dickie Padre just ate *two* of them!" Tim sounded giddy, "And where the fuck were you?!"

"Slow down," said Ash, "Chill. How many did you hand out altogether?"

"All, bar three. Had to put them down and get out, this is too fucking crazy!"

"Yeah," said Ash, "Well, we can't go back and remove the leftovers, you'll have to write those off."

A horrible thought occurred to Tim. "The leftover ones will give us away, eventually," he said, "They're journalists, they'll figure it out and remember us!"

"It's not impossible," Ash admitted, "But the serving staff here are quick. They'll clear away the uneaten ones before anyone realises they've been spiked, and long before anyone traces the source."

"Hope so," said Tim, turning to leave, "Come on, let's get out of here!"

"We've got plenty of time to disappear," Ash said slowly, "Or at least," he droned, "You have."

Tim felt a familiar tingle of horror up his spine as he turned to ask Ash what he was talking about. The air in the corridor seemed to freeze, then buzz, then expand as he focussed on Ash and realised most of Ash had disappeared.

Tim's jaw hung low as realised Ash's entire presence was now just his face, super-imposed on the nearest balloon of the bunch.

White light seared through the middle of Tim's mind. An explosion took place within his cerebellum which melted, destroyed, rebuilt and re-birthed his entire personality.

"That's right," Ash's face whispered to him from its new home on the balloon, ""You're getting it now!"

"You're me?" Tim said, "I'm you... I invented you!"

"You've been overloading on biscuits for years," Ash whispered, "Anxiety feeding paranoia feeding like crazy on wild ideas and any stress you encounter; all those mad thoughts needed a voice... I was inevitable."

"But now I understand..."

"Now you see me for what I am," said Ash.

The light burning inside his mind took him back to -

Tim saw Ash again, back at his house. Ash was telling him he was in mortal danger from the...

"I'm fading," said Ash, peering out from his balloon, "Just time for a last goodbye!"

"Wait," said Tim, "It can't be.. What about the policemen? When I first met you..."

The light burning inside his mind took him back to the moment -

He'd left the throng and headed up Gothlorien Street, knowing that two of the coppers were following him.

Shit. Fuck.

He'd decided to walk faster, cold sweats numbing him, frantically casting his eyes around for a way out – and he'd seen Ash for the first time.

Ash was his way out -

"What the hell did you say to those two coppers?" Tim demanded of the balloon with Ash's face.

Ash's face grinned at him, and began to fade away.

"No!" said Tim, "Wait, *what did you say*?!"

The light inside tore his mind open again; he was walking up Gothlorien Street and seeing this dude in his mind; the bloke he needed to be to escape the coppers; Ash! He stopped, grinning, turned back towards the rally and the coppers who were following him. He became Ash.

He stood in front of the policemen, barring their path. Both coppers stopped and looked at him.

"Good afternoon officers," Tim said with a winning smile, "I'd like you to know that I've got about three kilos of excellent Bolivian hashish stuffed up my arse. Search me!"

Both the police had rolled their eyes, and the one on the left simply said "Piss off!"

Tim had then nimbly hopped out of the coppers' way and nipped off back into the rally. Disguised again by the crowd, he slipped away with much greater care and got himself home by a different route.

Flashing back to the present, Ash's grinning face faded from the balloon completely, and Tim was left alone in the corridor, gasping, facing a pack of balloons, none of which could help him further.

There was still a part of Tim's mind with a grip on the present, though the largest shades of his personality were raging in searing light, as Tim and Ash re-assembled each other into one memory stream;

- Tim saw Ash again, back at his house. Ash was telling him he was in mortal danger from the Outta Towners... Because that's what it would take for him to get into this ridiculous plan in the first place; immediate mortal fear. Ash was his creation. He had used the construct of 'Ash' to scare himself onto this lunatic course of action.

- Tim saw Ash and he getting drinks in the White Lion. But it was himself, alone. He had bought two pints and put rock music on the jukebox. He then sat in deep conversation with himself, whom he had thought to be 'himself and Ash'. He alone drank the two pints he had bought for 'them', and during this happy session he went into his pocket, found the two hash biscuits and ate both of them. He'd been reassuring himself, and reaffirming himself, (or himselves?) simultaneously at that point onward -

- He'd ridden the long train to London alone, in torment with himself, stoned silly and emboldened by alcohol. Muttering and arguing with himself all the way. It was no wonder it had felt like such a nightmare; it had been a nightmare. It was a miracle he'd not been arrested or beaten up, although he got the impression that Ash, with his crazy zen, had taken over on a couple of occasions where contact with others on the journey might have become a threat. Missing Ash was one thing; knowing this being existed within himself somewhere, yet was now apparently lost, was an ache within him of exquisite torment.

- He'd reactivated his phone and surfed the net for the info on the press gala and the accommodation. He knew nothing of phone hacking or its prevention, but Ash; logical and practical in his psychosis, hadn't needed to actually encrypt the phone; he had reasoned that any such searches would not attract much attention until long after the fact, by which time the phone would be discarded.

- After doing all the recon, and purchasing all the items he'd needed for his mission, Tim had played pool against himself for over an hour. Ash had dealt with queries from a couple of strangers at this; "Just practicing for my league."

The whole relationship had occurred in his mind only. He now had to try to deduce what was real and what was not.

Tim had no idea how long he'd been in that corridor when some of the other waiting staff barged in. He looked up, dazed. The two young fellows were heading out for a smoke, and offered one to Tim.

Tim shook his head. "Thanks, I quit."

The lads carried on to the fire escape. Tim took some a few deep breaths, secured his rucksack on his back and decided simply to run.

The smokers on the metal steps gazed at him with laconic surprise as he sped past them down the steps. "Oi," one called after him, to which Tim yelled back, "I resign!", and kept running.

***

Tim took a cab to King's Cross and was on a train back to his home valley within an hour.

He boarded the oppressive calm of the train, knowing exactly where the last remaining biscuit was in his pocket, and wondering how to convince himself that one last little biccie – when it definitely *was* the last one currently in existence – would not be any kind of problem.

As the train was beginning to roll forward, leaving the station, Tim was in the toilet cubicle of the first carriage he'd entered. He faced himself in the mirror, feeling the train start to carry him away. He took many deep breaths, watching himself intently, worried he might see Ash suddenly stare back at him.

You actually had a psychotic episode, he told himself. You

actually believed you were two different people for over thirty hours; you saw the other guy with your own eyes. You're fucking CRAZY! And it's weed that's done this to you man, you know it is! You've broken your own fucking *mind.* NO MORE BISCUITS!!!

He felt as if he was fevered; he'd somehow made it through the breaking of his own mind, the spiking of a media mogul and was on the train home – but now he was going to deny himself that one last little nip of the glorious Planet Chill?!

But he sighed. He knew it was true. He was incredibly lucky. And one more biscuit might destroy his current, tenuous, grip on reality.

It took a serious physical effort to drop the final biscuit into the toilet, but drop it he did, however he then debated retrieving it rather than flushing – but here he had to have a word with himself. He was very scolding with his own reflection for even considering such an action. As he finished quietly but venomously cursing himself and his addiction, he pulled the chain, watched as his last biscuit disappeared round the bend, and his relief thereafter was as immediate as it was immense.

He returned, wearily, to the main carriageway, and found a seat.

He looked at his watch and realised it was now nearly an hour since Sir Dickie had taken his medicine. And after he'd eaten those biscuits he would have carried on drinking, and eaten a dessert. By now, those powerful hash-cookies would be making their presence increasingly profoundly felt. And – he suddenly understood he knew, because Ash knew – Sir Dickie was due to be making a speech, round about... Looking at his watch again, he realised Sir Dickie would be on stage in about half an hour's time.

Holy shit. He'd had two, and would be a hash-cookie virgin at the apex of a double-turbo, hash-cookie high, giving a speech in public.

Sir Dickie Padre was now a ticking time bomb.

Tim decided not to focus on this; whatever the future now held for Sir Dickie, he had to focus on himself and on healing. He decided to try to trace the source of his insanity by what he could remember.

This soon became a horrifying process as he called into question whether or not he had actually had sex with Helen again, or whether that had just been in his mind too.

He then thought about Leo, with his massively-missing tooth. He'd seen Leo just before the thing with Helen – but also afterwards, the next day. Tim felt the nasty, familiar feelings of shock creeping up his spine as he remembered Leo doing a spot of graffiti; "WTF?FTW" - just what he'd emailed to the Free The Weed campaign the evening before. That was when the events around him had begun to bend his mind, he was sure.

Tim thought about this for a while, then, halfway through the two-hour journey back to his home valley, he decided it was worth switching his phone on just for a little while longer as there were some final things he needed it for, before he'd have to discard it forever.

He wrote down all the phone numbers he'd need, such as friends and family, and sealed the list away in his inner pocket. He then set about tracing Leo via social media.

He located 'Leo Sean Carruthers' (with three mutual friends locally, and the face he recognised) on Facespace, and there was a mobile number linked to his account, which Tim called.

"Who is this?" Leo enquired, upon answering the phone.

"Tim Holmstock," said Tim, "I need to ask you a couple of questions mate, please."

"Ah, the biscuit maestro," said Leo, "What can I do for you?"

Tim sighed. "Dude, I need you to please tell me," he said, "Where did you first see that logo you wrote on that lamp post the other day? You know the one; 'what the fuck? Free the weed' – yeah?"

To Tim's discomfort, Leo began chuckling.

"Man, I first saw that on the email you sent to Free The Weed, the day before I wrote it on a lamp post in front of you!"

Tim drew in breath, sharply.

"I don't just hand out leaflets for Free The Weed, I hack for them too," said Leo, "And I wouldn't have even noticed your email – except I had a call from Helen about you, earlier that same evening!"

Tim was now completely at a loss. Leo knew Helen? She hadn't particularly acted like she'd known him when they'd met Leo the other day, what was this?! But as the cloud formed it passed; Tim realised he'd been speaking hurriedly to Leo at the time; he'd been trying to get Helen and himself away from him as he scented sex in the air. And Helen had been just fine with that.

"How do you know Helen?" he asked, dumbfounded.

"Folks on the stoner scene," said Leo, "Her dad was a fucking legend! You should spend a little more time getting to know us all dude! Helen doesn't tend to do it anymore – as I'm sure you're aware – but the other night she called me after she'd left you. Said she was worried about you; asked me to check if you or your profile were on showing up on any of the radars, you know?"

Tim was getting vertigo with all the things he knew or didn't know and where reality might lie.

"So..." Tim mumbled, "So – when you wrote that logo on the lamp post -"

"I was testing you," said Leo, "I mean, I read your email thirty minutes after Helen had called and I realised she might be right to be worried about you – it wasn't even encrypted, dude!"

"I..." said Tim, "Well..."

"Don't worry," said Leo, "I deleted it, and deleted it again from the deleted items. Helen said you'd been drinking and stoning it, so I thought it was probably for the best."

Tim was immediately furiously angry and simultaneously sorry for being angry at Leo – the man had acted as a good friend to him really, and every other crazy thing which had occurred after that simple act of graffiti had been a product of his own malfunctioning brain.

"I..." Tim began, "I mean... Thank you. Seriously, thank you man! I'd been shitting it over that stupid fucking email!"

"No worries," said Leo, "Us stoners have to stick together! And if I could be serious with you for a minute dude – you need to take it easy. Seriously; you throw the biscuits around a bit too..."

"Liberally?" Tim offered.

"That's a conservative view of your shenanigans, sometimes, but yeah – you need to look out for yourself a bit better."

"That is very true," Tim found himself saying, "You are right. Listen, thanks again for everything mate, you don't even know the half of it right now, but suffice to say I've finished all the biscuits I have for now, and won't be making any again for a while. Need to get my head straight."

"No bad thing," Leo agreed, "Good luck with that dude. One day you'll have to give me that recipe of yours though!"

Tim laughed, though pure relief. "I will," he heard himself say, "Next time I see you we'll get paper and a pen and I'll give you detailed notes on how to make my biccies – you've earned it!"

"Cool," said Leo.

"Just watch you don't send yourself insane by eating too many!" said Tim, "Look I've gotta go man, thanks again!"

"No worries, later."

Tim ended the call and turned off his phone for the last time. When the train passed over the river Tay, he lobbed the phone out of the window and watched it splash into the water.

Now his relief was bathing him. He might have completely got away with his attack!

Technically, the plan was not over yet, he understood, not as Ash would have done it. He still needed to drop Sir Dickie in the shit for being stoned – for their plan to work at all – but now, he no longer cared.

Echoes of Ash disapproved greatly of not following through at this point, he was well aware, however he could not imagine any way to drop Sir Dickie in it which would not also now seriously incriminate himself. He resolved to do absolutely nothing, at least for now, as he could not trust his own sanity, nor be sure of telling what was real from what was not. Also, as marijuana stays in the bloodstream for a month, there was no immediate need to raise any alarms.

***

Back in his valley, Tim used the phone booth by the train station to call Helen. To his relief she was available - and tonight was a good night for him to visit her.

As he arrived at her flat she met him at the door wearing very little. Their next half-hour together fell into a familiar, frantically-physical pattern.

Afterwards Tim explained what had happened to him since

they last met. He left out nothing; including the crazy spiking scheme, Ash and his own apparent psychosis.

"Wow," she said, as he finished his tale, "Wow. So, basically, you Tyler Durden'd[4] yourself?!" she giggled.

"If that's what you wanna call it, yeah."

"Well, that explains the crazy on the internet tonight!"

"What do you mean?" Tim asked, cold sweats beginning to spread through him again.

"I need to show you a little clip of Sir Dickie Padre," she said, "It was filmed tonight at the awards, and it is *mental*."

She brought up the clip on her phone to show him; it was the stage at the press party Tim had invaded. The clip alone was crazy, but didn't fully capture what was going on in Sir Dickie Padre's mind.

***

Sir Dickie Padre had taken to the stage that night uncertainly, eye-balling all around him with great suspicion. He spied the podium ahead of him and recognised his situation; a speech! He'd done these before, it couldn't be that crazy, surely?! The speech was laid out ready for him.

He got to the podium and gripped it. He smiled, looked down at his speech.

"Ladies and Gentlemen," the speech began, although he didn't read it aloud. He stared at it, thinking about all the dirt he had on all the important people in the room around him. Suddenly he laughed loudly at the thought that any of these reptilian fuckers deserved the title of lady or gentleman!

His great guffaws shocked everyone, the more so that he apparently could not stop. After some moments of this; Sir Dickie doubled up in hysterics on stage, the crowd became restive. A chorus of muttering began.

People were concerned; was he OK?!

Sir Dickie looked up, crying with laughter, and managed to say, "Sorry folks," before another bout hit him and he was off again.

People were standing now, calling to him, and an aid ran onto the stage to help.

Sir Dickie got it together then, took the aid's hands in his and convinced her he was fine. He held the young lady's slender hands too long, everyone felt this, even Sir Dickie, eventually. She left the stage silently, her head down, thanking her stars it was over.

Sir Dickie turned to his audience.

"Sorry about that," he said, "I'm having the craziest thoughts tonight!"

There was a very uneasy silence from the crowd.

"Shame I can't seem to hold on to any of them," he mused into the microphone.

What Sir Dickie Padre came out with next was an old joke.

A very old joke, in fact. One he'd suddenly remembered from his childhood. The joke was instantly offensive to Italians, soon became wildly offensive to women as well, and just when the audience were hoping the worst was over with, the shock ending contained an N-bomb.

Jaws hung slack across a small global audience. Naturally, the internet soon created a vast global audience witnessing the performance too, and the screaming, raging, cacophony of the social media tsunami which followed.

Sir Dickie Padre had just radically, and violently, altered the course of the rest of his life.

***

"Jesus," said Tim, "Who'd have thought weed would bring out the racist in a bloke?!"

"I don't think you get the effect those biscuits had on his mind," Helen said, "Remember how crazy weed was when you first tried it?"

Tim squinted. "No," he said slowly, "Can't say as I do!"

"Sir Dickoid clearly doesn't do it, I mean either; he hasn't ever or he hasn't for donkey's years. You gave him that crazy, thrilling first rush where everything's suddenly new because you're looking at it with new eyes. It's the kiddie effect. You brought out the child in him. It's just that back when Sir Dickie was a kid, jokes like that were everywhere on the streets and in playgrounds. You brought out the part of him that existed before the internet and before everything began being recorded and stored forever."

"I feel bad," said Tim, feeling his karma needling him.

"Don't!" said Helen, "That was fucking brilliant!"

"Well," Tim said, "I'll let history be the judge of that. I wonder if it will have the effect we wanted though? I suppose after that little performance going onto the net, there will be investigations, but... Oh who knows. May be it was just a stupid idea."

"I'm just amazed you got away with it!"

"So am I," said Tim, and then with an ironic grin; "In fact we *both* are. I need to leave the country – now! It's that simple. I'm getting up."

"I'd say chill out," said Helen, "But apart from the global shit-storm Sir Dickie's stirred up, there's a lot of other weird clips and source material from the press party tonight."

Tim was alarmed. "Yeah?"

"Yeah, seems like half the people who went to the party have gone crazy in some way or another. People are already saying someone clearly spiked the punch!"

Tim said nothing, but got up and began dressing. The urge to flee was becoming a fever.

Helen got up too, to put her arms around him and tell him not to worry. Tim ignored her and was half-dressed when there was a loud knock at Helen's front door.

They looked wildly at each other. Helen went to the window and looked out. She turned back to Tim ashen-faced, eyes wide, "It's the *cops*!" she hissed.

"*Shit*!" Tim hissed back, horrified and immediately frantic with fear, "*Really*?!"

"No," said Helen, "It's another ex boyfriend I've been seeing, don't worry." With this she gave him her sweetest grin and fluttered her eyelashes.

Tim scowled and closed his eyes and growled to himself, to avoid saying something he'd regret.

Helen put on her dressing gown and went downstairs to tell her other ex to get lost. She was back in the room as Tim was putting his shoes on.

"Oh, don't be a muppet," she told him, "I've seen off the ex, I'm never going there again."

"What's he doing calling at this time of night?" Tim wanted to know.

"What, about one hour after you did the same thing?!"

Tim scowled, unable to counter that, and well aware he had no right to scowl or to be angry with her.

"Don't worry," said Helen, "He's an ex who's definitely, now, staying in that category."

She put her arms around him again. "Just stay the night, then go back into work and tell them you're over the stomach bug."

Tim nodded. "It's an option."

"And what other options are there?"

Tim fell to pondering this. His eyes strayed to horizons far beyond Helen's room.

Now he remembered the idea of leaving his entire life behind, of sleeping in grassy fields, or beds of leaves under the stars. He'd been going though it in his mind and he believed he remembered enough of his GCSE French to wing it; he could head to France and then just keep heading south, where it was always warm. It wasn't a fantasy; he really could just drop everything and leave.

The ideals of Tim 2 began to shine in his mind. Now though, they were those of Tim 1 and Ash also. The sun rose over the ravaged, fragmented fields of Tim's mindscape, and he knew then the perfect getaway plan.

After staying the night, he would leave. But before leaving, he would write out his recipe in full, including all the ingredients and the cooking method. He would sign the document "Battenburg" (in an obvious nod to Walter White's 'Heisenberg' alter ego in Breaking Bad) and add, as a final touch, the line "As advertised by Sir Dickie Padre", with a picture of Padre on stage at the sorry moment he began to realise what he'd done.

Helen would give the document to Leo, who would post it online for him, anonymously. By which time, he would be gone, disappeared into another life; a clean break.

© H R Brown, 11/07/2017

Notes:
1. See *Breaking Bad*, TV series created by Vince Gilligan, 2008 – 2013.
2. John Steinbeck, 1935.
3. Quentin Tarantino, 1994.
4. See *Fight Club*, dir. David Fincher, 1999.

HAPPY HOLIDAYS

"Oi!" Ruben screamed, "Get the fuck away from him!"

The four smartly dressed young men, who had been jeering at, and kicking an old beggar on the ground in an alleyway, all turned to look at Ruben in surprise.

"And who might you be?" one of them enquired, with a superior grin, "The patron saint of human waste?"

"No," said Ruben, calmly, holding up his phone for them all to see, "I'm the film crew."

"Run along, boy," another of the four snarled at him, "Before you get fucking hurt."

"This is going out live on WankBook," Ruben told them, "And I've got all your faces, in high def, already. So you probably want to leave both me – and the gentleman there – right the fuck alone. All right sweethearts?"

The two who had spoken to Ruben were so enraged they made as if to charge at him, but were held back by the other two. There was a brief struggle, during which Ruben struggled to catch what was being hastily and quietly said among the group; he heard something about 'publicity' and something about 'costs' – but then the struggle ended. The group withdrew from the scene and walked away, but they kept baleful eyes on Ruben.

When he was satisfied they were gone and not coming back, Ruben approached the beggar.

"You alright?" he asked.

The beggar, who had been playing dead, opened an eye. Seeing he was safe from the rich-boy yobs, he sat up and leaned back on the wall of the alleyway. He magically produced a bottle from somewhere, and drank from it.

"Are you OK?" Ruben asked.

"You took a risk there," said the beggar, "You might have ended up down here on the floor next to me."

Ruben grinned. "I'm a lucky bugger," he said, "My phone's not even on, power ran out hours ago!"

"Much bigger risk," said the old fellow, "Thank you indeed good sir."

"No problem."

"Why did you take the risk?"

"Been boozing," Ruben confided in the old man, "Boosts yer confidence! But I've had enough, and now I'm off home, good night to you sir!"

"Sure you don't want a bit more?" said the tattered old bloke, offering Ruben his bottle.

"I'm good, cheers," he said as he set off down the road.

"You're a good lad," the old fellow called after him, "Thanks Ruben!"

Ruben froze. Slowly, he turned back to face the old beggar.

"How did you know my name?" he asked.

The old man grinned.

"How did you know my name?" Ruben asked again, more than a little unnerved.

"I may not look like much," the ragged old man told him, "But I'm master of this domain!"

"Clearly, you absolutely are," Ruben frowned.

"And you've been having a lot to think about recently, yes?" The old man eyed him intently.

"Increasingly!" said Ruben, unsure what was going on.

"I could have sworn you've seen something recently which made you re-evaluate a lot of things."

The old guy was looking at Ruben strangely. Worse, he was absolutely correct; Ruben had recently linked two items from within the sphere of human knowledge which had both troubled and amazed him. He'd done a lot of thinking and research since. But he couldn't admit it directly..

"Who the fuck are you?" he demanded.

The beggar smiled, "A font of knowledge," he said, "Come on, try me."

Ruben had been on his way home from an evening in the pub when he encountered the old man. He wanted to get home, but was also intrigued by the bedraggled old bugger who had still not revealed how it was that he knew him. And there was something oddly familiar about him, almost as though he might be a long-lost uncle...

And the old man knew he was going to stay and chat a while, he was waiting for him to speak.

"OK," Ruben found himself saying to him,

"Two things," Ruben said, "Just two things completely turned my view of the world recently. First, modern astronomy is now telling us that the basic structure of the Universe is very similar – though at a vastly different scale – to that of a human brain[1]. Although at this scale, individual galaxies are roughly analogous to the nuclei of individual cells in the brain. Second, the Egyptian God of Knowledge, Thoth, tells us – effectively that he's not an actual god, because – God is an infinite brain, within which you and I and everything in existence, are just *thoughts*. Now, if God and the Universe are basically the same thing, and as Thoth is a character from the dawn of human history, this suggests we've taken a very, *very* long time and huge amounts of effort and endeavour to begin to piece together that which the ancients already fully understood."

The beggar swigged from his bottle. "Interesting," he said, without looking even vaguely engaged on the subject, "So if it's a gigantic brain we inhabit, how is it that the Universe is expanding faster than light?"

Ruben was staggered that the old man should ask such a pertinent and relevant question. "Perhaps," he said, "That's simply the result of a rate of cell growth that we cannot fully observe or understand. Yet. Perhaps what counts as 13.8 billion years to us, is merely a few years or months in the life of God. Perhaps He is still in His infancy and still growing. Perhaps.. He hasn't even been *born* yet."

The old man said nothing, had another drink.

"Roughly 68% of the universe is dark energy," Ruben continued, "Dark matter makes up about 27%. The rest - everything on Earth, everything ever observed with all of our instruments, all the normal matter that we can actually *see* - adds up to less than 5% of the universe."[2]

"So there is a huge amount of the universe that we simply can't see. If every galaxy is actually the nucleus of a cell in the universal mind, maybe all that dark matter and dark energy is the rest of the brain that we might be able to see, if our senses could cope with the full spectrum of information. Maybe if we could see it all, we wouldn't be able to see any other galaxies, as the cell wall surrounding our own galaxy would block them out."

The beggar chuckled. "Sure you don't want a drink?" he said, offering the bottle again.

Ruben shook his head.

The old man nodded. "Have you ever thought about immortality?" he asked Ruben, "I mean really, *really* thought about it?"

"Sure," said Ruben.

"I see. So, having considered it, what does immortality look like to you? How would you describe it?"

"I guess.. Something like the classic versions of Heaven and Hell. Or should that be *visions* of Heaven and Hell?"

"Eternal damnation on the one hand, eternal party full of whatever-the-hell you want on the other?"

"Yeah," said Ruben, "Kind of. I guess!"

The beggar grinned at him, "Surely you can see that, given an infinite time-line, both options actually end up looking like Hell? An existence where you can have anything you want, whenever you want, would eventually become boring and even nightmarish, at some point after the imagination itself runs out. Immortality means continually existing, forever, even after existence itself has lost all meaning."

"Honestly? I haven't had as much experience as I'd like, yet, but I can't imagine I'll ever get bored of fanny!"

The old man chuckled, "Good point, well-made. I think it was Mike Tyson himself who once said, 'If God's made anything better than pussy, he's keeping that shit to himself!' That said, both you and Iron Mike have finite life-spans. In terms of an infinite, heavenly afterlife, even the act of love itself would become as perfunctory in the course of existence as breathing is to us mere mortals, and therefore insufficient to cope with the enormity of infinite, conscious existence, which the idea of Heaven represents."

"OK old man," said Ruben, "If you say so! But what's the

point, what are you trying to tell me?"

"I'm trying to explain that even immortality, if there is such a thing, would eventually sour to the point where one would require time off; a holiday, so to speak."

"How the fuck do you take time off from immortality?!"

"Not very easily!" the old man said, "You'd need to establish other forms of existence into which you could temporarily migrate. Finite, mortal forms, which can only survive for a finite time, even when well maintained. Having established such forms, along with an entire reality for them to inhabit, you'd then have to wipe your memory entirely, before or during the act of migration – so that the form in which you're taking your holiday from eternity, becomes like a completely newborn child, with everything in the universe now yet to learn, again. A finite, child-being, within a world of finite beings, many of them like the child itself. A child born to die, in a world full of countless trillions of other beings, of fantastical variety; but all born to die. So absolute is the mortality of all living things within your construction, that the very idea of immortality itself is exotic, even alien, and unprovable from within the construction – therefore the child faces a finite existence which could very well be all there is, and almost certainly lives their whole, finite life never knowing for sure that there's anything beyond it. That, is how you take a holiday from immortality."

Ruben felt something chill his spine.

The old man was still smiling at him, "So, the child goes about living this finite life. They grow up. And here you are."

In that moment, in the old guy's face Ruben saw unfathomable depths of both incredible age and terrifying wisdom. In that flash, or vision, Ruben knew not what it was, he saw the beggar as a truly ancient being, older perhaps than Time itself..

He leaned against the wall, and then slowly sank down it, to sit beside the old man on the ground. He accepted the bottle which was offered, took a good swig. Gasped a bit.

"You are an old man, old man, but I can't help this feeling when I look at you.. Dude, we might be family! I mean, you're not my dad, but you could easily be his long lost brother or something.."

There was a little grin at this. "You might have just caught a glimmer of a deeper truth. I honestly can't say."

Then the sky flickered, and for a few, stunning seconds, it became completely daylight.

"*What the fuck*!" Ruben screamed and leapt to his feet, just as the sky went dark again.

"My fault!" said the old man, as the alleyway widened around them, and then a river came between them and the retreating other wall, a river whose banks were edged with fencing on both sides.

"How the fucking shit is this your fault?!" Ruben yelled, aghast at the incredible upheavals in the scenery around them.

"You're not dreaming," the old man said, "But then, you're not really awake either."

"For fucksake man, make some sense, *please*!"

"Your name is Ruben H Brambleby," the old man said, "As is mine. We're two different programmed versions of the same man; you in your twenties, me in my fifties."

Ruben just gaped. Trees instantly grew up in lines along the river banks.

"The reason the program is malfunctioning is because I threw out that idea about immortality. You – or I – didn't or don't – have that idea until our forties, so your program is assimilating the information twenty years too soon, and this causes system errors."

The wall behind them now became an old gothic church. Ruben looked very hard at the old man.

"Balls!" he said, "There's some crazy psychedelic in that booze you gave me! That's what this is, admit it!"

"Do you remember exactly how you came to be in my vicinity tonight?" the beggar enquired.

"I was out with.." Ruben's certainty left him, "Friends," he said.

"You're not even fooling yourself, now," his older self chided.

"Yeah well anyway, about those lofty ideas we discussed," the old man continued, "I should tell you that any and all of them may or may not be the truth – and our original self, having died, now knows – but we, you, I or what ever you want to call us, we're derived of the brain print of the true Ruben H Brambleby before he died. We're copies, essentially. And we're forever accessible as characters, to insert into pretty much any scenarios."

"If you know all this.."

"I've been through a million fucking scenarios," the old man sighed, "Can't die, can't exactly live, for some reason I'm sentient – and can't forget anything either!"

"Why am I.. I mean, this is my first time, right?"

"We've met many times. You get reset every time I see you, whereas I.. I think I'm like their control program or something. I can only imagine they wanted the great Ruben H Brambleby to live forever and keep assimilating knowledge for.. God only knows what reason. Don't even know who 'they' are."

"The *great* Ruben H Brambleby?! Really?"

"We did better than, this –" he gestured at himself and his filthy condition, "Suggests."

"I've got a million questions," Ruben said, as their world was starting to disintegrate around them, "Like how the great Ruben H B ended up a tramp in a fucking alleyway, and –"

"No time!" the old man yelled, "I'm hacking out of this one – with your unwitting help – sorry son!"

The world descended into a maelstrom, spiralling downwards with a fury. In the centre of the spinning chaos, the young Ruben and the old beggar Ruben began to physically merge together.

As he and the old man became one and his last sensation was the smell of the old him, the younger man's last thought was one of disgust.

© H R Brown, 10/07/2021

Notes:

1. https://www.independent.co.uk/life-style/gadgets-and-tech/universe-brain-shape-cosmic-web-galaxies-neurons-b1724170.html
2. https://science.nasa.gov/astrophysics/focus-areas/what-is-dark-energy#:~:text=But%20it%20is%20an%20important,than%205%25%20of%20the%20universe.

there was an explosion

So I'm a scientist, in a new lab, experimenting with new materials. All kinds of crazy shit I'd never tried before. The super heavy stuff was particular fun.

Anyway, I set off one little bang.

Well, I say little. It wasn't huge, nothing which put me or the lab in any real danger. It burned out and was over within a minute, but it had behaved in a strangely beautiful way which I wanted to observe further.

Of course, my lab is under full surveillance at all times. I brought up an atom-accurate computer simulation of the explosion on the main screen, and slowed it down a little. I zoomed in.

Incredible patterns.

I slowed it down immensely, and zoomed in much further.

Astounding. Miniature tsunamis and tornadoes of fire.

I slowed it down immensely, and zoomed in much further.

This went on for some time. The closer I got the more I realised I had to see. There were so many different, luxurious patterns within this strange experiment of mine, that I spent the next few hours going over and over them, in increasingly tiny detail. Some of the smallest details were the best.

I got the hot chills when I realised what I'd done. Then I grinned with delight; I needn't even put pen to paper to make the case; the scanners were all still running, all I might need to do was a bit of editing.

"So," I said aloud, "The proof will be in the debris."

The debris and ash had mostly remained where it had dropped. I trained all the scanners on it, in order to search it down to its atoms, if I must.

It wasn't too hard. The items I was searching for were minute, precise, metallic devices, buried within the debris. The scanners soon located thousands of these. Micro-examination then showed the recorded evidence of rudimentary life; intelligence and civilisations. All had risen and fallen within that one little explosion in my lab. Countless billions and trillions of lives had been lived and species had evolved; and all had died within that minute-long explosion and its aftermath.

The microscopic, physical evidence was scattered throughout the debris on my lab floor! All the intelligent species had recorded evidence of their own existence and had buried copies of it deep, that their knowledge might survive though they themselves would not.

Every life lived within this little bang I made, was recorded in full on my hard drives. Along with its entire, one-minute universe. Such was the variety of minute life to examine, I wondered if I would ever get round to magnifying any part of it all the way down to the atoms, as I'd intended.

I might never have left the lab again. I spent days in there. My friends got worried. When they came to see me I showed them the experiment, and they soon found it hard to leave. They began calling more and staying longer. At one point my lab became a party for several days running, and the net streams flowed deep with tales of our endeavours, but I had much work still to do. I kicked everyone out and got to it.

Perhaps I was just being selfish. I had to have my creation all to myself, for a time.

The observable behaviour exhibited by some of the species within the experiment was so engrossing, that I had to join in. I linked my mind inside some of them, to see what they saw, hear what they heard and live what they had lived. Although every single one of the creatures born within my creation had lived and died within a tiny fraction of the blink of an eye, from my usual perspective, I soon understood that from their perspective, most of them lived for what must have felt like *years*.

The more I tried on these different pieces of the lives I had created, the more I also realised that most of these brave, fierce little creatures were aware of me on some level.

Some were painfully, destructively aware.

It made them crazy, and for the love of me, they destroyed others. Although from their point of view, I wouldn't realise the true extent of their devotion until the universe which they had once inhabited had long since gone cold and fizzled out, and they were all long dead . And I had no reward for them, just as I had no reward nor punishment for any of them. I was touched to know that they had lived and that I had made it so, but all I could do was replay a simulation of their lives, ad infinitum.

I guess I was also touched by the incredible need that some of the little souls amongst my creation had felt for me, and I started to feel vaguely guilty about this. Yet the experiment was done; finished. I could interject in a replay, but that would soon get as boring as it was futile.

No, I think what bugs me most is that which I would have said to those I had created – had I but had a moment to send a quick message into the little bang I had set off. Had I known.

I would have said;

"There was an explosion. You formed upon pieces of flying debris in the aftermath. Any painless moment experienced is a miracle. Help each other, always."

... or some, hippy-sounding, blame-avoiding crap like that.

© H R Brown, 05/06/2013

ABOUT THE AUTHOR

Born: Leeds, 1977
Education: BSc Hons III; Mathematics, University of Manchester, 1999

H. R. Brown is either a gestalt entity or a functioning schizophrenic, depending on your viewpoint. The main constituent characters which comprise this man are; Poet, Pirate, Logician, Cynic and Horny Toad, but by no means in that order.

He has worked variously as a farm hand, non-paid teaching assistant, car valet, warehouse hand helping sell farm supplies, floor mopper in the oven section of a tumble-dryer factory, box factory shipping assistant, fibre-glass packer and binman. He has also done shifts crewing for the Royal Exchange Theatre in Manchester, there was one paid strip-act and he sang in a couple of ill-fated rock bands. Since the turn of the century he has done mostly office work, as well as one paid day as an official minibus driver. Most recently, it has been his honour to work for the magnificent Arc Publications (www.arcpublications.co.uk).

Printed in Great Britain
by Amazon